Sister of the Bollywood Bride

Nandini Bajpai

POPPY

LITTLE, BROWN AND COMPANY
New York   Boston

Poppy
Little, Brown and Company
Hachette Book Group
1290 Avenue of the Americas, New York, NY 10104
Visit us at LBYR.com

Originally published in 2013 by Scholastic India Pvt. Ltd. in India
First U.S. Edition: May 2021

Little, Brown and Company is a division of Hachette Book Group, Inc.
The Little, Brown name and logo are trademarks of Hachette Book Group, Inc.

Poppy is an imprint of Little, Brown and Company.
The Poppy name and logo are trademarks of Hachette Book Group, Inc.

The publisher is not responsible for websites (or their content) that are not owned by the publisher.

Library of Congress Cataloging-in-Publication Data
Names: Bajpai, Nandini, author.
Title: Sister of the Bollywood bride / by Nandini Bajpai.
Description: First U.S. edition. | New York : Little, Brown and Company, 2021. | "Originally published in 2013 by Scholastic India Pvt. Ltd. in India." | Audience: Ages 12 & up. | Summary: Seventeen-year-old Mini plans a magnificent Indian wedding—from their deceased mother's jewelry to a white wedding horse—for her older sister Vinnie, a medical resident, but a hurricane threatens to destroy it all.
Identifiers: LCCN 2020043604 | ISBN 9780316705424 (trade paperback) | ISBN 9780316705431 (ebook) | ISBN 9780316705400 (ebook other)
Subjects: CYAC: Weddings—Fiction. | Sisters—Fiction. | East Indian Americans—Fiction.
Classification: LCC PZ7.1.B335 Sis 2021 | DDC [Fic]—dc23
LC record available at https://lccn.loc.gov/2020043604

ISBNs: 978-0-316-70542-4 (pbk.), 978-0-316-70543-1 (ebook)

Printed in the United States of America

LSC-C

Printing 1, 2021

For Mum and Kiki.
I'm lucky to be the link between you two.

Chapter One

The silver key resting on my palm looked pretty ordinary, but what it unlocked was not. I dropped it back into a tiny envelope that read CUSTOMER KEY, BOX NUMBER: 311 and handed it to the teller.

"You'd like to open your safe-deposit box?" The bank teller's eyebrows shot up at my request—it clearly wasn't every day a teenager asked for access to the bank vault.

"Yes, thanks." I tucked a strand of hair behind one ear, acting casual, though my heart was pounding like a Punjabi dhol.

"Follow me, please."

The teller came around the counter and led the way to the other end of the small lobby.

Who knew our little Bank of America branch in Westbury, Massachusetts, even had a proper bank vault like in a heist movie or something?

She unlocked two massive doors—one with steel bars, the other studded with gears and bolts—and let me into the strong room. It was insanely solid.

"Three-one-one," she said under her breath, looking for the matching key in a metallic drawer, then read the numbers off the deposit boxes until she found mine. Both keys had to be inserted and turned simultaneously for the box to open. She pulled the box—long, metallic, coffinlike—out of the locker and handed it to me.

"You can open it in there." The door she pointed to led into a private closet-sized room.

I shut the narrow door, deposit box clutched tight—and took a deep, deep breath in the tiny space. Probably exhausting its entire oxygen supply, for I was suddenly breathless.

I lifted the lid.

Oh. My. Three hundred and thirty million gods.

Jewelry boxes with clear lids stared back at me, the brilliant yellow of Indian gold gleaming richly through them.

Vinnie was never going to believe this!

Vinnie, my older sister, was the reason I was standing in that bank vault. Always the steady, serious type, Vinnie had recently lost her head, had fallen in love, and was getting married this summer. Also, she had just graduated from medical school and was starting a three-year emergency medicine residency at a hospital in Chicago—which meant she had no time to plan her wedding here in Boston.

Add to this the fact that our dad, still in shock over the whole thing, said he was not paying for a big fat wedding. His five-year fiscal plan involved frugal living and aggressive saving in the year between Vinnie's graduation and me going off to college—spending lavishly on a wedding did not enter into it in any way, shape, or form.

But getting married she was, and whatever the budget, I was going to make sure that my sister looked fabulous—Indian style.

The only problem? There's one thing an Indian bride can't do without—gold. Twenty-two-karat gold. And a couple of ounces of that stuff probably cost more than my secondhand car.

Not to worry, Dad said—evidently Mom left us some jewelry, information no one bothered to share with *me* before—*just take the safe-deposit box key and check it out.*

I untied the strings of a deep blue velvet pouch and emptied its glittering contents into my cupped hand. More jewelry. I *knew* this stuff. Some of it was heirloom old—passed down from my nani. Some of it was new. Kind of. Mom had had it made for Vinnie and me.

I opened a box. A note with my name and a date in Mom's neat handwriting—strange how I recognized it instantly—was tucked under the necklace. I touched the dainty peacock with turquoise feathers and ruby eyes with one finger. Mom's design. The date was seven years ago. Only two months before Mom...My throat was suddenly tight.

This is for your wedding, Mini.

For something so delicate, it felt heavy. The price of gold back then was not astronomical, apparently. Talk about return on investment. Well played, Mom, well played.

I opened another box. Earrings with missing pairs. Broken chains. All gold, though. The note in it said matter-of-factly: *Junk, but it has value—sell it if you girls ever need money.* I had to smile. Mom was nothing if not practical.

I closed the lid on the broken jewelry and picked up the necklace Mom had designed for Vinnie. What would Mom think of a simple civil ceremony with twenty guests? The answer to that was staring me in the face. She wouldn't have saved and scraped for such fancy jewelry if she hadn't wanted a proper Punjabi wedding. That's what she would have liked. Lots of family, food, flowers, music. Vinnie in a gorgeous lehenga. Her groom in a red turban on a white horse, like in one of those Bollywood movies.

No way was that happening, the way things were.

I stroked the peacock pendant with one finger. Maybe...

I bundled the jewelry into my messenger bag and zipped it up carefully. Stepping out of the tiny room, I knocked on the glass pane between the teller station and the vault and gestured that I was done.

The younger teller, clearly Indian and recently married—going by her glass bangles and the red sindoor powder in her neat, straight-down-the-center parting—sized me up in one glance. Tall, by Indian standards—thanks to Dad's genes. Lean—thanks to cross-country running and the fact that neither Dad nor I could cook as well as Beeji, my grandmother, who had returned to India four years ago. Long dark hair, olive skin, brown eyes—pretty, I've been told. I've been mistaken for South American/North African/ Middle Eastern, but not by other Indians.

I smiled back and wondered if she'd bring up region, caste, or marital prospects.

"You're Gujarati?" she asked. There it was.

"Punjabi," I said.

"Oh!" she said. "In senior year?"

"Starting in the fall," I acknowledged. Good guess.

"You're Mr. Kapoor's daughter!" She looked proud to have placed me. "Your sister is doing medical, I heard?"

"She just graduated in May," I said.

"Very good! You must be a good student too, like Winnie?" She looked to me for confirmation.

I smiled at how she pronounced *Vinnie* with a *W*, the way Beeji did. "I'm okay, I guess." Something made me add, "She's getting married. In two months!"

"That's great," the teller said, genuinely happy. "Is she marrying an Indian boy?"

"South Indian," I said.

She nodded in sympathy. Gujaratis and Punjabis, though different, are at least both not *South* Indian. "Well, it's better than, you know..." Her spread hands encompassed the plethora of humanity that is not Indian at all. "He's a doctor too?" she asked, and smiled her approval when I nodded. *That* is almost as good as being Gujarati!

"It would have made your mummy happy," she said. Apparently nothing is a secret from bank tellers at the intersection of Routes 30 and 27. "If there's anything I can do, only ask," she added, awkward yet sincere. "Okay?"

"Okay," I promised, but automatically stuck her offer in the forget-about-it-zone of my brain.

They always meant well, the people who wanted to help because they knew about Mom—but they just totally embarrassed me instead. The extra weight in my bag dragged down more than my shoulder as I walked to the parking lot, but my mood lifted as I caught sight of what was waiting there like a faithful pup—my one-week-old pride and joy on wheels. One-week-old for me, that is. The car was actually a 2010 model—though Dad had made sure it had low mileage, no accidents, and only one owner—but it totally rocked.

"She was always so level-headed, you know?" Dad said. He was still grappling with the notion that Vinnie was getting married—whether he liked it or not. "No dating in high school or anything. I never expected her to rush into something like this. She should be thinking of her career. She's much too young to get married!"

He looked like his hair had gained some extra gray since Vinnie had announced her engagement. That and the worry lines on his brow were the only physical changes in him in the last decade.

"Dad, she's twenty-five!" I said. It was hard work being a Vinnie apologist.

Given that my parents' loving marriage of twenty years was a match made in the *Times of India* matrimonial section, I didn't expect Dad to understand about dating. Mom was a pretty and popular good-girl type who only crushed on guys from afar. And Dad was seriously uncool in high school. I mean, dork-glasses, skinny-frame, peach-fuzz-mustache uncool. Let's face it. They needed the help. Vinnie did not.

But from sophomore year all Vinnie thought about was grades—and Mom. There was no time for dating when Mom, in the final stages of cancer, was fading away before her eyes. That was also the reason Vinnie didn't want to waste time now.

"I tried to explain it to her. And you know what she said?" Dad was still going on. "She said there will never be a good time. First she had seven years of medical school, now there's three years of residency, and then she'll probably do a subspecialty fellowship in pediatric emergency medicine. She said if she's old enough to help deliver a baby, she's old enough to get married."

"She's kind of right," I pointed out.

"I don't know...." He scowled at the picture of Vinnie and Manish that I had framed and set on the mantel: Vinnie in her graduation gown and Manish in a suit and tie with his arm around her—both glowing with happiness. "He's from *Bangalore....*" He paused. "They're...you know."

"What?" I asked, and watched with amusement as he tried to articulate his misgivings without coming off as insufferably North Indian. Funny how he was usually so openhearted but the tiny difference between Punjab and Tamil Nadu was too much for him.

"Th-they're...," he spluttered. "They're just..."

"Not Punjabi," I said. Yeah, that was it.

Dad nodded, worry lines etching deeper.

"She doesn't care," I said. "It's not like we live in Punjab or something."

"She got into the honors program in medical education at Northwestern," Dad said, changing tactics. It was true. My sister, the genius, got accepted into the seven-year, straight-from-high-school medical program for gifted students—Mom had known before she passed away that Vinnie would be a doctor. "And he went to UMass."

"*Dad!*" I said. "Not everyone can afford to go to private school. It's not like he isn't super smart—he got into Feinberg, didn't he? The same school as Vinnie!"

They had met at medical school—Manish was a year ahead of Vinnie—and they clicked because they were both from the Boston area. Their first date was a baseball game where they were the only two people at Wrigley Field rooting for the Red Sox. I heard about him from Vinnie off and on, of course, but I had no idea how serious they were. When Dad and I went to Chicago for her graduation and Vinnie told us they were engaged, it was a seismic-level shock to our family—but I could see that Manish made her happy, and that was good enough for me. Dad, meanwhile, was still struggling to comprehend our new reality.

"She's putting him before everything," Dad said. "She was going to come back here, and now . . ."

We had always expected that Vinnie would come back to Boston for her residency—there are so many good hospitals here. But when she placed at University of Chicago's emergency medicine residency program on match day, the same place where Manish was a second-year resident, it was clear that things had changed.

"Dad, it's natural, isn't it?" I said.

"And on top of everything, he's allergic to dogs." Dad played the trump card.

I sighed, my hand going instinctively to the furry head planted on my knee. Our dog, Yogi, was never more than five feet from me when I was home. I had to admit that Manish's allergies were a horrible disappointment. Still, I racked my brain and made an attempt.

"Maybe he'll try allergy shots?" I asked. Weak, I admit, but valiant. "They do work on some people."

"Who knows what the family is like," Dad mumbled ominously. "We haven't met them even once."

"I'm sure Vinnie has spoken to them plenty of times," I said. She probably had. I pushed back my chair.

"Dad, we just have to deal with him," I said. "He's going to be family."

"Well, I'm not paying for a lavish wedding out of *your* college fund," Dad said.

"It doesn't have to be lavish," I said. "But we have to do *something* special, Dad—it's Vinnie's wedding!"

"It's not just the money," Dad said. "She doesn't have time to plan it. I don't have the bandwidth either—you know how things are at work!"

"I have time, Dad!" I said. Something about holding the jewelry Mom had left us made me want to make sure Vinnie had a rocking Punjabi wedding. One Mom would approve of. "*I* could do it." It was true. I had over two months of summer vacation!

"Nonsense," he said. "You might be taking the SAT again; that's much more important. And you have math tutoring, college visits, the common app, and supplemental essays to draft and whatnot. You're not responsible enough to plan a whole wedding—you're seventeen!"

I bristled at the words, but it was no use arguing with him right now. Plus, thinking about getting my SAT score back in approximately two weeks actually made me feel ill.

"You're not wrong," I said, very calm. "But who knows, I might have gotten a good score on my first try, right?" I felt *okay* about it but definitely not 100 percent confident. "Can we just wait and see?"

Chapter Two

"I am not interested in doing my math."

The kid's solemn eyes could have melted the iceberg that sank the *Titanic*. For a five-year-old, she articulated every word ridiculously well. But what do you expect from a preschooler who can do multiplication?

"Come on, Kylie, it'll be fun," I wheedled, but she darted out from behind her desk and made for the door. I chased her down, tackled her, and carried her back to her work sheet.

Where's her nanny? I mouthed at Sonal. She was checking algebra work sheets for a bunch of pimply middle schoolers. Sonal shrugged and pointed to the wall.

Nannies sometimes dropped kids off at math tutoring and took off for a coffee next door.

I didn't sign up to be a summer camp counselor like half my friends, just to avoid wrangling teeny kids. No younger siblings or cousins in the country meant I had no experience with little kids. Who knew that math tutoring would be full of them? More than half the kids who went to Ace Tutoring were elementary age or under. I felt bad for them—doomed to daily math torture for all of summer vacation. At least I got paid for it, and the kids were actually sweet. Turns out I'm not half bad at handling them.

My sister Vinnie and I are nothing alike, but we do have math in common. In high school she played every sport she could fit around her course load—field hockey, soccer, volleyball. I stuck to art, speech team, and drama club—painting sets, designing costumes, and putting makeup on Oompa-Loompas, Munchkins, and the lost boys from *Peter Pan*. But we're both math whizzes. She always was, and I became one because Dad would have been crushed if I wasn't, so I tried extra hard.

But I don't have the same nerd gene they do, the kind that makes them drop everything to watch *Nova* specials on things like the Andromeda–Milky Way collision or the structure of DNA. I'd rather watch an art restoration video on YouTube or a K-drama instead.

Kylie slaved through her multiplication tables, to both our relief.

"Gimme five," I said, and drew a smiley face on her work sheet. She slapped her dimpled hand into mine, ran over to the corkboard that said TODAY's GOOD JOB!, and pinned her work sheet to it.

"Hi, Mini Kapoor," said an apple-cheeked seven-year-old. Wide brown eyes gazed into mine, pools of unquestioning trust.

"Hi, Rahul Singh," I said. Rahul, my favorite student, had no problem being interested in doing his math. His mom told me he had trouble relating to his teachers at school, due to his Asperger's, but Rahul and I got along just fine—probably because math was his favorite subject. No surprise; Rahul breezed through his work sheet wicked fast and sat smiling at me as I marked it—he had gotten everything correct.

"Is this getting a little too easy, Rahul?" I asked.

"Yes." He nodded solemnly. He tapped his digital wristwatch. "Only took three minutes and forty-two seconds for twenty-four problems."

"That is fast!" I said. It was definitely time to move him up to something more challenging. I walked over to the huddle of moms and nannies in the waiting area and searched for Rahul's mom. Some of the Indian moms were in the middle of an animated discussion about the merits of the latest Bollywood blockbuster, starring Koyal Khanna, the newest sensation to hit the silver screen.

"Have you seen *Meri Bollywood Wedding*? Where Koyal is a simple girl from Bhatinda who wants to have a real designer lehenga for her wedding and she runs away to Delhi to try and get one at a charity auction by the top designers. And she falls in love with this boy she meets there...."

"Yes, and that Mallika Motwani lehenga she gets finally was drop-dead gorgeous. Better than the Sabyasachi, and that's saying something! There's even a cameo of the designer walking around looking bossy."

"She didn't look bossy, she looked busy and preoccupied. She's a genius, that woman. All her clothes sold out, and they cost a fortune! I heard even Bollywood stars and celebrities have to beg to get one of her outfits."

I scowled. Busy and preoccupied was Mallika Motwani's natural state—I should know.

"Ahem!" I cleared my throat, not wanting to interrupt their conversation.

"Is everything okay?" Preet asked. Preet Singh was cheerful and outgoing, and completely devoted to her son.

"Oh, yes, super," I said. "I was actually wondering if we could skip ahead, move him up a notch. Rahul is ready, I think. He can do this without even trying."

"Oh!" She beamed. "Yes, if you think he's ready, then I've no problem." She had a pretty accent and an elegant head waggle to go with it.

"Yes, he's ready," I said. What a lovely hand-embroidered shirt she had on, I thought, and the woman beside her too. Gujarati mirror work, if I wasn't mistaken. I hadn't seen so many Indian outfits since my mother's one-year memorial.

So many Indian outfits! I looked around the waiting room. If someone here didn't know everything about Indian wedding vendors, I didn't know who would. Was it worth asking them? Meanwhile, Rahul had grabbed his mom by the hand and was tugging her toward the door.

"Preet!" I said. "I have a question...."

She looked at me inquiringly.

"My sister is getting married in two months," I blurted out. "I have to help her organize everything, and my dad...he's not much help. I don't even know where to start. Do you know how to find a good wedding decorator, or DJ, or caterer?"

"Your mom is not taking care of it?" she asked.

Was there any way to avoid telling her? I wondered, dreading the usual awkwardness that followed when I mentioned what had happened to Mom. If it'd been anyone but Preet I'd have found a way to avoid answering directly.

"She..." I squared my shoulders. "She passed away. Years ago."

Suddenly all the chatter around me hushed. Crap. What a dumb idea this was. Great way to identify myself as the clueless, motherless freak show. I wanted their help, not their pity.

The first one to speak was not one of the Indian moms but my boss, Sonal Saxena.

"Mini," she said. "I'm so sorry. But don't worry, *ya*? We'll help you."

The Indian moms unfroze into a chorus of me-toos. It was hard to make sense of all the chatter since everyone was talking at once, but apparently Preet's cousin owned a restaurant and catered at very reasonable prices, Pinky's sister had a bridal boutique in Cambridge, and the Srinivases' niece got married last month and they knew all the best wedding vendors.

Wow, they were more useful than two days of Googling. I grabbed a handful of Ace Tutoring of Westbury business cards from Sonal's desk and wrote my email address on each one. "Please email me any leads. Thank you!" I said, handing them out.

"So sorry, kutti," a very pregnant lady said to me with a tight hand squeeze. I nodded and squeezed her hand back and gave her a card.

"I know a lighting guy, honey," Kylie's nanny piped up unexpectedly. I promptly gave her a card too.

Time to get back to work. When I left an hour later, no-nonsense Sonal Saxena gave me a hug. "I don't want you to stress," she said. "If you need time off work, just tell me. And if you're not sure of anything, just ask. We'll help you." I walked out to my car. I'd look into their leads, of course. Their quick offers of help had nearly downed my automatic defenses. Nearly.

Yogi pounced on me when I got home—all licks and wagging tail. From the reception I got, you'd think he'd been locked up all day instead of having been walked once already and having had Dad for company as he was working from home.

"All right, all right," I told the beast. "At least let me get changed."

I got out of my responsible math tutor outfit—dark-wash jeans, dip-dyed T-shirt, teal Converse lace-ups—and changed into my new capris and crop top. Over it I threw on a ripped T-shirt made by my friend Shayla—she had dyed a regular cotton tee, shredded its sides into strips, and knotted them to fit me perfectly. If I had to walk the creature in a heat wave and get all sweaty, I planned to do it feeling comfortable and looking fine. Good thing my math tutoring and Etsy shop brought in enough cash to support my fashion habits. God knows Dad didn't give me enough of an allowance to buy anything decent.

The capris were a weathered purple—Mom would have called it baighani—and the top was a soft vintage tea-washed pink—Shayla is a genius with color. Silk, cotton, chiffon—she can dye them all. We have a sweet deal that I alter anything she needs tailored—hem jeans, sew pockets in dresses, custom-fit T-shirts—and she dyes fabric for me. I slathered on the moisturizer, the sunscreen, and the bug spray and added a slick of lip gloss, just in case.

The whimpering had turned into deafening barking. Yogi was clearly losing his mind.

"Let's go, Yogi," I said, and a blur of white fur streaked off for the garage.

A towel covered the back seat—my lame attempt at keeping the car fur-free. In spite of this, stray bits of white hair stuck to the mats on the floor. I'd have to vacuum them. Again. It wasn't easy to love a living shedding machine.

I backed out carefully into the street and headed for the campus. When I got my license Dad and I negotiated the places where I could go dog-walking. Dad shook a bunch of news reports (about girls who tragically vanished in the woods while walking their dog) under my nose and threatened to impound the car if I didn't comply. It wasn't fair that he never put restrictions on Vinnie. To be fair, she has a black belt in Kempo, while I only made it to a junior yellow with a stripe.

The town we live in is Westbury, not to be confused with Weston, or Sudbury, or any other of the extremely expensive towns in MetroWest Boston. No, Westbury is a middle-class enclave, best known for having the biggest and most upmarket mall in the Northeast, where the residents of the surrounding affluent towns can shop without fighting traffic gridlock in their own streets. Point being, except for the town woods there aren't many options for walking Yogi off-leash in Westbury.

But one of the spots Yogi and I loved was Lake Waban in our neighboring town of Fellsway. Half of it lay on the campus of Fellsway College. Given that the Fellsway student body is 99 percent female, though it's not called a women's college anymore, Dad felt better about my safety there than in the town woods.

Unleashed, Yogi took off up the track, fur bristling with happiness. I followed at a slower run, knowing he'd come back to me if I called.

Yogi and a brown-and-brindle Catahoula hog dog circled each other nose to tail as its owner and I exchanged a quick "*is he friendly?*" check. It was sweltering hot. I peeled off my top layer and stripped down to my crop top. I'd waited till five to take the dog out and it was still too hot. If I didn't love the blasted mutt, you couldn't have paid me to go out. Yogi leapt up a steep incline like a mountain goat, struck a gallant dog pose at the crest of the hill, and grinned down at me, radiating happiness. I grinned back and charged up the hill after him. Anything for Yogi.

When Mom and I picked Yogi out, he was a gangly puppy, all legs and floppy ears and whipping white tail. She knew by then that she didn't have much time, but when they leveled with her about her prognosis she went straight to the animal shelter. Did she know that with her gone, Vinnie in college, and Dad's long hours, I would need someone waiting for me at home? That I'd need something upbeat to talk about when everyone acted awkward around me? Other people with her condition would have gone all hyperclean and germophobic, but Mom got a not-yet-housebroken puppy instead.

Dad and Vinnie took Mom to the hospital for her surgery, chemotherapy, radiation, physical therapy. Mom and I took Yogi to Zen Dogs for obedience training. The nurses taught Vinnie to give Mom shots of painkillers, and how to operate the oxygen machine. Mom and I taught Yogi to fetch, sit, and stay. Okay, he never really got *stay*, but we tried. They brought the hospital bed into Mom's bedroom. Mom had the dog crate brought into my bedroom. Every morning when Yogi was let out of his crate he ran to Mom's room, jumped on her hospital bed, and spent an hour curled tight next to her. Until I called him to go for his morning walk. Then, one day when I called him, he didn't come. I walked into Mom's room in my pj's and found him curled up by her, not moving an inch. Just curled tight with his nose in his tail looking at me with sad, sad eyes. Mom's hand lay on his back, cold and still, her gold bangle gleaming against his snow-white coat.

I threw myself onto both of them and screamed. I could hear footsteps in the hallway as Dad, Vinnie, and the hospice nurse ran to us. Yogi stayed still. He didn't flinch or bark. If I'm brave enough to think back that far, I can still feel his warm tongue licking my face.

Now, I blinked away tears behind my sunglasses. Why did that memory surface just now? What was even the point of going there? Yogi was seven years old. We had all moved on.

A black dog bounded out of the undergrowth with a menacing growl. There was no owner in sight. Not again! If you think poodles are little lapdogs, you've never seen a poodle in a bad mood. We had run into this particular critter before. Who hurt her, I don't know, but for some reason she had it out for Yogi.

"Yogi, come." I didn't like the poodle's body language one bit. Yogi turned to me with cautious sideways steps, his eyes never leaving the dog.

He was nearly up to me when the poodle launched herself on him with a savage snarl. Yogi dived behind me. "Hey, hey," I said, keeping my voice gruff and my stance wide. "Cut that out!"

The poodle's white teeth snapped less than an inch from my ankle.

This was so not going to end well!

"Shadow!"

Finally! It was the owner.

"Get over here," she said to the dog. "She's not like that usually," she said to me.

Sure, lady. That was *another* animal who had attacked us the last time we'd met. And the time before that. Shadow retreated. "Come on, Yogi," I said as calmly as I could. "Let's go."

The magic words unfroze Yogi from cowering behind me, and we took off up the dirt path. The poodle and her person headed in the opposite direction.

I pulled out my cell phone with shaking hands.

"Hello."

"Shayla," I said, relieved to have someone to unburden myself on. "A dog just jumped Yogi."

"No way!" Shayla said. "Are you okay?"

"I'm fine," I said.

"What kind of dog?" Shayla asked.

"A poodle," I said, only to hear *laughing* at the other end. "It's not funny, Shayla!"

Meanwhile Yogi decided to run through the trees and assume the I'm-about-to-take-a-dump position on a manicured lawn with a series of signs nailed to the tree above it.

KEEP OFF THE GRASS

DOGS MUST BE LEASHED

NO TRESPASSING

I was so rattled I forgot that we had entered the on-leash section of the trail.

"Wait, Yogi! Yogi, STOP!" I yelled.

"What's up?" Shayla said. "Is the poodle back?"

"Call you back," I said, and herded Yogi off the grass. The lawn was unsullied by Yogi doo-doo. Whew.

"Go. Potty. In. The. Woods," I explained carefully. I think I may have made helpful hand gestures to help him understand.

"Good advice." There was a laugh hidden in that deep voice, even though it was trying to be deadpan.

"Thank you." I nodded civilly at the runner who tossed that at me as he jogged past.

But when he vanished into the leafy distance I freaked and screamed silently at fate.

Really, Universe, really?

Did *that guy* have to pass me at that exact moment?

This was even worse than our first meeting—and *that* is saying something!

I'd first seen mystery guy three weeks ago. I had taken Yogi out early that day, around 7:30 AM—it was that freakishly hot week in June when the temperature was into the eighties by nine. So there we were, having a nice cool early-morning run along the lake, with the sun just coming up, when what should we see but a cat—an enormous gray Maine Coon—just sitting in our path like it owned the place.

Now, Yogi is a sweet, friendly dog—he even gets along with cats if they're introduced to each other indoors—but he is, after all, a *dog*. And when a dog sees an unknown cat, he is morally obligated to chase it.

Next thing I knew, Yogi had bolted after the cat. The cat had morphed into a yowling, bushy-tailed puffball that sounded like it was being skinned alive. I chased Yogi, who chased the cat, and suddenly there was this great big hulking guy looming over us all. And then the cat jumped into his arms and magically calmed down.

I had grabbed Yogi's collar and was fumbling around trying to untangle his leash, so I didn't at first get a good look at him. Then I straightened up, fully apologetic about my dog's antics, and realized that the guy was wearing Burberry plaid pajamas and a Dr. Who T-shirt, and that he was barefoot, sleepy, slightly stubbly, and—even with a bad case of bedhead—utterly gorgeous. Also, he looked completely baffled.

"I'm *so* sorry," I said. "Is the kitty okay?"

The cat had attached itself firmly to his shoulder and was lashing its tail.

"He's in one piece, I guess," he said—and what was that accent—British?

The cat let out a bloodcurdling yowl that was straight out of a horror movie, and Yogi's hackles shot up from neck to tail. He tugged the leash so hard I slid to the ground and landed in a shallow puddle, splattering mud all over myself.

"Whoa! You all right?" the guy asked, keeping a firm grip on the cat.

"Yes," I said, getting to my feet red-faced and wiping a muddy hand on my shorts. There was definitely dirt on my face as well. "I'm fine."

"Nothing bruised or broken?"

"Nope!" I was too winded to say anything else, and it wasn't smart to stick around anyway. "Come on, Yogi!" I dragged Yogi away from the scene of the crime, jogging off with as much dignity as I could muster around the bend in the trail.

So there you have it—our first meeting—wherein my generally sweet-as-petha dog chased down his poor defenseless pedigreed cat, forcing him to come to its defense barefoot, in his designer pajamas, and me to trespass on private property to leash my dog before landing butt-first in a mud puddle and beating a hasty and disheveled retreat.

Not exactly a proper introduction, huh?

After that I saw him 3.5 times (the .5 was a day when I saw him but he didn't see me), and each time we simply nodded and smiled as we ran past in opposite directions. And now this. Not much of an improvement, frankly.

"It's all your fault, Yogi," I said. "Again!" And it was. But Yogi pricked his ears and cocked his head so trustingly that I couldn't stay mad. Time to call it a day—it had been a long one. I trekked back to the parking lot, feeling hot and sticky and cranky, and reached for my car keys.

Only, they weren't there.

Whaaat?

They weren't there!

Yogi whined, waiting for me to open the car door, and I had nothing. I racked my brain. I must have dropped them when the poodle incident happened.

Oh, crap.

Chapter Three

"They were right here!" I wailed, cell phone clutched to my ear. "Shayla, I swear!"

"I believe you, okay?" she said. "But I can't ditch my camp kids at River Bend and help you search. Just . . . keep looking."

"Will you give me and Yogi a ride back?" I begged. "I have a spare set at home I can try to find. If Dad realizes I lost the keys he's never going to believe I'm responsible enough to plan anything."

"I'll come get you, I promise," Shayla said. "Got to go."

I stuck my cell phone into my pocket and started over, slow-walking from the hill where the poodle had jumped Yogi, all the way to the lawn, eyes scanning the ground, searching for any glint of metal.

Straight into a sweaty chest. One that I would have seen if my eyes had not been glued to the ground.

I sprang back. "Excuse me!"

Way to go, Mini. Looking dorky twice in an hour to the same guy was a record even for me.

"You've lost something," mystery guy said. The deep voice sounded matter-of-fact, and yes, the accent was definitely British. "These, maybe?"

He was holding up my car keys.

Yes! I was not in trouble. I didn't need to call AAA. Or tow the thing back to the house and pay for a new set of keys. Dad didn't even have to know! I could kiss this guy. Well, he was pretty kiss-worthy anyway.

"My keys!" I said. "Thank you! I didn't think I'd ever find them."

"Hey, no worries," he said, dropping them into my grateful hands. "We've met before. Your dog chased my cat, right?"

I nodded. "For the record, that was totally out of character. Yogi's a really good dog normally."

"I can see that." He held out his hand. "I'm Vir, and you?"

Okaaay. Who shakes *hands* when they introduce themselves? No one I know under the age of twenty. And Vir—that was Indian, wasn't it?

"I'm Mini," I said.

"What kind of dog is Yogi?" I could tell by the way he said *dog* that he knew perfectly well that Yogi was a mutt.

"He's a rescue," I said. "A sato, from Puerto Rico."

"What are they?" he asked. "A designer breed?"

"*Sato* means 'street dog,'" I said. "There are too many strays in

San Juan so they fly them here. The dogs have a better chance of getting adopted."

"Makes sense," he said. I realized that he'd fallen into step next to me and seemed to be headed the same way as me, back to the parking lot. "You know what he looks like?"

"What?" I asked.

"A coyote," he said. "No—a dingo!"

"He's white," I said. "Dingoes are usually brown, aren't they?"

"He looks like a dingo that's been dipped in bleach," Vir said.

I laughed. "But his ears are brown," I said.

"He looks like a dingo that's been dipped in bleach and pulled out by his ears," he said.

"Okay—stop! That's just..." I spotted the amusement in his eyes. "You secretly think Yogi's awesome, don't you?"

"Who wouldn't?" he asked. "He reminds me of street dogs in India too, by the way."

"Are you Indian?" I asked.

He nodded. "And you?"

"Yeah," I said. "It's Mini Kapoor."

He still didn't crack a smile, but his shoulders were shaking with silent laughter. "You own a Mini Cooper," he said, pointing to the logo on my key chain, "and your name is Mini Kapoor?"

Didn't miss a thing, did he?

"Guilty as charged!" I said. "But if your dad's into British cars and you like Mini Coopers, you may as well own one, right? It would be silly not to."

He tilted his head, as if conceding a point. "You sure he didn't name you after the car?"

"My name is PADmini," I said. "Mini is just short for it."

"Nice name," he said. "And the car fits you, Padmini Kapoor."

"Thanks," I said. I could tell by the way he pronounced my name—he did it better than I could—that he had spent way more time in India than I had.

"Did you drive a long way to get here?" he asked.

"I live over the town line," I said. "In Westbury. And you?"

"There." He waved over his shoulder to the graceful old house on whose manicured lawn Yogi had nearly done his business.

"There?" I asked. "Wow, that's some house. I love the architecture! It's a Georgian Revival, isn't it? What is it—hundred and fifty, two hundred years old?"

He shrugged. "We only live there because my mom works at the college."

I stared at him with dawning realization. "Is your mom the dean?"

"Yes," he said.

"You're Gulshan Chabra's son?" I asked. "She's amazing. The first Asian American woman to be dean of Fellsway. The youngest woman to be provost at Harvard. I thought she was unmarried."

"She is," he said. No silent smile this time.

Awkward. But by now we had reached the parking lot.

"Oh, no!" I spotted a splat of bird poop on the windshield. Couldn't have that blocking my view! I unzipped a tiny pocket in my capris and extracted a Clorox wet wipe sachet I kept for emergencies.

"Could you please hold Yogi?" I handed Vir the leash and wiped off the icky stuff carefully. Done! I dropped the wipe in the garbage bin by the car.

Vir had been watching the proceedings with interest, Yogi's leash firmly in hand.

"If you have a pocket in those pants," he inquired, "why don't you put your *keys* in it?"

Because the towelette fitted flat and didn't look like I'd grown a lump, that's why.

"The keys don't fit," I explained.

"Really?" He leaned over to stare at the pocket, which, unfortunately, was located on my butt. "That material looks pretty stretchy."

I snapped straight, turning that part of my anatomy away. "I could stuff it in, but it would look like I've grown a lump or something," I said. "Look, it doesn't matter."

"Does your dad have other British cars?" he said, changing the subject smoothly. The silent laugh was back in his voice.

"A 1991 Lotus Esprit," I said.

"Sweet," Vir said. "Bond car, right?"

"Yeah," I said. "Most people don't know that, actually!"

"But it was legendary!" he said. "It turned into a submarine and took out a helicopter with a surface-to-air missile while *submerged*."

"I can see you know your cars," I said.

"As do you," he said.

"Didn't have a choice," I said. "I got dragged to the car shop whenever Dad wanted to tinker. He took me to all the car shows when I was a kid too—you know, at the Larz Anderson Auto Museum. Italian car show, German car show, but especially the British car show—Jags, Rolls-Royces, Aston Martins, they have everything. But I liked the Minis best."

"They suit you," he said. "The pocket rocket."

Was that a crack about my size, about the pocket, or something else? "I'm not exactly small!" I said, standing tall. He was still a head above me. Dang.

"That's what they call the car," he said.

"I know!" I said. It was way past time to end this conversation. "Listen, thanks for finding my keys. You've no idea how much trouble I'd be in if I lost them."

"Anytime," he said. "See you around the lake?"

"Sure."

"Dude," Shayla said. "Who was that guy?"

"What guy?" I asked. My cell phone had lit up five minutes after I left the parking lot.

"The guy hanging out with you in the parking lot," Shayla said. "Holding Yogi's leash and staring at your butt."

"You saw him?" I asked, mortified.

"I came by to pick you up," Shayla said. "Like I promised.

But you were standing there with the keys in your hand talking to him."

"Why didn't you come over?" I asked.

"Didn't want to break up the cozy chat you were having," Shayla said. "God knows you don't talk to many guys."

"I talk to Peter, and David, and Isaac. . . ."

"AP study group is not talking!"

"He found my keys," I said. "That's all. He wasn't, like, chatting me up, or anything."

"Sure he wasn't," Shayla said.

Shayla and I met in kindergarten, and we've been close since sixth grade. Back then we took Yogi for a walk every day after Dad got home from work. I rode ahead on my purple bike with the blue and silver handlebar streamers, and Dad and Yogi followed on the sidewalk. That was my favorite part of the day, way better than school, where people stared and walked on eggshells around me (Her mom, like, *died*! It's *so* sad!), and more fun than the quiet dinner and homework that came later.

Shayla's mom, Sue, always waved to us on our walks—which led to us stopping to chat, which led to invitations to cookouts at their house. The Siegels, Rachel's family, were usually there too. Shayla, Rachel, and I rode Razor scooters in the driveway while Dad tried to cope with stilted conversation that tiptoed around Mom's passing. I found out later that Sue's niece had died of cancer. All the people in our unofficial support group had been affected directly or indirectly by the disease. Shayla's cousin, Rachel's grandmother. They understood.

Anyhow, that's why Shayla knows me well.

"I mean it," I said. "He's not my type."

But I don't think I was convincing her.

"Look, I'm home now," Shayla said. "Can you come over? I want the deets!"

"Sure!" I said.

Chapter Four

I dropped Yogi home before going to see Shayla.

Who was in full-on interrogation mode.

"So he has a cat?" she asked. A Camp Woodtrail headband held her dark, springy hair out of her pretty green eyes—the better to quiz me with.

"Uh-huh," I said.

"And his mom's a dean, and he's into cars?" she said.

"Yeah," I said.

"Hmmm." Shayla analyzed the available information with care. "So, he's probably smart—because of Mom; kind—since he likes animals; he's athletic, he's cute . . . but is he seeing someone, or not?"

We both decided he must have a girlfriend. He hadn't made the slightest attempt to ask for my number.

"Well, at least you've talked," Shayla said, strategizing. "So *next* time you can—"

"No!" I said. "I may be prepping for the SAT again. And I've got too much to do for Vinnie's wedding. I'm not getting involved with anyone."

"But you finally found someone you LIKE," Shayla said. "It's like a miracle!"

"What's a miracle?" Sue, Shayla's mom, popped into the room and we dropped the subject. Sue, an avid quilter, is my sewing guru. She wanted to know all about what Vinnie was planning to wear to her wedding and fifty other things. I wished I had answers!

When I got back, the house was quiet.

No dog at the front door. No Dad either. But Dad had to be home because the minivan was sitting in the garage—he and Yogi were probably out for a walk.

I checked in the garage, just in case. God, Dad really *had* to clean the garage before the wedding! It was full of junk—car tires, garden tools, old files, computers. Even if he did, I'd still have to park my car outside. The Lotus was too delicate, and there was no question of putting the minivan outside.

I looked at my key bunch. Did I still have a key to the minivan? Yeah, I did.

On impulse I opened the door and turned the engine on. Familiar scents cocooned me. In the rearview mirror I could see the weathered Northwestern University bumper sticker that Mom had proudly placed on the back window when Vinnie had been accepted to Feinberg. Dad knew I wanted the minivan to be around to see me off to college and let me add my bumper sticker next to Vinnie's. Only then would he donate the minivan to benefit

WBUR, as Mom wanted. But it didn't feel right to be sitting in the driver's seat. I left the minivan in park and climbed over the armrest into the second row.

The thing was a time machine, I swear. If I closed my eyes I could go back to being ten years old. I could almost imagine Mom sitting in the driver's seat....

My eyes snapped open. No, the radio channel was wrong. I leaned over the armrest, turned off Dad's talk show station, and put on WBUR, Boston's National Public Radio station. A measured voice filled the van, talking about the Senate race. Yeah, that was right. I smiled, remembering the time when Mom called the number and got on air. How amazed I was that she could be right there in the car, driving me home from karate, and people all over Boston could hear her on their radios.

In here, I could admit it. I still missed Mom so bad that it hurt. And I was terrified that Vinnie was getting married. I was ten when she went away to college. That first summer...I wouldn't have made it without her. When she left for college, the house felt so empty with just Dad and me and Yogi. I always thought that when Vinnie finished med school I'd get her back. Then she met Manish, and now she was getting married—soon she'd be gone forever, or that's what it felt like, anyhow.

"Hey." Dad knocked on the window.

I rolled it down sheepishly. "Hey," I said. "I made sure the garage door was open so I wouldn't die from fumes."

"Good. But do you have to sit there with the engine idling?" he asked. "I thought you cared about global warming."

He knew very well why I camped in there once in a while. When Vinnie left, he sold his other car and made the minivan his daily driver. This is a man whose other car is a Lotus Esprit.

"I do," I said. "Just need a minute in the van."

He nodded. "I'm going in," he said. "Don't stay out here too long."

I rolled the window up and went back to listening to NPR.

"Our guest tonight is Shoma Moorty of Namaskar," the voice on the radio said. "Shoma, thanks for joining us today."

"My pleasure." The husky voice had a clipped New Delhi accent.

No way. That sounded just like Mom and Masi. What the heck was Namaskar?

"So what brought you into the wedding decorating business, Shoma?" the host asked. "And why only Indian weddings? Is there even enough business there to keep you afloat?"

"Enough business?" The rich laugh sounded familiar too. "We're so busy, David, that I have to turn events away. I'm booked solid months in advance."

"Really?" David asked, sounding intrigued. "I had no idea that Indian weddings were so big in New England."

"Most Indians here like to spend on two things, David," Shoma Moorty said with confidence. "Education and weddings. They may cut corners on everything else, but you won't find them letting their kids take out massive student loans or have slipshod weddings. Indian weddings are big business."

"How do you spell *Namaskar*?" David asked.

"*N, A, M, A, S, K, A, R, Namaskar,*" said Shoma. "You can find us online."

I slid open the minivan door, turned the engine off unceremoniously, and zipped into the house.

"Dad, pen!" I said. "Write this down."

"What?" he asked.

"*N, A, M, A, S, K, A, R, Namaskar,*" I chanted. "They're a local business."

"No need to shout," he said. "I know how to spell *Namaskar.*"

He typed it onto the iPad screen. "Here it is."

I grabbed the tablet from him and stared at the web page he'd brought up. It had a tasteful design with mango leaves, gold drapes, and a white horse wearing red wedding livery. I smiled at the image of the horse. "Jackpot."

"What are we looking at?" Dad asked.

"Wedding decorator," I said. "I found one."

Dad snorted. "It's going to cost us."

Us? That was a change! I looked at him questioningly. Could it be that he had finally seen sense?

"I guess we've got to do this right," he said gruffly.

"We do," I said.

"I used to know a Shoma Moorty," he said, reading over my shoulder. "When we lived in Brookline."

"Good," I said. "Because we need her to fit Vinnie into her booked-solid-for-months schedule."

"We have nearly two months," he said.

"Not enough," I said. "Not even close to enough."

"Speaking of Brookline," Dad said, "they're having the British car show this weekend. Do you want to go?"

"Do I want to go?" I said. "Do Louboutins have bright red soles?"

"Do they?" Dad looked doubtful.

I rolled my eyes at him.

"Yes, they do."

Chapter Five

I clutched the phone.

It was time to stop staring at the computer screen and actually, like, *call* the number I had up on it, but I was nervous.

The average budget for a wedding in Massachusetts was $35,000, as per Shoma Moorty on NPR, and the typical desi wedding, she said, was probably triple that amount. But Dad had only approved the baseline 35,000. How was she going to take that news?

Worst case, she'd blow us off.

I had a notepad and pencil out on the coffee table. The dog had been walked and fed and given a rubber toy to chew. I dialed. The call was immediately picked up.

"Shoma Moorty here," the voice at the other end said.

"Hi," I said, my voice a bit shaky. I cleared my throat. "I'm calling about a wedding in August," I said. "We need a quote for decorations." Could she tell it was a teenager at the other end?

Apparently not.

"What's the date?" Shoma said briskly.

"August twenty-one," I said. "Tentatively..." They hadn't set a date yet but I had to give her something.

"I'm sorry, I'm booked for that day," she said. Great, the conversation hadn't lasted even a minute and she had already panned me. "Can't do the twenty-seventh of August either, that's the Patel-Bernstein wedding," she added. "How about August twenty-eighth? I've had a cancellation."

"Sure!" My voice was squeaky with relief. "August twenty-eighth would be great!"

"What's the venue?" she asked. Was she taking notes?

"We have some places in mind," I said, fibbing freely, "but we haven't booked a place yet."

"Sure, sure," she said. "Are you the bride?"

"No, the bride's sister," I said. Guess my grown-up act was going over pretty well.

"And your name?" she asked.

"Mini, um...Padmini Kapoor," I said.

There was a pause at the other end. When she spoke, her voice had lost its impersonal, businesslike tone. "You're not Megha Kapoor's daughter, are you?" she asked.

"Um, yes," I said. Guess Dad was right about knowing her. "Dad said you were our neighbor in Brookline, but I wasn't sure you'd remember." I was glad she'd made the connection.

"Of course I remember!" The warmth in her voice sounded

genuine. "So it's Vinnie that is getting married? Why isn't *she* calling?" She remembered Vinnie's name too.

"Vinnie is in Chicago," I said. "She can't really get time off her residency to come here. So Dad and I have to."

"But you're just in high school, no?" she said.

"I am," I said, trying not to sound defensive. "But there's no one else."

"What about your grandmother?" she asked.

"Beeji and Bauji moved back to India," I told her. "The winter was getting too much for them."

"Are they coming for the wedding?" she said.

"Well," I said, "they don't know about it yet. It was all kind of sudden."

"Who's the boy?" she asked. "He's Indian, isn't he?"

Guess the number one reason not to tell the grandparents about a wedding is that the boy or girl isn't Indian.

"Manish Iyer," I told her, settling her suspicions on that score. "He grew up in Newton."

"Oh, Manish!" she said. "I've known him since he was little. Very nice family. They're from my community, Tamils, you know."

Wow—I would never have guessed! Shoma sounded more Punjabi than any South Indian—Tamilian, I guess I should say—I'd met. Maybe she grew up in Delhi or something.

"We don't really"—I hesitated—"understand their customs properly."

"Yes, yes, Tamil weddings are quite different from Punjabi weddings," she said. "Have you talked to his parents?"

"No," I said. "We've only met once."

"His sister got married last year," Shoma said. "I decorated for them, of course. They spent *lavish* amounts of money on her wedding. It was at the Hyatt in Boston. Huge mandap, three priests, four-day event. Very expensive."

"Three priests?" I said. "That seems, um, excessive. Anyway, we really don't have that kind of budget."

"Oh," she said. "Well, I can work with any budget—it just reduces the options. Just tell me what you want to spend and I'll work with that."

"Dad just founded a new technology start-up with two of his friends." I backpedaled, trying to set low expectations so she wouldn't be shocked. "He's the CTO, and he's putting money into it right now, not the other way around. If things work out he may start paying himself, but for now..."

"All these techie start-up types." She sighed. "Wasn't Vinod with some big corporation?"

"He was. But this start-up was made for him. So he locked down my college fund before investing in the company," I said. "That's why, for the wedding, it isn't going to be more than thirty, thirty-five thousand total." About the price of one semester of college, according to Dad, and all he was willing to spend right now. Better let her know what she was dealing with!

She whistled. "That's going to be hard," she said. "But we can do something, beta. Listen, why don't you come to my office and we'll run some numbers, okay?"

At least we were on board with one of the top wedding decorators in New England. And she knew Mom. Vinnie would be so impressed with how well I was doing.

"Sorry, Sonal!"

I was late for work again.

Ten hours a week of part-time work isn't a lot, really, but it felt like I hardly had time for it anymore.

"It's okay," Sonal said. "Just call me next time you're late. What's new with the wedding?"

"I've found a wedding decorator!" I said. "An Indian one!"

"Namaskar, or Ayojan?" Sonal asked without lifting her eyes from her paperwork.

"Namaskar," I said. "I didn't know about the other one."

"Oh, there are more than two!" Sonal said. "But Shoma Moorty has been around the longest. She does the Miss India New England pageant, you know? And she was the *India New England* Woman of the Year—twice."

"Yeah, and she knows my dad, apparently," I said.

"She knows everyone!" Sonal said.

Rahul ran in and took a place at a desk. He was early today—the center had just opened.

"So sorry we're early," Preet said, following him in. "We have to go to my cousin's daughter's birthday party in the evening. I'm going to tell him everything about the wedding, Mini. Did you call him?"

"Um, no," I said. "Not yet."

"Call him," Preet said. "Sher-e-Punjab on Route Nine. I know it doesn't look like much, Mini, but trust me. Bhai makes the best food outside Punjab, I promise. And he will give you the family rate, I promise."

Rahul fixed solemn eyes on me and said, "Rajinder Singh makes the best samosas in the USA." I smiled. That child spoke only the truth, this I knew.

"If you're recommending him, Rahul, then I'll definitely call," I said. "I promise."

My second job—not a proper job, actually—is at my friend Rachel's mom's business, a fashion consignment store called the Turnabout Shop. I work for Amy there on weekends, sorting and evaluating clothes and accessories, and I do alterations if someone needs a garment fitted. It's pretty high-end for a secondhand shop—we only take new or lightly used designer wear from the past two seasons. I can basically set my hours because it's hard for Amy to find people who know fashion like I do.

I don't get paid for my hours, only for the alterations, but I do get dibs on new stock and a 50 percent staff discount! It's not easy to find things in my dress size, but I can usually alter anything to fit, if I really like it. I find it fun to take apart a high-quality garment and decode how the pattern is pieced together. When I explained it to him once, Dad said it's like engineering in fabric. He even got hopeful for about a nanosecond about my following in his tech footsteps before I put that to rest. I've scored a ton of cool accessories too. Last month I got "paid" by buying an almost-new handbag—spearmint green, bow-bedecked, and totally awesome—*every* girl should have one quality accessory with a stylized version of a bow. And I got a pair of bright red ballet flats. All for a grand total of $15. Total win!

I missed Rachel, though. Of my two friends, Shayla's more like Vinnie—there are some things she'll try with her look, but mostly she plays it safe. But Rachel is an experimenter—she takes *risks* with style. Sadly, she was in Israel for the summer with her pals from Camp Micah. It wasn't half as much fun finding a gem of fashion at Turnabout without her around.

I still liked being there, though. Amy always has fresh flowers and lit candles and bowls of candy at her store. It's so nice that people like to come in just to browse. She also stocks hand-crafted jewelry from local artists and vintage items—my staff discount applies to those as well.

"Mini, there's a bunch of pants that need hemming," Amy said. "I pinned them to the right length, could you do them today?"

"Sure," I said, and took the stack of clothes from her. "Any news from Rachel?"

"Nothing new," Amy said. "But she'll be back soon, so we'll get it firsthand."

I nodded and went into the office, where the sewing machines were set up next to racks of clothes that had to be sorted through before being moved up to the shop floor.

"Hey, Bobbin." I patted Amy's cat, who was also the Turnabout Shop's store cat. He stretched and came over to watch me sew. He found scissors, thread, pins, and fabric endlessly interesting.

"Nicely done." Amy put a cup of freshly brewed tea next to me and looked over my shoulder.

"This is a bargain," I said, checking the price tag that was still attached to the pants I was sewing.

"Making fashion affordable, that's us." Amy smiled. "I'm taking Bobbin home; he needs his dinner. Will you close up the shop when you're done? And have a look through the new stock, in case you like something."

"Sure," I said, grabbing Bobbin off my lap where he had settled and handing him to Amy.

Later I went through the boxes of new stuff, folding and organizing and putting aside a couple of things I liked. Amy would look them up and price them and if they were in my price range, I might get them.

Honestly, I would much rather buy one expensive versatile piece, new or used, than twenty bits of fast fashion. Not that there's anything wrong with basic clothes, especially once I've altered them! I'm more against the horrible way workers down the supply chain get treated and how wasteful consumerism is in general. Thrift stores recycle fashion and give them a second life, and I'm so there for it.

Speaking of being there, I had to hurry home—I'd promised Vinnie I'd video chat her after work.

Vinnie *still* hadn't seen the jewelry.

She had been so busy lately she hadn't even found time to call. She was packing up her old apartment and moving in with her friend Shinu, also a first-year resident, until the wedding. Shinu was closer to the hospital and to Manish's apartment.

I turned the laptop on and waited.

Vinnie was in shorts and a cami. Behind her I glimpsed a room crammed with packing boxes. I grinned—it was good to see her!

"Hey, Vinnie," I said.

"Hey," she said. "Awww, Yooogi!" She made kissing sounds as I pointed the laptop webcam at the dog. He whined, because he had no clue how Vinnie's voice was magically coming out of my computer.

I put the computer back on the table.

"How did it go at the bank?" she asked.

"Great!" I said. "Wait a sec and I'll show you." I ran to my bedroom and grabbed the jewelry boxes, which had been lying on my SAT prep papers ever since I unearthed them from their hiding place in the house. "Here, look!" I carefully unwrapped the beautiful necklace tagged with Vinnie's name and held it up to the webcam.

"Wow!" she said. "Hold it closer, Mini. Turn it a bit? Oh, I remember that necklace so well! And the bangles and the earrings!"

"Me too," I said.

"But you were so little...," she said.

"I still remember," I said. "And Mom left notes in each of the boxes. Look at this...." I clicked open another jewelry case and unfolded the note inside it. "'You won't believe it, girls, but this necklace is actually one of your nani's anklets,'" I read from it. "'She had them made into matching necklaces for your masi and me. Anklets are supposed to be silver. In the old days you were not allowed to wear gold on your feet—unless you were Rajput.'"

"That's so cool!" Vinnie said.

"She says I can have it," I said. "She based your necklace design on it. See how the pattern repeats all the way around, just like an anklet? And it has tiny bells!"

"Show me more!" Vinnie said.

So we played dress-up for a bit, with me modeling all the heirloom jewelry like a five-year-old with a Disney Princess Dress Up box and reading out Mom's notes to Vinnie.

"Where are you keeping these, Mini?" she asked suddenly. "What if the house gets burgled?"

"Don't worry." I grinned. "I used Beeji's trick."

Beeji, our grandmother, sealed her jewelry in a Ziploc bag and buried it at the bottom of the basmati rice bin—I wasn't her granddaughter for nothing.

I put the jewelry away—it was time for business.

"Listen, I talked to a wedding decorator and her rates are pretty reasonable. But we need to get her a date and a venue and a head count, ASAP. Have you figured out what day works for you and Manish?"

If the twenty-eighth didn't work for her, we were sunk.

"It'll have to be a weekend at the end of August," she said.

"How about August twenty-eighth?" I asked. "It's a Sunday."

"I *think* that'll work," Vinnie said.

"Good." I grinned again. "Because it's the only day she can fit us in!" Guess it was meant to be!

"Awesome!" Vinnie said. "Having an actual date makes it seem so real!"

"How many days will you have off?" I asked.

"Only three days and the weekend," she said. "So we can fly out on Wednesday of that week and be back Monday."

"No honeymoon?" I asked.

She shrugged. "We're cool with that."

Knowing Vinnie, I could believe it.

"So, what about the guest list?" I asked. "You want to make sure that your must-have guests can make it."

"I'll call everyone," she said.

"How about Beeji and Bauji, and Nanaji, and Mallu Masi?" I asked. "Dad hasn't called them, you know."

"I'll talk to them," Vinnie said. "Masi already knows...."

"You talked to her?" I was amazed that she'd told Masi before our grandparents.

"Yeah," she said. "Hey, we should send out a save-the-date card."

"I've got it," I said, making a note on my sketchpad. "Aaaand, the venue! Shoma said Manish's sister got married at the Hyatt on Memorial Drive—would you like that? Or do you want me to scout other places?"

"It's a nice hotel, I guess." Vinnie hesitated. "But it's so beautiful in Boston in summer—I wish we could have an outdoor wedding. I've no idea where, though. And I don't want to make more work for Dad...."

"I'll ask around," I said. "And see what's available. But we have to move fast, Vinnie. These things are usually booked solid months in advance."

"Sounds like you're doing everything," she said. "Is Dad going to help?"

"He will," I said. "It's just that he's busy. And he's still coming to grips with it, you know. It was kind of a shock."

"Yeah," she said. I could see by the unhappy shadow that had come over her face that this was troubling her.

"What about a wedding outfit?" I asked, changing the subject. "Will you wear a lehenga?"

She hesitated. "I thought we could ask Mallu Masi...," she said. "She does work in fashion."

"Really?" I said. She was going to ask Mallu Masi, Mom's flaky sister. The one who was so busy and preoccupied that she didn't even show up for Mom's funeral. I knew Vinnie spent a lot more time with her than I did, but, *Really?*

"Look, you don't remember her much," Vinnie said, "but I do. All those vacations in Delhi, before she moved to Mumbai, when she was just starting her business, she was so fond of both of us. She always said she's the one who should have had the girls, not Mom."

"She hasn't bothered remembering us since you went to college," I said.

"She's never forgotten my birthday," Vinnie said.

"She's never remembered mine," I said. It was true. She was oh for six on getting it right.

"I'll be at orientation, or sleeping, during waking hours in India all week." She gave me the Look. "Maybe you could talk to her?"

Me? I cringed at the thought. But she was right that no one else but Mallu Masi could get us a wedding dress from India. I didn't trust Beeji to pick out anything remotely suitable. Mallu Masi was our only safe choice.

"Look," I said. "I'll talk to her—for you. But FYI, there isn't enough money in the budget for a Mallu Masi dress. They are insanely expensive even if she gives us a discount."

"Oh! I was thinking," Vinnie said, tucking a hank of hair away from her face, "that I might even fit into Mom's instead!"

"Mom's wedding lehenga?" I asked.

She nodded. "Can you get it out of the attic?"

"You're sure it's in the attic?" I asked. It could be anywhere. It could even be gone—Dad had given away boxes and boxes of old clothes to Goodwill recently.

"I remember Mom and Dad packed it away," Vinnie said. "Just check it out. It's worth a shot."

"Okay, I'll look," I said. I didn't want to put a damper on

Vinnie's idea by telling her about Goodwill. "Vinnie, put your hair down!" I said. She had it up in a scraggy ponytail, as per usual.

"Why?" she said.

"Just do it!" I said. "I want to see how much it's grown."

She dragged the hair tie out of her hair and her thick hair sprang out, framing her face. She had actually let it grow!

"I know, it's a mess!" she said, snaking a hand through it self-consciously. "I haven't gotten around to cutting it for months."

"If you *dare* snip an inch of it, I will personally fly to Chicago to murder you," I threatened her. "Don't you touch it until after the wedding."

"Okay, okay!" she said. "Jeez!"

"How's Manish?" I asked. I didn't see any sign of him anywhere.

"I've been talking to him," Vinnie said, "about the guest list."

"And?" I prompted.

"He's got a huge amount of family and friends in Boston," she said.

I groaned. I didn't like where this was going. "Okay, so?" I said.

"His sister just got married a year ago and they invited four hundred people," she said.

My jaw hung open. "Four. Hundred. *People?*"

"He said they could keep it down to one fifty for our wedding," Vinnie said.

"One hundred and fifty people!" I said. "You know how much that would cost?"

"I know, I know," Vinnie said. "Look, we can just get married on a beach out in the Caribbean. As long as Dad and you are there, I don't need anyone else."

"No way! What about Beeji and Bauji?" I said. "What about Nanaji? What about your Mallu Masi?"

"*Our* Mallu Masi," Vinnie said. "They can come too!"

"So, bottom line: We have to include everyone, or you're getting married on a beach?" I asked.

"At least half of them?" Vinnie said. "And Mom's old friends from dance school, and Beeji and Bauji's friends."

It was completely crazy! "If we invite all of them we'll have a hundred and fifty people of our own!"

"Somewhere there," Vinnie admitted. "But you know, Mini, not everyone will be able to come! There's going to be at least twenty percent who won't make it."

"We can't do anything until we have a head count," I said. "Not even send out save-the-date cards. Can you and Manish put together a guest list? And I'll start on everything else."

"And just talk to Mallu Masi," Vinnie added. "I'd do it, Mini, but honestly I have no time!"

"Yeah, yeah. Fine!" I squared my shoulders. "I'll talk to her."

Chapter Six

I hate her. I totally hate her!

I paced up and down the immaculately vacuumed carpet and then threw myself onto the couch. It was not going to be easy, but I'd promised Vinnie.

How ironic! There was a time when I couldn't wait to see Masi, when I hung on her every word. But that changed the winter after Vinnie left for college.

I flipped open my battered MacBook and adjusted the screen. I had spent the whole morning obsessively cleaning the house, as if someone were actually coming over. I'd even washed and waxed my car—washed the dog too, since I had the garden hose out. But it was only a virtual visit—she was going to see my face and shoulders, and approximately ten square feet of wall behind me, total. I put my bottle of Poland Spring down by the laptop, clicked my Zoom window open, and waited for the tone to ring.

I couldn't even exchange ten words with the woman, and now, for Vinnie, I had to beg her for handouts.

The singsong tone rang loudly, nearly making me choke on my gulp of springwater.

The video chat window popped open. "Answer with video?" it asked politely, and I clicked OK.

I expanded the video window to full-screen and waited for the screen to refresh.

"Mini? Are you there?" a familiar voice said. It killed me how much she sounded like Mom, when no two women were ever less alike. "I can't see, beta."

"Just give it a minute, Mallu Masi!" I said. "It'll come up soon."

And there she was. Mallika Motwani, in the flesh. Dark shoulder-length hair with classy caramel highlights, her fine-featured face a younger, feminine version of Nanaji's. She had a huge pair of very stylish glasses perched on her nose. Hello? Who wears sunglasses indoors? Apparently she wears anti-glare glasses so she can bear to look at a computer screen.

She pulled them off to reveal wide brown eyes, just like Mom's—and mine. I noticed Masi's had a few more lines around them than I remembered.

"There you are! Mini!" She smiled. The office behind her was tastefully decorated. Was that a real M. F. Husain hanging on the wall? For all I knew, the master artist had been a personal friend of hers or something. She certainly didn't have to spend an hour vacuuming and mopping and picking up, like I did. No, Mallu Masi had a live-in housekeeper, a driver, a cook, a gardener for her penthouse terrace garden, a massage lady (I kid you not), and sundry other specialized servants. Some of this isn't out of the ordinary for even middle-class India, but Mallu Masi was definitely not middle-class.

I nudged the wet mop gently away with my toe so it wasn't visible leaning against the ten square feet of wall behind me.

"You look great, Mini," she pronounced. If I didn't know better I'd have said that her cheerfulness sounded a bit forced, just like mine. I wiped the sulky look off my face and tried for a genuine smile. It wouldn't do to look rebellious if I was trying to get something out of her.

"Thanks, Masi," I said. "So, Vinnie's wedding is most probably going to be on August twenty-eighth." No point beating about the bush. "And she really needs a wedding lehenga. I know it takes months to custom-embroider one—but is it possible to get one off the shelf?"

She ignored me completely and asked a question instead. "Who is this boy Vinnie is marrying? Why didn't anyone tell me about him?"

"*We* didn't know about him either, Masi." I forced myself not to sound impatient. Vinnie had been over this with her, surely. "Vinnie kind of sprang it on us, you know?" I tried to steer the conversation back to the lehenga. "Um, Vinnie is going to be home next week. Could we pick a few options for her to look at? And did you get my email with her measurements?"

"Yes, yes." She waved one bejeweled hand. "I got the email. Don't worry, we'll fix Vinnie up. And we can look at everything I have in stock next week—whatever she wants. But what about the boy? Is he...nice?"

"Yes, he's nice." I didn't know Manish well enough to give him a ringing endorsement, so I went over his basic résumé instead. "He's a doctor. He's twenty-seven years old. He was one year ahead of Vinnie in med school. He's a second-year resident, at the same hospital where Vinnie is doing her residency."

"But where is the family from?" she prodded. "Has anyone checked them out?"

She called Vinnie exactly once a year, and now she wanted to "check out" the family of the guy she was marrying. What next? Was she going to arrange a marriage for me?

"They're from Newton, Masi," I said. "Newton, Massachusetts."

"No, no, where are they from *in India*?" Masi said.

Oh, that.

"They're, uh…Tamil?" I said, trying to remember what Shoma Moorty had said. "His name is Manish Iyer."

"Iyer!" she said, her face clearing. "Yes, they're Tamil. TamBrahms."

I probably looked confused because she added, "It's short for Tamil Brahmins."

"Okay," I said. Not that I cared about caste or anything, but it felt oddly nice that someone had a clue about where Manish's folks were from, geographically speaking. Apart from Newton, Massachusetts, that is.

"They'll probably want her to wear a Kanjivaram sari for the wedding," she said.

"What's a Kanjivaram sari?" I asked. I'm always interested in fabrics, and though I knew a lot about saris I hadn't heard that term before.

"They're very rich handwoven silk saris," she said. "Like a South Indian version of Benarasis. You know what those are, right?"

I did. Mom had some. One of them even had real gold thread woven into the border.

"Aren't they kind of heavy?" I asked.

"They are," she said. "I'm not sure Vinnie can handle that. She should wear a Punjabi lehenga—one of mine, of course—I can make it as light as she wants. The wedding customs should be from the bride's side of the family, no? After all, we're hosting."

"About that," I said, remembering how the moms at Ace talked about the movie where some girl was hell-bent on buying a Bollywood lehenga from designers like Masi—*Meri Bollywood Wedding*, or something. "Mallu Masi, how much would the lehenga cost? Or that sari you're talking about. We can't really afford an expensive lehenga, you know."

"Cost?" Mallu Masi said. "You think I'm going to charge my own niece for her lehenga? It hasn't come to that yet!"

I fist-pumped just out of the camera frame, startling Yogi. I had been hoping she'd say that. But it was a relief nonetheless. Vinnie could have a gorgeous Bollywood-style lehenga—for free!

"Thanks…Mallu Masi," I said.

"No problem, Mini," she said. "Just tell me when you need it. Did you look at the link to the latest bridal line I sent you? Which one does Vinnie like?"

Shayla and I had spent a half hour looking at the bridal line and being shocked at the insane prices.

"I'll send you a short list of lehengas to pull," I said. "I'd love to see her in the A-line lehenga on page four. She doesn't think she'll like gold, but she'd look totally hot in it, if you ask me." I stopped for a second—no point getting all excited in front of Masi.

"She will," Masi concurred. "Good choice, beta. That lehenga was actually featured in a movie recently. I do have one or two pieces left I could have fitted for her."

Funny that we were sympatico on this when I couldn't remember ever having a grown-up conversation with her—about anything.

"Then her bridesmaids could wear saris too, in a complementary color—it'll look so nice in all the pictures," I said.

"Aren't you the bridesmaid?" Masi asked.

"Yes," I said, "but you can have multiple bridesmaids here. People do—all the time. She has friends from high school she wants to include."

"American girls?" Mallu Masi said. "You sure they'll wear saris? Who's going to tie it for them?"

I suppressed a flash of annoyance. "I will," I said.

"You know how to tie a sari?" she asked.

"It's not that hard," I said, feeling defensive. "When I was nine Mom taught my whole Girl Scout troop how to tie them. I'm pretty good, actually."

"Oh!" she said. "And Vinnie?"

"Vinnie never learned," I said. "She was too busy with sports and studies to do Girl Scouts."

"One time I came to visit," Masi said, "and your house was full of cookie boxes. Hundreds of them."

"Mom was cookie mom that year," I said. The memory almost

made me smile. "We had to sort them out and collect the money for the whole troop."

"I should have just stayed in New York," Masi said. "She had no time for me and I put on two kilos from eating those things. Caramel deLites, no? They were good!"

Mom had no time for her? That was rich coming from the sister who didn't even visit Mom on her deathbed. I fumed inwardly but bit my tongue.

"I remember, Masi," I said with a tight smile. "Can we talk next week when Vinnie gets here?"

"Of course we can. But you know, Mini," she said, "the best thing would be if she came down here for a fitting. That's the right way to get a custom fit."

"She can't do it, Masi," I said. "But don't worry, I've taken the measurements very carefully. And if something needs fixing we can get it altered here. But we need it here in good time to do that."

"Okay," she said. Someone appeared at her elbow and put down a tea set. The kind in period dramas, with a pot in a tea cozy, and a fine bone china teacup and saucer. And a creamer and sugar bowl. "One sugar," she said absentmindedly to the person next to her; I could only see the torso.

"What about you, Mini?" she said. "What will you wear for the wedding?"

"I haven't thought about it, Masi," I said. There wouldn't be enough money left for a pair of shoes after we were done, to be honest. Forget about a full wedding-worthy outfit.

"I can pick something out for you," she said. "Something that will complement Vinnie's look but not overshadow it." Her face brightened up. "In fact, I have just the thing for you, Mini."

"No, really, it's okay," I said. The whole thing was awkward. What if she picked out something hideous and I was stuck wearing it? "You don't need to bother."

"No, no," she said. "What size are you? Same as Vinnie?"

"No, I'm about five inches—" I said. Her cell phone rang.

"—bigger? Got it," she cut in, glancing at her cell phone. "I have to go, beta. Sooo sorry. But I have to take this call. That's the waist size, right? Lehengas are free-size anyhow, so it should fit if it's in the range. Okay, done!"

The screen flickered off.

"Five inches *taller*," I said to the empty screen.

I felt drained. I flipped down the lid of my laptop and punched the air. Arrgh! Why does she get under my skin? Why is she so... Both my hands formed into fists.

Who knew what old junk she was going to send me? She did have good taste, though, however irritating and preoccupied she was. Truthfully, I was a teeny bit excited to see what she could possibly think was perfect for me.

The day of the British car show dawned sunny and clear.

Dad was relieved because he didn't like to take the Lotus out in the rain. We headed out to Brookline right after breakfast. Yogi and I stuck our heads out the window as we flew down Route 9—our hair (or fur in his case) flapping in the wind.

The Larz Anderson Auto Museum has the feel of a castle on a hill. It's a stone building overlooking a vast green park with an outstanding view of the Boston skyline. I'd been to these car shows many, many times with Dad, but it was always fun to ride over to the showground in Dad's Lotus, even with Yogi stuffed beside me into the passenger seat. You're ridiculously low to the ground, and the engine (even with only four cylinders) has enough oomph to launch you into orbit around Earth. Maybe not actually, but you get what I mean.

Once there, Dad parked the Lotus in a carefully selected shaded spot, and we walked around and looked at all the cars, and the people, and the dogs. Personally I liked the dogs almost as much as the cars. There were always lots of them at the car show.

Dad ran into Ernie Uncle, one of his friends who owns a garage that specializes in exotic cars. He's always fixed all our vehicles—even Mom's minivan, though he rolls his eyes about it. I wandered off with Yogi to get myself some guilty treats—warm honey-roasted nuts and a stick of cotton candy. Something that shade of neon pink couldn't possibly be good for you, but it tasted wonderful!

I was busy eating the cotton candy or I would have seen that Dad was now talking to that guy. Because it was him—you know—whatshisface from Fellsway.

"Hi, Mini," he said. He looked great in cargo shorts, a T-shirt, and Teva sandals. I wasn't surprised. A guy who looked good in pajamas with a stubble and bedhead could look good in anything. Meanwhile, I was a fashion disaster.

In my defense, even someone who gives a damn about personal style doesn't dress up when they're going out with their *dad*. I wore well-worn cutoff jean shorts, a Red Sox T-shirt, and $1 flip-flops and had my hair up in a goddamn *ponytail*. Tiny Percy Jackson and the Olympians–inspired earrings that I had owned since sixth grade dangled from my ears. In other words, I looked like a twelve-year-old, and I carried, as you might recall, a bright stick of cotton candy that was just then probably the same color as my face.

"It's Vir, right?" Apparently I could still talk while in shock, and remember stuff.

"Yogi's behaving well, I see," Vir said.

"Thanks," I said. "He's been here every year since I was ten, so he knows the rules. And he does behave well most of the time— you just haven't seen him at his best."

"I was just talking to your dad," Vir said, "about his car."

He leaned in a little and smiled, causing momentary confusion and tongue-tiedness in me. "Are those Ferrari earrings? No, those are Pegasuses...or should that be Pegasi?"

"They're from when I was younger," I explained. I was so going to bury these at the bottom of the basmati rice bin!

"You liked mythology?"

"Just Rick Riordan, to be honest." I'd read all the books. Mom had read most of them to me, actually.

"Same!" Vir grinned. "Blackjack, right?"

I nodded and smiled back.

"I'm sure Dad liked talking about his car." I sneaked a look around to scope if he was here with anyone. No girlfriend in evidence as far as I could see.

"He did," Vir said. "Actually, I had one more thing to ask him."

He walked back to Dad and the Lotus. I stood there for a moment—undecided—then shook my head and went off to get some lunch instead of following him. Yogi whined as I pulled him away.

"You'll like a hot dog better than him," I told Yogi, and got a sizzling-hot one for him and one for Dad. By the time I got back to the car, Vir had vanished.

Dad took the hot dog from me.

"I just met the nicest boy, Mini," he said. "He knew more about cars than most kids these days. Remembered the Esprit from *The Spy Who Loved Me* and everything."

I'm sure he did, Dad. I'm sure he did.

Chapter Seven

It was the farthest I had driven on my own—ever.

Since I could pretty much stay on Route 27 all the way to Shoma Moorty's office, Dad said it was okay for me to go by myself. I even put on the radio station instead of driving in total silence, fists clamped around the steering wheel, the way I used to last year.

It was easy to find the little strip mall. There were a real estate agent, a dental office, and a florist on the bottom level. Namaskar was in a suite on the second floor. I smoothed my hair down once nervously and rang the bell. "Coming!" Yes, that was Shoma Moorty's voice, all right.

She opened the door. She was very tall. Her kohl-rimmed eyes had hanks of spiky hair falling into them. Yoga pants, sweatshirt. Lots and lots of gold chains. Barefoot. Huh! I mean, I hadn't expected her to be wearing a sari or anything, but this was not what I had visualized either.

"Come in, come in, Mini," she said. "You have Vinod's height, but you look just like your mama."

"Really?" It was a compliment—we both knew it. "Thanks for saying that."

"Your sister takes after your dad," she said, "soccer player and smart, and all."

"Hey, I'm smart," I said.

"Yeah," she said. "But"—she gave me the once-over—"you have style. Like I said...you're like your mom."

Couldn't argue with that.

"Masala chai?" she asked.

"Sure," I said, looking around the large, sunny space.

She padded off to a kitchenette.

Her office was hung with giant pictures of wedding mandaps. They looked like Bollywood sets, glitzy and *completely* over the top. No way Vinnie would get married in something like that.

"So, Vinod doesn't want to pay for Vinnie's wedding?" she said. "I should call him and straighten him out."

"You have Dad's number?" I was shocked.

"*If* it hasn't changed," she said. "It's been years, though. How's he doing? Since Megha passed, he's not been in touch with anyone."

I guessed that by anyone she meant anyone Indian. "I know," I said. "He didn't really feel like going to, you know, Indian get-togethers, for the longest time. Dad doesn't cook, for one thing."

"Or return phone calls," she said. "No, I understand. It's always the women, beta, that keep the social circle going."

"Vinnie kept in touch with some of her Indian friends," I said, a bit defensive. Vinnie had grown up in and out of all these Indian people's homes because Mom was around for practically her whole childhood. It was me who was stuck with Dad and his lack of desi social skills. After Dad stopped going to the gatherings Mom used to take us to, and hosting any of his own, we gradually stopped seeing any Indian people at all.

Vinnie kept in touch with her friends via emails and Facebook, and she made even more Indian friends in med school, but my friends gradually became school friends and neighborhood friends. It didn't help that I dropped Indian dance too. Without Mom or Vinnie to ferry me there after school, and no one close enough to carpool with, it was too hard to stay in the class.

Dad still feels bad about that, I think, since that was another one of the things Mom and I shared.

"Never mind, beta," Shoma Moorty said. "At least she found an Indian boy. That's more than so many of our girls are doing now."

"I guess," I said. Though what was wrong with a non-Indian boy, I couldn't fathom.

"So where are you thinking of booking?" she asked, handing me a cup of steaming masala chai that she had conjured out of her kitchenette. "Does she want to be closer to Newton or Westbury? There's the Newton Grand, or the Crowne Plaza, and the Westborough Villa has really reasonable rates."

But Vinnie wanted an outdoor wedding. The picture she'd sent me that morning of her and Manish on a hiking trail at sunrise flashed before my eyes. Vinnie was SO not a cookie-cutter, five-star-hotel-ballroom-wedding kind of girl.

"I don't think a hotel will work for her," I said. "Someplace natural and green, and outdoors. All this"—I gestured, somewhat apologetically, at the walls of glitzy Bollywood sets—"this really isn't her style."

If Shoma Moorty wasn't willing to offer anything other than the mandaps on display, I would try making one. A basic bamboo structure and a ton of fresh flowers ought to do it. Rachel's aunt had had a homemade canopy for her wedding—I think the Jewish name for it was huppah. We could probably even rent one from a temple, come to think of it.

But to my surprise, Shoma Moorty didn't look at all offended. "I give them what they want," she said. "Most people want what they see in the movies. All gold-shold, and tamasha." She shook her head. "What to do? It isn't my job to judge."

"Really?" I said.

"Yeah. And don't rule out hotels, beta," she said. "Most outdoor locations don't have waitstaff, or linens, china, and silverware—you have to truck everything in. Some insist on their preferred caterers, so you can't have Indian food. But hotels usually allow Indian caterers, and some have gardens available for the ceremony. That can work out really well."

"Do you have a list of hotels I can research?" I asked. "Dad and I can shortlist them for Vinnie, and she can pick the final one."

"Sure, I'll email you a list. What's this?" She pointed at my sketchbook. She had a good eye, that woman.

"I have some ideas about mandaps, Aunty. Can I call you Shoma Aunty?"

"Of course," she said. "I'm older than you, aren't I?"

I opened my little folder and pulled out a sketch or two. "These are some of my ideas. This one is a basic bamboo structure draped with sheer tasseled silk drapes. And another idea is to have four real trees be the basic structure of the mandap and have flower garlands to connect them together."

"Hmm," she said. "I could do the first one really easily. I have a simple mandap that we could cover with silk. I have the sheer drapes in old gold and I'd add a cranberry-red fabric for a pop of color. Can I keep this picture?"

"Sure!" I said. I was thrilled that she was open to trying it.

"How much would it"—I gulped, dreading the price tag—"how much would it cost?"

She tilted her head and considered. "For the mandap, and the wedding garlands—I have them flown in fresh from India—and some table centerpieces, and a guest book..." She paused. "Five thousand, beta, for you."

I was frozen to the spot because it was a lot less than I expected. She must have given us a huge discount. "Okay, I'll let Dad and Vinnie know."

It was hard to start narrowing down venues when I didn't have a final guest list—but I had to make a start somewhere. From the list of hotels Shoma Moorty sent, I marked off three venues that fit Vinnie and Manish's requirements:

1. Reasonable cost.
2. Close to Westbury and/or Newton.
3. Catering by an outside vendor (Indian) allowed.
4. Outdoor garden or patio for the wedding ceremony.

This last one was the hardest. Most hotels didn't have a garden large enough for a mandap and all the guests. The ones that did tended to be in Cape Cod or Western Massachusetts—too far to work for us—but after a dozen phone calls and massive amounts of Googling I found three that looked promising. I set up appointments for us—Dad was supposed to come check them out with me, but of course he canceled.

So there I was at the Newton Grand grown-up and organized (I hoped) in a sleek blowout, dress pants, and pumps.

I clutched my folder nervously and approached the front desk. I had taken ten pictures of the parking lot and the lobby. Evidently Ragini Aunty, Manish's mom, liked the Newton Grand, and it was halfway between Westbury and Newton, so at least it worked location-wise. But how much would it cost?

"I have an appointment with the event manager," I told the receptionist.

"Mini Kapoor?" she asked, and I nodded. "She'll be right down."

When the event manager showed up I was relieved to see that she was quite young. Right around Vinnie's age.

"Hi! Is it Mini?" She took me under her wing. "Let's start at the ballroom, shall we?" And soon we were examining the ballroom, which could accommodate two hundred to five hundred guests, and yes, the linens, silverware, and waitstaff were included in the price. We could book hotel rooms for out-of-town guests at discounted prices, and they would throw in a room for the bride and groom for free. My head was spinning with the details she tossed out—how on earth did she have everything memorized?

I took notes and snapped pictures diligently. It was right on the highway, but that probably made it easy to get to, and Vinnie would love the view over the Charles from the big windows!

"Where is the garden?" I asked. The garden would make or break the deal.

"Come right this way," the event manager said. We took the elevator down to the ground level and walked outdoors.

A neatly mowed strip of grass rolled gently down toward the river. It was small—that was my first impression. There were pretty azalea bushes, and tall pines overhead, and the water of the Charles lapping the end of the lawn, but when you turned away from the river the hotel loomed over everything. I tried not to let my disappointment show. It could work—maybe—but it was far from perfect. I clicked a bunch of photographs, angling the shots away from the building.

"Nice, isn't it? We've had lots of Hindu weddings here." Her upbeat attitude was starting to annoy me. Especially since two mosquitoes had bitten me on the ankle in the five minutes we'd been standing there, even though I was wearing full-length pants. The pretty backdrop of the river definitely had a downside—it turned the garden into bugsville. "This space works really well for the moondaap."

"Mandap," I corrected automatically.

"Right!" she said. "Would you like to go over the rates now?"

The pumps might have made me look older, but they killed my feet. I limped back to the parking lot, got into the car, and yanked off the heels so I could massage my ankles. I had to get going if I didn't want to be late for work. Luckily the hotel wasn't too far from home. Well, if you drove like a normal person—which I didn't! Couldn't wait for the day driving would feel as natural as walking. Definitely wasn't there yet.

That's how I took the wrong turn at the intersection with Route 128 and ended up on the highway instead of going over it—it was confusing, okay? Next thing I knew, cars were zooming alongside me at warp speed and I was either going to have to speed up or get run over. I shifted into fourth gear and caught up with the rest of the roaring traffic. I looked for the next exit, but I was in the wrong lane and there was a huge tractor-trailer in the next lane blocking it. Dang! I kept going. How far could it be to the next exit?

I stepped on the accelerator and suddenly I was enjoying myself instead of panicking. I liked the feeling of zipping along in my Mini. That thing could go! I turned up the volume on the radio.

However, the gas gauge was dipping into dangerous territory—*way* less than a quarter tank of gas—even though my reserve light had not as yet turned on. I had to get off the highway and figure out how I was getting home. And get some gas, in case I was actually, like, lost. And call Dad so he wouldn't freak. And also break it to my boss that I wasn't going to get to Ace.

I managed to get into the rightmost lane, in position for the next exit. The reserve tank light was now on—blinking red on the dashboard. Great—now I had less than a gallon of gas left!

I pulled off onto Route 2. Where was that—Lexington? I grabbed the cell phone—no bars, no service whatsoever! Where was I, and why hadn't I brought the GPS like Dad had asked me to?

I kept driving, and a street sign went by that looked familiar. Wasn't Ernie Uncle's garage somewhere here? Sure enough, there was the sign for ERNIE'S AUTOMOTIVE—the place where I learned to change oil and a flat tire and helped Dad fix the radio on the Mini. The red neon sign that said OPEN was like a homing beacon.

I pulled in, parked, and got out on shaky legs.

I wandered onto the shop floor—a couple of cars were up on the lifts getting some work done—and opened the door to the office. "Anyone there?"

"Heeey, Mini." It was Ernie Uncle, wearing neat blue overalls, his broad face lit up in surprise. He did a double take when he saw my outfit. "Whoa! You look fancy! Car doing okay?"

He had no idea how happy I was to see him.

"Car's fine, but it could do with some gas," I confessed. "It's running on fumes!"

"Minnnni!" he said reproachfully.

"Look, I'll be more careful in the future, okay?" I said. "And my cell has no service. Can I use your phone?"

"Sure you can," he said.

"Thanks!" I dipped a hand into the candy he always keeps on the check-in counter, feeling like a kid again. "Dad?" I said when he picked up. "Dad, don't get mad! I'm at Ernie Uncle's. I took a wrong turn onto the highway. No, I'm fine. I just want to let you know because I'll be late and I didn't want you to worry. No, Ernie Uncle is filling up my gas; will you pay him next time you're here? ... Yes, I know how to get home from here!"

I also called Sonal, who was far more understanding than I deserved, then left the office to find Ernie Uncle.

He was all excited about some Indian car he'd just been working on.

"It was an Indian SUV," he said. "The Mirchandani Stinger. Am I saying it right?"

I shrugged. "Don't ask me!" I said. "I've heard Dad talk about them, though. They use them in the army, I think. The Indian army."

"Neat little thing," Ernie Uncle said. "It's no Hummer, of course, but it's well-built. Anyway, what I want to tell *you* about is the guy!"

I raised my eyebrows. "What guy?"

"The guy who brought it in. His dad owns Mirchandani Motors, dude!" Ernie Uncle said. "Good-looking kid—can't be much older than you. He's coming back on Saturday." He rocked back on his heels, looking proud of himself. "Want me to introduce you?"

"No way!" I said. "Will you please stop acting like my grand-mother? She wanted to set me up too—with Chintu Patel."

Ernie Uncle waved off Chintu Patel impatiently.

"This guy isn't just Indian, he's nice, incredibly smart, and probably very rich," Ernie Uncle said.

I laughed. He really was acting like my grandmother, which was both hilarious and endearing. "I really appreciate the thought, but. Not. Interested!"

"Fine," Ernie Uncle said, resigned to my indifference. "Hey, do you need any help with the wedding? Anything we can do?"

"No, we're good," I said.

He nodded. "You're all set with the car. Give me a call when you get home, okay?"

"Thanks," I said. "I will!"

I could see him grinning in my rearview mirror as I turned back onto the street. I had to add three more names to the guest list—Ernie Uncle, his wife, and his daughter. That made 183. Yikes!

Chapter Eight

"Well?" I waited for Vinnie's reaction.

I had just uploaded two hundred pictures of the Grand onto Facebook Messenger for her to see. "Do you think it'll work?"

I didn't mention the mosquitoes—yet. Why muddy the waters before giving the place a chance?

"It's nice." Vinnie didn't sound too thrilled. "It would be really convenient, and the price isn't bad...."

"But...?" I said. I could tell there was a *but*.

"But it's not really atmospheric," Vinnie said. "You know?"

I sighed. "I know," I said. "Onward, I guess."

"But it is such a good rate," Vinnie said with forced cheerfulness. "Maybe we should just book it anyway?"

"Not yet," I said. "Let me check out the other options."

"But it's taking up all your time," Vinnie said.

"So?" I said. "We're not booking anything until we find the perfect place, okay?"

"Okay," Vinnie said, and that was that.

I Googled venue options until I was cross-eyed, and fell asleep exhausted. This was so much harder than I thought it would be.

In another week things were no better.

The Westborough Villa had the most delicious chocolate walnut cookies on the planet, and a really cute patio, but though it had some pretty flower beds, it was completely paved over with no grass lawn. It also had a fabulous view—of the parking lot! The Four Seasons and the Boston Taj were just too far from Westbury, and too damn expensive. The Hyatt was where Manish's sister got married a year ago, and though I loved driving down Memorial Drive to look it over, and it had a lovely view of the Charles and the Boston skyline, it really didn't have a garden option, so it wasn't for Manish and Vinnie.

By the time I had been through five hotels and their event managers, I was feeling like a pro.

But still no deal.

It was thanks to Yogi that we cracked the venue in the end.

I came home from yet another venue-scouting trip to find Yogi looking all hangdog and miserable. Usually he jumped up and fawned all over me, but today he barely lifted his head. Guess he thought I was going to ignore him again.

"Aww." I stroked his soft ears. He gave me a look of utter resignation. That settled it. I was exhausted, but I couldn't let him down again.

"Just give me a minute!" I dragged myself off to my bedroom and changed into shorts, a tee, and running shoes. I slapped together a sandwich in the kitchen and wolfed it down with a glass of cold milk, then grabbed Yogi's leash. He leapt off the couch, ears up, tail lashing. Now he got it. He could smell honest intent a mile away.

"Where to?" I asked as we set off. "Fellsway College or River Bend?"

We hadn't been to River Bend in a while, what with work, wedding research, and SAT prep. Shayla probably thought I'd abandoned her for the summer.

I cut through the scenic but narrow Pond Street and turned into the River Bend reservation—the home of the Massachusetts Botanical Society. There was a pretty little bridge over the Charles before a long one-way loop took us past the stately old manor house—its last owners had donated their estate to MassBot—and finally to the canoe launch site's parking lot. The place is really beautiful and peaceful—usually. Not that day, though. Camp Woodtrail was in full swing and the grounds were overrun by kids, kids, and more kids. I slowed down to ten miles an hour so they could see me coming.

"We—are—TI—GERS!" chanted a bunch of ten-year-olds. "Mighty, mighty TI—GERS!" I peeked around the crowd of kids and spied Shayla leading them on, along with a couple of other camp counselors. She was yelling louder than the rest of them, her face red with heat and effort.

I slowed to a stop, rolled down the window, and waved at her frantically. "Shayla!" I said. "Here!"

She jogged over to the Mini. "Where've you been?" she said. "I haven't seen you in days!"

"Wedding stuff," I said apologetically. "It's driving me nuts!"

"You brought Yogi-wan-Kenobi!" she said. "Want to walk with us? Wanna go walkies with Shayla Aunty?"

"With all of you?" I scanned the kids milling around her. "Is that a good idea?"

"Sure!" she said. "The more the merrier."

I parked the car and Yogi bounded out grinning like a wolf. A couple of kids looked alarmed. "He's friendly, see?" I put Yogi in a sit and let them pet him. He was really patient, putting up with ten hands at a time patting.

When we got to the wooded trail along the river I let him off-leash. He bounded away and raised his leg at a large pine tree. A couple of kids broke ranks to chase after him. "Timmy," Shayla yelled, "get back here. Stay with the group."

Yogi quickly figured out that staying a hundred feet ahead of us meant he'd be unbothered by the kids and promptly took the lead.

"So, tell me what's up," Shayla said. "You've nailed everything down yet?"

"We—are—TI—GERS!" The kids kept up the refrain as they marched.

"Nailed down?" I wailed, yelling above our background noise. "Are you kidding? I don't even have a venue yet."

"I thought you looked up tons of places," Shayla said. "Is Vinnie being fussy?"

"Not really," I said. "She wants an outdoor wedding, that's all, and all the places in our budget have the lamest gardens." I shook my head. "Or they're on Cape Cod or in Western Mass or something. Nothing close!"

"What about here?" Shayla asked.

"Here?" I asked. "What do you mean?"

Shayla crossed her arms and stared me down. "I mean River Bend!"

I stared at her stupidly. "What?" I said.

"River Bend!" Shayla repeated. "Don't you know they do weddings?"

"NO WAY!" I said. "I did NOT know that! How come it doesn't show up on any of the wedding sites?"

"Because it's members only," Shayla said. "But membership at the Massachusetts Botanical Society is only ninety bucks a year. Not bad, huh? And they have different options—you can put up a tent in the gardens, or have it in the Italian Garden by the manor house. You know—the one with the big fountain? I've seen five weddings here since camp started!"

My heart was suddenly hammering. Yes! That felt right. River Bend was where Vinnie spent half her school years, playing soccer and field hockey and whatnot. Mom even came here for one of Vinnie's big games. She had the biggest smile on her face as Vinnie pushed her wheelchair around the field for a lap of honor. She had on her brand-new wig, a lovely Audrey Hepburn–esque pageboy style, made of thick, beautiful hair—Vinnie's hair. If you didn't know that Mom had lost her hair from chemotherapy, you'd never have guessed it was a wig. Vinnie looked strangely grown-up in her new bob—she had always had hair halfway down her back before then. Afterward, she never grew it long again.

Indian men sometimes shave their head in mourning after the death of a close family member. It was almost like Vinnie kept her hair short in mourning for Mom. That's why I was so determined not to let her trim her hair again. She had to grow it out—thick, long, and beautiful—in time for her wedding. Mom would have wanted her to.

"Do they have an indoor space?" I asked. "In case of rain?"

"I think they use the Carriage House," Shayla said. "You know, the one where they have the Christmas tree festival."

I remembered the space. It was a huge hall with really high vaulted ceilings. With some draping and lighting and decorations, it could be epic.

"Shayla, you're a genius!" I said. "I'm going over there right now!"

"You're welcome!" Shayla said.

I called for Yogi and took off down the trail in a run. Behind me I could hear the chant of the kids fade away. "Mighty, mighty TIII—GERS!"

You'd think Vinnie might have seen it in all those years she played soccer at River Bend—but no. It was so well hidden by the tall hedgerows on either side that unless you knew the way in, you'd never even guess it was there.

Chapter Nine

Venue finalized, it was time to move on to other vendors.

I had been trying to get a response from Vinnie's preferred caterer, Curry Cuisine, for over a week. Sondhi Jr., the dude I kept reaching, wouldn't give me a quote without Papa's input, and Papa seemed too busy to write up quotes.

Vinnie wanted them mainly because Manish's mom had recommended them. They had catered Manish's sister's wedding. So if I could get them to return my calls, we were probably going with them—even though Sher-e-Punjab, the guy Preet had told me about, was much more reasonable.

But since Curry Cuisine was still dragging their feet, even after five messages, I decided to go over to Sher-e-Punjab. Just in case.

I knew where it was, of course. It's the kind of place you pass before stopping at the next fancy new restaurant that has popped up on Route 9. Those fancy restaurants vanished as quickly as they appeared, but Sher-e-Punjab never changed its signage or paint or decor and yet stuck around year after year after year. It was a mystery, really, how it stayed in business.

I was surprised. It was bright and cheerful inside, in spite of the plastic flowers on the tables and the backlit Golden Temple poster on the wall—or maybe because of them. I could hear Gurbani music playing in the kitchen and voices chatting in Punjabi. There was no one in sight—I guessed they had only just opened for lunch—but the buffet was well stocked with glistening, aromatic curries that made my mouth water, not to mention warm, crusty garlic naans, fragrant rice, and heaps of red tandoori chicken. It smelled wonderful—as good as my Beeji's kitchen, and that's saying something.

"Hello?" I called out.

The curtain parted and a middle-aged man with a beard, a handlebar mustache, and a prosperous potbelly appeared behind the counter. He wore a Sikh turban in a delicate shade of periwinkle blue. So the picture of the Golden Temple wasn't only for decoration. I hadn't realized that Preet was Sikh because Rahul's hair was short and he didn't wear a turban.

"Yaas?" the man asked, his accent as thick and earthy as makke di roti made of the finest Punjabi corn.

"I wanted to get a quote on a catering order," I said.

"Okay," he said. "What would you like?"

"You have a catering menu?" I asked.

"No," he said. "We've been meaning to get one, but"—he shrugged helplessly—"it's very hard to do everything."

"I can tell you what I'd like," I said. "We'd like to have a vegetarian meal. Rice, naan—"

He cut me off. "For how many people?" he asked.

There it was again—our stumbling block.

"About one hundred and eighty," I said after some mental calculations. "Give or take thirty or forty people."

He raised his eyebrows. "I'll have a firmer count soon," I promised. "We're working on it."

"It's okay," he said. "No problem. You can check what you'd like on this menu?"

I grabbed the piece of paper and looked it over.

"Tussi Rahul di teacher heinna?" he asked in Punjabi, surprising me.

"Haanji," I said automatically before switching back to English. "Rahul's mom said you have the best Indian food in Boston." How did he know Preet had sent me?

He chuckled. "Maybe not the best Indian food," he said modestly. "But the best Punjabi food, we have it, yes."

Not so self-deprecating after all.

"Preet said so many times you would come," he added. "Unne appko describe kiya si, that's why I could recognize you. She's our sister, cousin sister. We give you the best food, and the best rate. Family rate."

"Oh, thank you." I was floored by his warmth after getting the runaround for days on end by that snooty Curry Cuisine. "I'm sorry I can't order from you for the wedding, but I need catering for the mehendi also."

I was going to give Sondhi Sr. one more day. If I didn't hear back from him in twenty-four hours, we were booking with Sher-e-Punjab.

Vinnie was swamped, what with her orientation at the hospital, and Dad had a conference call with Intel Capital ("It's really important, Mini!"), so I finally ended up totaling it myself.

If I included the cost per person, the waitstaff, the dosa chef, the china and linens charge, and the gratuity, we were still under $9000. It was another $1500 if we brought the guest list up to 180 people—which was the maximum number of people the Carriage House at River Bend could hold for the wedding reception.

Dad and Vinnie would hire whatever vendor I recommended. They were just too busy to do any of the organizing themselves. I was tempted to have them check out Sher-e-Punjab. Thanks to Preet, the rate they were giving us was out of this world! But there was the whole business of the South Indian food, and the recommendation by Manish's family...It was a lot to think about.

Also, today was the big day when I was getting my SAT results back. How I did was going to decide how I spent the rest of my summer: slogging to retake the test or finishing up planning for Vinnie's wedding. I checked the time on my cell phone. One hour before I could log in to College Board and get my result. I covered my face with my hands and screamed silently but looked down when I felt a paw on my knee.

Chapter Ten

Yogi was right, the best place to look up my test score was outdoors walking, with just him for company.

I grabbed the leash and my car keys and headed out the door.

Just turning into the parking lot by the athletic field and seeing all the tall pine trees in the distance made me feel better.

I unclipped Yogi and he ran off ahead of me. We both knew the path well by now. First there was the gentle uphill, then a steep descent with a spectacular view of Lake Waban. Then a wooden boardwalk over wetlands, filled with rushes, ducks, and wetland birds, followed by a long, level stretch along the south side of the lake. After that we entered PRIVATE PROPERTY, where the NO TRESPASSING, DOGS MUST BE ON A LEASH signs were nailed to a gazillion trees.

I didn't want to have to bother with holding on to Yogi, so I veered off up a hill track away from the lake. After a steep incline, it went along the spine of the hills surrounding the lake. Great view, cool breeze, no bugs, and Yogi could run free—what could be better? I could even scream out loud if I got a horrible score.

I found a cool, shaded rock to sit on. Yogi was still unleashed, but he never wandered too far from me.

I checked my phone—still half an hour to go. Better put that time to use, who knew how much time I'd have after I checked College Board. I pulled out my notebook and pencil and started to make a list.

- Date: Sunday, August 28th
- Venue: River Bend/MassBot
- Wedding decorator: Shoma Moorty of Namaskar
- Guest list: Finalize numbers, get addresses.
- Invitation cards: Have Vinnie approve design.
- Food (Indian vegetarian): Sher-e-Punjab for mehendi, Curry Cuisine for wedding
- Wedding cake: Check out the bakery recommended by Amy.
- Wedding dress: Masi
- Priest: Krishna Ji, Sherwood Temple?
- DJ/Lighting: ???
- Photography: ???
- Hotel rooms & transport to MassBot for out-of-town guests: Westbury Plaza
- Alcohol/bartender: ???
- Licenses: Wedding license, alcoholic beverage license, etc.

I went back to chewing the end of my pencil. Time to pencil in some numbers. Next to *Wedding decorator: Shoma Moorty of Namaskar*, I put $5000. Next to *Venue: River Bend/MassBot*, I put $7000. Next to *Wedding dress: Masi*, I put FREE. Next to *Food (Indian vegetarian): Curry Cuisine for wedding...* I put $10,000. I had three quotes, and two contracts signed and ready.

"Hey." The warm voice was just next to my ear.

I dropped my notepad. I knew that voice, that accent—it was Vir.

"Hey," I said.

"Haven't lost your keys today, huh?" he said.

Running shorts and shirt and muddy sneakers again—and he still looked hot.

I picked up my notepad and looked away. "Not today," I said.

"What's that?" he said, looking over my shoulder.

"That's private," I said, clutching the notepad to me.

He held up both hands, laughing. "Okay!" he said, heading back to the walking trail.

Oh, no, he was going away!

It would be weird to tell him about the wedding or the SAT, but I wanted him to stay. Let's face it, I needed distraction.

"I'm just sketching, actually." I turned the page hurriedly to a sketch of Yogi I had done the other day.

"Wow!" he said, examining the page closely. "That's amazing. You're really talented!"

"Thanks," I said.

"Are you in art school or something?" he asked.

"I wish!" I said. "I'd like to apply to design school, but I have to convince my dad it's not for deadbeats first."

"It's your life," he said. "You should apply. Totally!"

"He's paying for college," I said. "He wants to make sure I manage to get skills I can earn a living with."

"Like what?" Vir asked.

"You know—engineering, medicine, law." I counted them off on my fingers. "The usual things you're allowed to do if you're Indian."

Vir laughed. "But you've clearly got talent." He turned a page to another sketch. "That's awesome!" He flipped another page. "What's that?"

I snatched back the notepad. "Nothing!"

"It said 'Wedding checklist'!" He looked surprised. "What does that mean?"

"It means that it's a checklist for a wedding," I said. He wasn't the only one who could be sarcastic.

"Aren't you a bit young for that?" he said.

"Vinnie's wedding," I explained. "My sister?"

"Your sister's wedding!" he said. "Of course. How come she isn't planning it, then?"

"She's starting residency on July first," I told him. "In Chicago. And her fiancé is a second-year resident. They don't have the time to plan it, so I'm helping out."

"So big sis got into medicine, huh?" he said. "Is that why you're not applying to design school?"

"I never said I'm not applying," I said.

"Okay, I'm confused...."

"It kind of depends"—I checked my phone. Yikes, my test score had been out for fifteen minutes already!—"on what I get on my SAT."

"Oh, when do you find out what you scored?"

"Right now." I took a deep breath. "They just released the score, but I haven't looked...yet."

"Aah," he said. "Nervous?"

I nodded.

"It will be fine," he said. "Really! Just look, okay? Do you want me to go?"

"No!"

"No?"

"I'm going to sign in," I said. "But I'm terrified to look. Can you...check it for me? If it's over 1490, give me a thumbs-up, if it's below, a thumbs-down."

"There's nothing wrong with being below 1490!"

"My sister scored 1590, for context...."

"Damn. What a beast!"

"Yeah. But I'm not anywhere near her level. Okay, I'm logging in...." I handed him my phone. "Check!"

He took my phone without a word, his face serious. I stared at him as he tapped through the screen.

"Sooo?"

He broke into a sudden smile and held his hand up for a high five. "Sorry, thumbs-up, right?" He gave me an enthusiastic thumbs-up. "It's 1510! Look!"

"I scored over 1500?" I grabbed the phone and checked for myself. It was true. "Yes! Thank goodness! I'm so happy!"

We grinned at each other.

"Congratulations." He held out his hand and pumped mine in a handshake. "Well done you!"

"Thanks, and what is it with you and handshakes? Honestly?"

"School culture?" he said. "Speaking of which, where do you go?"

"Westbury High," I said. "And you?"

"Nowhere," he said. What? I must have looked confused because he added, "I took a gap year. After being stuck on a boarding school campus in the Thar Desert it was nice to have a break, you know?"

"Cool," I said. "What did you do?"

"Worked in Mumbai for ten months," he said. "And traveled—Australia, Singapore, UK…"

"That explains the British accent." I nodded wisely.

"Very funny!" he said. "The British accent is from living in England. I grew up there. Lived in other places since, but it kind of stuck."

"So, are you going to school in the US?" I asked. If not, he'd be leaving soon….

"Yes," he said. "Starting in fall."

"At Fellsway?" I asked.

"Yeah, right!" he said. "No way I'd go there!"

"It's officially coed!" I said. "I've read their prospectus!"

"Any college where my mum is dean is not for me," he said. "Ever!"

"Where *are* you going?" I asked.

"MIT," he said.

"Impressive," I said. "Wait, so what did you get on your SAT?"

"Same as your sister." He grinned. "Also 1590. Weird, right?"

"Now who's a beast?" I said. "And after telling me not to stick to the doctor/lawyer/engineer mantra, you want to be an engineer?"

"Why not?" he said. "It *is* what I want. That's what matters!"

Shayla was right about him being smart as well as cute. He had that casual aura of self-assurance that comes from having it all.

"I guess!" I said. "Congratulations. It's really hard to get into MIT. What's their acceptance rate? Like nine percent or something?"

"Where are you applying?" he asked. "Do you have a college list yet?"

I could actually think about finalizing a college list now that I had my SAT score, though I still had to wait to see how I scored on my AP Studio Art portfolio and my other AP exams.

"Fellsway, for one," I said. "Put in a good word for me with your mom, will you?"

"Fellsway doesn't have a design program," he said. "You should be applying to Parsons, or FIT, or Rhode Island School of Design, or—"

"I know what the good design schools are," I said, raising an eyebrow. "But Fellsway is close to home, so I can still see Yogi—my dog, you know—and my dad too. Why are you dissing the school, anyway, when your mom runs it? Jeez!"

"None of my business, I know," he said. "But you have talent, clearly. Don't sell yourself short!"

"It's not like I haven't thought about it," I said. "I have a portfolio from my AP Studio Art classes and I'm hoping to finish some new pieces over the summer. I'm definitely going to apply. And if I get in—I'll see how I feel then."

"Good plan," Vir said.

"You must have been in some Indian weddings," I said, changing the subject. "Any tips for me?"

He made such a horrible face that it made me laugh.

"Like weddings that much, huh?" I said.

"I didn't mind so much when I was a kid, but now...," Vir said. "Hey, why aren't your parents planning it?"

I rolled my eyes. "Dad's hopeless," I said. "And Mom's not around."

"Oh." He didn't ask for details. "I'm sorry."

"It's okay," I said.

"Divorce?" he asked. "Not that it's any of my business." Funny he assumed that.

"It isn't that," I explained. "She passed away." I'd had a lot of practice saying this, and it had gotten easier to say. "It's been seven years. Right around the time my sister took her SAT, and she still got a 1590. If not for that, she would have scored a 1600 for sure."

"That's amazing," he said.

I nodded. I was so proud of Vinnie. Not only was she smart, she was genuinely committed to helping people.

"So, your father hasn't remarried?" Vir asked.

"Nah," I said. "Mom was the love of his life, evidently."

"He's lucky to have had her," he said. "It must have been hard."

"It was years ago," I said. "It's fine now. We're over it."

"Uh-huh." He wasn't buying my we're-fine line, I could tell.

"Okay, so maybe we're not," I said, surprising myself. Weren't we? "I mean, how do you get over something like that?"

He said nothing, just tapped my list. "You still need a DJ?" he asked. "Hire me."

"You're a DJ?" I said. "What do you charge for a gig?"

"Charge?" He looked blank. "Oh, I'll give you a discount on whatever's the going rate. I just haven't had a chance to, you know, cost it out."

I raised an eyebrow. "You have references?"

"Not in Boston," he said. "Like I said—I'm trying to get the business started."

"You're making this up, aren't you?" I said. "What kind of DJ are you that you don't even know what to charge?"

"The cut-rate kind." He grinned. "The kind people pay with free dinner."

I didn't know if he was being serious or not. "I'll think about it," I said.

He grabbed my notepad and wrote *Vir* and a phone number next to the DJ line.

"I'll do a good job, I promise," he said. "Try me."

His eyes smiled into mine and made me feel warm from head to toe.

"Okay, I'll think about it," I said.

"Let me know what you decide," he said. "I better get going." He turned to head off down the trail. "I'm a good DJ, remember," he flung over his shoulder.

I stared at his retreating back, flabbergasted. (His back was also nice to look at, let's be honest.) How on earth had I just spent an *hour* talking to some guy I barely knew about my mom, and my college applications, and my sister's wedding? After letting him check my SAT score for me? I'm really not the kind of person who spills everything about their life to strangers. What was happening to me?

"Spill!" Shayla ordered over the cell phone. "You can't just say you're thinking of hiring that guy to DJ Vinnie's wedding without a proper explanation. I want to hear everything."

"Aren't you going to congratulate me on the score?"

"Congrats. But, duh, I always knew you'd do fine! And you let him check your score? What was that about?"

"I was just scared to check it myself!"

"Why, I'll never know! But why is he DJ'ing the wedding, again? How did this even come up?"

"Well." I dithered. "I was making a checklist for the wedding. By the lake, you know."

"Very romantic," Shayla said encouragingly.

"Shut up!" I said. "Or I'm hanging up."

"Fine, fine—continue," Shayla said.

"And he happened to run by, and he saw me, and so he stopped to chat, and then it came up," I said. "So he mentioned that that's what he does, and he's starting up here and he'll give me a discount. That's all."

"But he's starting at MIT in September!" Shayla said. "You don't launch a DJ business the year you're going to MIT!"

"Maybe he did DJ'ing over his gap year. To help pay for college tuition or something!" I suggested. "Not everyone taking a year off goes backpacking, you know. Shayla, he gave me his number—should I call him or not?"

"You should definitely call him. But I think he's offering to help because—" Shayla said.

"No. I don't want to hear it!" I said.

"—he likes you," Shayla said, fulfilling her need to have the final say, however delusional her conclusions.

So, I went down to the Indian grocery store to pick up some supplies—a crate of mangoes, creamy Indian-style yogurt, cilantro, ginger, lentils, a few boxes of KDH spices, and freshly fried samosas from the little café kitchen they had in the back of the store. And I picked up a bright flyer for wedding horses. Apparently, it's possible to hire a decorated wedding horse for weddings in the state of Massachusetts.

BARAAT WEDDING HORSES
by Springmeadow Farms

We provide decorated white horses for your weddings.
We serve Massachusetts, New Hampshire,
Maine, and Vermont.

Our horses are well mannered and gentle.

Our staff is experienced, courteous, and professional.

We have provided horses for many Baraat/Hindu
weddings & matrimonial events.

Safe, fun, and memorable

Fully insured

Please contact us for more information,
quotes on our low prices, or for reservations.

To see more pictures of our horses,
please visit our website.

"It sounds legit," I said to Shayla after reading it to her over the phone.

"It sounds nuts!" Shayla said.

"Wait, there's more," I said. "It says here: 'Elephants available on request.'"

"Elephants?" Shayla said, her eyes round like Ritz crackers. I'm guessing this, obviously, since she wasn't actually there.

"Elephants," I confirmed. "They have pictures."

"Get out of here," Shayla said.

The elephant was out, of course, because (a) Vinnie and Manish weren't nuts, and (b) as per the rates on the pamphlet, it cost a shitload of money to rent one.

The decorated white horse, though. That might actually fit in the budget!

"Hello." The deep voice with the British accent was Vir, all right. He sounded distracted.

I nearly panicked and almost hung up.

"It's Mini," I said. "Mini Kapoor. We met by Lake Waban?"

"Mini!" His voice warmed up immediately. "What's up?"

"I'm calling about my sister's wedding," I said. "You said you could DJ for it?"

"Sure can," Vir said. "If you give me the date, I'll put it on my calendar right away. And if you like, we should probably meet to go over the music, and the lights, and the schedule of events—that kind of stuff."

He said *SHED-ule* instead of *SKEJ-ule*—it sounded sweet.

"Um, we're having a meeting at the venue on Tuesday with some of the vendors. Could you come to it?" I said. "My sister will be there too. We could go over everything then."

"Where is it?" Vir asked.

"The River Bend reservation. You know, MassBot," I said.

"I don't," he said. "But I'm guessing that MassBot is not, as it sounds, a robot of some sort."

"What?" I said. "No! It stands for Massachusetts Botanical Society. It's right by Fellsway College."

I gave him the time when Vinnie and I were meeting with Shoma Aunty, Sondhi Sr. of Curry Cuisine, and Jen Courtney of MassBot.

"Okay, then," he said. "I'll see you Tuesday!"

I was smiling as I hung up.

Chapter Eleven

My sister was finally coming home!

I hummed a happy tune as I drove down to the airport to get her. Yes, me—all by myself, all the way to Logan Airport. And why was I even allowed to do this after my last driving debacle, you ask? Because Dad was in meetings all day long, and unless he wanted her to take the Logan Express Bus Service to Framingham, or pay for a taxi, there was no one to get her but *moi*.

Only, this time Dad had made sure I was prepared. Gas tank? Full. GPS? Functioning. Cell phone? Charged. Mass. Pike E-ZPass? Velcroed to my windshield. I was good to go.

I didn't feel guilty about leaving Yogi at home either, because he'd be psyched when I got home with Vinnie. Not that we were planning on hanging out at home for too long. We had to hit the ground running—there was a ton of wedding stuff to cover in the three days she was there. The best part would be taking her back to River Bend—I couldn't wait to show her the gorgeous Carriage House!

I made it to Logan without screwing up, and also backed into a super-tight spot in central parking without incident—huzzah! Vinnie had told me to park so I wouldn't get stressed about trying to spot her on the curb and find a place to pull over. She was waiting by the baggage carousel, even though she had no baggage.

"Mini!" She grabbed me in a bear hug. "I'm getting married!"

"Vinnie!" I hugged back as we hopped in excitement, arms locked. "I know!"

People were staring at us, but I didn't really care and neither did Vinnie. We didn't have to wait for bags—she just had a carry-on—so we were out of the airport in no time.

Sadly, she didn't seem to share Dad's confidence in my driving abilities.

"Slow. Down," she said. "I want to live to see my wedding day. And have babies and stuff."

"Hey, I drive well," I protested.

"You drive way too fast," she said. "Now slow the hell down. Or stop and let me drive."

"Okay, okay." I eased off the gas. Jeez! "Relax, I'm doing the legal, I promise!"

She unclutched her fingers from around her armrest.

"So what are we doing today?" she asked.

"We're talking to Masi to pick out your wedding outfit," I started. Might as well get the worst part over first. "Then tomorrow evening we have an appointment with the caterer, the wedding decorator, and the DJ/lighting dude at River Bend. And the Dover fire marshal is coming too."

She didn't know about Vir being the DJ/lighting guy. She didn't know about Vir, period. What would she think of him?

"Mini, if it weren't for you, Manish and I would be getting married in our scrubs in the hospital parking lot or something," she said. "Seriously, thanks for doing this!"

"Aww." I smiled. "You're welcome!"

"And-watch-out-for-the-car-in-your-blind-spot-before-changing-lanes!"

"Okay, okay...don't panic!" I said, and did a head check.

"Why is the fire marshal coming?" she asked after I switched lanes and got off at the exit.

"Because there's a fire at the wedding ceremony," I reminded her. "The fire department has to okay it. Also, we might want to get a dosa chef to make fresh dosas for your TamBrahms."

"Why?" she said. "Won't that cost extra?"

"Not much more," I said. "We have some South Indian dishes on the menu anyway, so why not dosas too?"

"They really like Punjabi food, actually," Vinnie said.

"Good, then let's have Sher-e-Punjab cater," I said. "They're cheaper anyway."

"Who?" Vinnie asked.

"Another restaurant," I said. "Look, it's fine. Dad's already okayed it. We also have to meet the mehendi lady and the bridal makeup lady, and pick out the flowers and wedding garlands."

"Also, we're meeting the Iyers tomorrow," she said.

"The IYERS?" I said. "You mean Manish's parents? I didn't know we were seeing them."

"They invited us to lunch after Manish gets here tomorrow morning," she said. "I think it's time we all met properly."

"Okay," I said. "We have a lot to do tomorrow, then. You should have warned me about the Iyers so I could have prepared Dad."

"What's the use?" she said. "He's determined not to like them. Hey, how's Yogi?" she asked.

"See for yourself," I said, because we were pulling into our driveway and there was a frantic dog at the front door, who knew via some finely honed canine instinct that the second-most-important girl in his world was home.

It was midmorning in Massachusetts and evening in Mumbai. The pink glow of the sunset over the Arabian Sea lit up Mallu Masi's office windows, even on our computer screen. She must have a kick-ass webcam on her computer because Zoom was never that clear. Mallu Masi herself was dressed in linen capris and a kurti shirt in pale green, and looked as cool as a cucumber. She was also smiling a lot more today because Vinnie, her favorite niece, was here to chat with her.

"Vinnie, beta, congratulations!" she said. "You're ready to see the lehengas we pulled?" Why did she always talk so loudly? Like she thought the webcam wasn't picking up her voice or something.

"Yes!" Vinnie said, all excited. "Thanks for pulling them, Masi!"

"I've an assistant, Ria, who's about your size—Mini sent me your measurements. The models were all too tall," Masi said. "Ria is going to try the lehengas on so you can see how they look worn."

"That's awesome!" Vinnie said. "Let's go, I can't wait!"

"Okay, here's lehenga number one," Masi muttered at someone off-camera, and the webcam was expertly trained on the model—I mean, the assistant.

The lehenga was brilliant, and I don't use that word loosely. Among the people who can afford to buy this stuff—Bollywood A-listers, celebrities, billionaires—Masi is known for her gossamer laces and light-as-air lehengas and saris that still include traditional embroidery like zardozi and dabka. She has workshops full of craftspeople working on them—some of them months ahead of time. She doesn't sell anything ready-made; every single piece is custom-tailored to her wealthy clientele. Seriously, she's booked solid a whole season in advance, just like in that movie. Unless you're lucky enough to be her niece. This lehenga was classic Mallu Masi—which meant it was awesome, but not necessarily that it was perfect for Vinnie. It was a subtle moss-green silk contrasted with rich red velvet—traditional wedding colors, but it would look too Christmasy on Vinnie, I thought.

"Ooh," Vinnie said. "It's beautiful!"

The girl walked around and did a slow turn, then spread the chunni out to show the intricate embroidery on it. After we'd examined every bit of the outfit, thanks to Masi's camera assistant, we moved on to the next dress. And the next. They were all gorgeous but not quite Vinnie.

"It's really nice, Masi," I said after checking out the newest dress Ria had modeled, which had to be the understatement of the decade. "But I think the A-line lehenga will look spectacular on her. The one with the antique gold lace?" I consulted the catalog in my folder. "It's on page four. Remember we talked about it?"

"Yes, the *Meri Bollywood Wedding* lehenga," Masi said. "Ria, can you change into this one?" She pulled out the gold lehenga from the stack of garments on the table.

"Masi, Manish's parents have invited us for lunch tomorrow," Vinnie said. "Do we have to bring them gifts or anything? I don't know what the etiquette is...."

"You've already had an engagement, right?" Masi asked.

"Manish gave me a ring and we took our friends out to dinner, and his friend Sol took engagement pictures for us," Vinnie said. "That's about it. Mini and Dad and his parents and sister weren't there."

"What I don't understand is why you kids don't do anything properly!" Masi wasn't impressed by Vinnie's short and sweet engagement. "You live in America, not in a jungle. You're supposed to have a godh bharai, when the boy's family comes with gifts and formally accepts the proposal. And then your dad and uncles and brothers go with gifts to the groom's house for the tilak ceremony."

"That's ridiculous!" I said. "What do the parents have to do with it? Those two are getting married, not the parents!"

"I'm not saying it makes sense," Mallu Masi said. "I'm just explaining how it's always been done."

"Not in his family!" Vinnie volunteered. "They have this thing called a janvasam at the temple. The girl's father announces the wedding date to everyone there. And then they parade around the temple with the groom in a decorated car and invite everyone they see to the wedding."

"Everyone they see?" I was horrified.

"It's a holdover from when everyone lived in one village and knew everyone else," Vinnie explained. "It's not like everyone at the temple thinks they're invited, unless they also get a card."

"Are you going to do the ceremony?" Masi asked.

"Good luck dragging Dad into a temple." I snorted. "Have you leveled with Manish about us? He should know he's marrying into a family of raging rationalists."

"Of course I have. And Manish isn't really religious or anything," Vinnie said. "I don't know about his parents, though. I think they might be a bit orthodox."

"Hmmm," I said. This meeting was going to be a disaster. I could feel it.

"Here she is!" Masi said, and Ria the assistant sashayed into the room in the antique-gold outfit. I was trying not to get too excited about Mallu Masi's designs while she was watching, but I couldn't stop smiling at how incredibly perfect for Vinnie this lehenga was. I felt like standing up and applauding.

"Wow!" Vinnie was speechless. "What do you think, Mini?" At least as far as style is concerned, she always looks to me.

"It's outstanding." I gave her two thumbs-up, smiling from ear to ear. "I knew that one was right. I just knew it!"

"Will it look like that on me?" Vinnie asked. I leaned over

and whispered in her ear, so I wouldn't offend the helpful Ria. "It'll look better on you, I promise. Your arms and shoulders are so much more toned and tanned than Ria's. That old-gold color always looks amazing on you. And it's made to go with Mom's jewelry."

"Really?" Vinnie's eyes were shining.

I gave her a squeeze. "Really."

"What are you girls whispering about?" Masi demanded via video chat. "D'you like it or what?"

"I LOVE it, Masi," Vinnie said. "That's the one—I'm sure. Could I please, please have it?"

"Of course you can, darling." Masi smiled magnanimously. "Get this one altered to the measurements I gave you," she ordered some poor off-camera underling. "It has to be couriered to this address. Quickly, okay? They need it NOW."

"Vinnie, read this!" I clicked on a bookmark in my web browser. "We can order your wedding garlands from India via Fancy-Flowers. Shoma Aunty said it might be easier if we order the varmalas ourselves."

Apparently, a florist exists that ships handstrung garlands straight from India to Canada and the US every week. Vinnie could choose from dozens of wedding garland designs. Who knew?

"Niiiice!" Vinnie said. "But I hate this one!" The garland Vinnie hated was made with banknotes as well as flowers! "And what is this one?" Another garland, this time with twenty-four-karat gold-plated beads threaded in with the flowers.

"We can order jasmine strings for the mehendi!" I said, inspired by the gorgeous flowers and reasonable prices.

"We're having a mehendi?" Vinnie asked.

"We most certainly are!" I said. "You can skip some ceremonies if you like, but how can you have a Punjabi wedding without a mehendi and sangeet?"

"How can you have an American wedding without a bachelorette party?" Vinnie countered.

"We're combining them," I said. "And having it at home! Unless you think your girlfriends won't want to do the mehendi?"

"Oh, they will!" Vinnie said. "But won't it be expensive?"

"Sher-e-Punjab is giving us a great rate," I said. "And the mehendi lady's rate isn't bad either."

"We can't fit everyone into the house!" Vinnie said.

"I'll get tables and chairs from Talbot Rental. There's plenty of room if we set them up outdoors," I said. We had a one-acre yard, much of it level enough for tables.

"TamBrahms don't do mehendi," Vinnie said.

"*We* do!" I said, and set my jaw stubbornly. I was not budging on this one, Iyers or no Iyers. There was no way we were skipping it.

"Okay, fine—let's do it," Vinnie said. "If you think it'll fit in Dad's budget. By the way, who's coming to River Bend? Is it just the decorator and the caterer?"

"And Vir...," I added. "I mean, the sound and light guy. I

haven't hired him yet, but he said he had to take a look at the venue to give me a proper quote on the lighting and all."

"All right," Vinnie said. It's a testament to how distracted she was that she didn't pick up on how awkward I sounded when I mentioned Vir.

"I don't even know if I should hire him, but he's really, really cheap," I said in a burst of guilt.

"Mini, is he cute or something?" Vinnie asked, finally clueing in.

"No!" I said, but my face was flaming red.

"Really?" Vinnie raised an eyebrow. "We will see!"

Chapter Twelve

The Iyers—Ragini Iyer, PhD, and Venkat Iyer, JD, PhD—lived on Commonwealth Avenue in Newton in a pretty little colonial with well-maintained rosebushes currently in full bloom outside, books stacked on every available bit of space, and musical instruments—both Indian and Western—scattered throughout the house. The instruments looked well used—seemed like anyone in that family could pick up any of those and play at a pro level, including Manish and his sister.

"Come in, come in." Mrs. Iyer was the tiniest woman I'd ever met. Vinnie at least didn't tower over her, but Dad and I definitely did. "Sooo nice to see Vinnie's family." I hunched down automatically—Dad did not.

Mr. Iyer stepped out from behind her. "Welcome, welcome," he said, beaming. Awww. He had the sweetest face. Manish obviously got his charm from his dad.

Dad was trying not to scowl, or step on an instrument or book or something. He looked like a bull in a china shop. Along with the instruments, there were also brass statues of Ganesh, and Laxmi, and various other deities. They were adorned with fresh flowers and kumkum, so clearly the Iyers were believers. Dad's scowl deepened even more.

"Heyyy!" There was Manish. He put an arm around each of his parents. I had thought he was of medium height, but he was clearly the tallest person in this family.

"We got you some flowers." Vinnie looked lovely in the salwar kameez I'd fitted for her. It was a gift from Mallu Masi for me when I was fourteen. I was way too tall for it by then, but she had no clue, unsurprisingly. But after I tweaked it a little it fit Vinnie's petite frame perfectly. It wasn't one of Masi's couture pieces, just something sweet and summery that she had specially made for me when she still bothered doing such things.

"Yashasvini, you look so pretty!" Mrs. Iyer said. "I've never seen you in Indian clothes. You should wear them more often—they suit you!"

"Thank you," Vinnie said. "Can I help with the food or anything?"

"No, no," Mrs. Iyer said. "I want to tell you, Mr. Kapoor—Vinod, isn't it?" She looked at Dad for confirmation.

"Yes," he said.

"I want to tell you, Vinod, that we're so glad these two found each other," she said. "We've had so many proposals for Manish...."

"*Mom*," Manish said.

"It's true," she said. "So many people had sent proposals from our community, you know, but he had decided long back that it was Yashasvini and no one else for him."

Dad cleared his throat. "I think they're going a little fast myself," he said. "I tried to talk some sense into them. Why not wait and finish with their residencies before getting married?"

"Very correct," Mr. Iyer said, in brotherly solidarity. "I was thinking that also."

"Nonsense," said Mrs. Iyer. And it was suddenly crystal clear who was boss. "There is never a good time to get married. This way they can start a family when they're done with residency."

Dad looked like he was about to explode.

"Yeah, yeah," Manish said. He didn't seem at all upset about his mom's comment. "We'll decide that, okay, Mom? Let's just take it one step at a time."

"Ragini Aunty," I said, "we've booked the River Bend reservation for the wedding."

"Yes, Manish told me," she said. "It sounds very nice."

"We're thinking of booking Curry Cuisine to cater."

"Curry Cuisine is exccccellent," Mrs. Iyer said, brightening up. "They catered for our daughter's wedding. That Sunny Sondhi makes better payasam than anyone. So delicious. He did a great job for Mohini's wedding. We had three priests and four hundred people. It was a very grand wedding, very grand."

Her enthusiasm made me smile. Would Mom have been that stoked for Vinnie's wedding?

"We're getting Shoma Moorty to do the wedding decorations," I added when she paused for breath.

"Shoma is my oooold friend," Ragini Aunty said. "We've known her so long, since when Manish was a baby. Manish is like a son to her. She did the decorations for Mohini's wedding too. We had a grand entrance and a huge mandap—it could fit eight people—did I mention?"

"Yes, you did," I assured her. "Aunty, we were thinking of having Krishna Ji from the Sri Balaji temple in Sherwood to perform the ceremony."

"Krishna Ji is wonderful, of course, but how about Sundaraman?" Ragini Aunty asked. "Manish really likes him. He always said to Manish that I will be the one to marry you."

"We've known Krishna Ji a long time," Vinnie said quietly.

It was true. Granted, we had not seen him for years, but he had visited Mom throughout her illness. Even Dad had tolerated him because it was clear that whatever she believed or did not believe, he brought Mom comfort.

"But he's Iyengar, you see," Ragini Aunty said. "Sundaraman is Iyer. Of course it's up to you, but it's better if Sundaraman does the wedding."

It clearly meant a lot to her, and what did we care about priests?

"Sure," Vinnie said.

"What is your family?" Ragini Aunty asked, her face shining with trust and anticipation.

"We're ath—" Dad stopped short as I stomped without mercy on his foot.

113

"Arya Samaj," I said, glad I remembered the name. "We're, um... Arya Samaji." It was a semitruth—my Beeji had been a leading light of the New England Arya Samaj scene when she lived here. I smiled brightly before continuing. "There was a lady priest my grandmother liked very much, Pandita Gayatri Vohra, but we've lost touch with her."

Beeji would have preferred that the Pandita visit with Mom too, but since Gayatri Ji had a full-time job as well as her other priestly duties, we'd had to turn to Krishna Ji instead.

Meanwhile Ragini Aunty was looking rather stunned. Too late I realized that Arya Samaj was scandalously liberal, by their lights.

But at least I had prevented Dad from blurting out the even more shocking truth—that after Mom passed, Dad, Vinnie, and I had been nothing but your simple garden-variety Massachusetts atheists.

"Well, you could get Krishna Ji to be your family priest, even though he's Iyengar, and Sundaraman could be ours," Ragini Aunty said. Evidently even Krishna Ji, the Iyengar, was better than a Punjabi lady priest.

"How many priests does it take to marry two people?" Dad said. "Let's just go with your guy!"

"How many...?" Ragini Aunty said. "Oh, that's funny, Vinod! How many priests! Your father is a real jokester, Yashasvini!"

Thank heavens Ragini Aunty took everything in such good humor! Vinnie probably looked okay to everyone else, but she was inwardly cringing, I was sure.

"I'll go help Uncle," she said. In the time we'd been talking, Mr.

Iyer had made tea for everyone and was carrying in a tray of snacks that looked bigger than him. What a sweetheart! I hoped he had brought up Manish to be as caring as he was.

"We're going to do what Vinnie likes, Mom," Manish said. "She doesn't like over-the-top movie set decorations."

"Or their prices," Dad mumbled into his tea. I hoped I was the only one who had heard him.

"Do you have pictures of Mohini's wedding, Aunty?" I asked.

"Yes, yes, of course!" Ragini Aunty said. "Would you like to see?"

"No," said Manish, Mr. Iyer, and Dad simultaneously.

"You stay with them, Yashasvini," Ragini Aunty said. "I'll show Padmini the pictures."

"The clothes, the flowers, the food!" I said. My mind was blown, clearly. "The GOLD!"

I was still trying to digest the pictures that Ragini Aunty had shown me. Apparently it's common practice for men to wear only a veshti and be bare-chested at Tamil weddings. So the guys with good bods looked amazing, and the ones without—not so much. "Manish would look great, though, right?"

"Right," Vinnie said. "But we should look nice together for the pictures and how will that work if I'm in Masi's gold lehenga and he's wearing some minimalist Tamil outfit?"

"Maybe we could buy him an outfit," I said.

"No, your clothes are supposed to come from your mother's brother's house," Dad said with an air of authority. I had no idea if we could trust that piece of information, given that it came from Dad.

"*Now* you want to buy them presents," I said to Dad.

Dad had the grace to look embarrassed. He had vetoed all my attempts to buy gifts for the Iyers, saying it smacked of tacit dowry demands. As if!

When Ragini Aunty presented gorgeous Kanjivaram saris to both Vinnie and me, and a thick gold bracelet to Dad, he felt awful. Luckily I had fitted in a trip to our local Indian jewelers—Kay Jee Jewelers—and traded in Mom's broken and mismatched gold for a gold chain for Manish.

"Mom didn't have a brother," I said. "But Masi is Mom's sister. That's close enough, isn't it? We should pick out his outfit! Then we can make sure that he'll complement your lehenga. Okay, done! Let's get his measurements and send them to Masi."

Forty minutes of driving later we were at the mehendi lady's salon. It was a tiny place with a small selection of gifts and jewelry up front and a proper beauty parlor at the back. I grabbed a handful of glittery stick-on bindi packets and a few stacks of glass bangles in vivid pinks, blues, and greens. No telling when we'd need some bright accessories.

Usha, the woman who ran the place, came out to talk business.

"We will have about forty people, I think," I said. "Most of them will get henna, but they'll be fine with simple patterns. Just a central motif and a few decorations on the fingers, maybe. How much will that cost?"

"I'll do the bride's henna myself," Usha said. "And bring an assistant for everyone else. The bride's henna will be five hundred dollars. And we'll charge by the hour for the assistant."

"How long does it take to do a pair of hands?" I asked.

"Pick a pattern and I'll have her do it," Usha said. "You can time her. Here's the pattern book."

It seemed like a good plan to try out the mehendi before we hired the service. I volunteered to be the test subject.

I picked a pattern from the design book. "This one."

The assistant henna lady worked quickly. She had a plastic cone filled with dark green henna paste from which she squeezed a thin string of henna onto my palm. It was like watching someone ice a cake. In no time she had finished an intricate paisley pattern with a peacock feather beside it. It was amazing.

Vinnie looked at her clock. "Seven minutes for that design!" she said. "Wow!"

We put down a deposit. The mehendi was on!

Vinnie had to drive my car because my hand was covered in slowly drying green paste. The design was amazing, though. When we were little, Mom bought us premade cones of mehendi at the

Indian grocery store and we tried doing our own henna. It isn't too hard, actually, if you have patience, a steady hand, and a good eye for design. We weren't as good as Usha and the other mehendi ladies, of course—there's a reason they charge the rates they do.

And it was so weird to me that the mehendi was not an essential part of TamBrahm weddings. In Punjab, where our family is from, *get her hands colored* is a phrase synonymous with getting a girl married. Not something that can be skipped.

"So your SAT and all your AP and SAT subject tests are in the bag, right?" Vinnie said as she drove. "Have you started on your essays?"

Vinnie had written an amazing essay about Mom back when she applied. That was definitely not something *I* was going to do. The medical stuff was irrelevant for me, unlike Vinnie, and I didn't want a pity party.

"Don't worry about that right now," I said. I had made no progress whatsoever in coming up with ideas for my essays.

"You should at least think about it." Vinnie frowned. "Next thing you know you'll be staring at deadlines and have to rush to get them in."

"Okay, fine," I grumbled. Vinnie always checked on me, however busy she was. When I was freaking out about taking AP World History, my first AP, she talked me down from rescheduling it. This was when *she* was dealing with taking the USMLE Step 2 and actually doing rounds in hospitals and stuff.

By the time we got home, the paste was nearly dry. Good thing too, because I had to get changed. What was good enough for the

Iyers and the mehendi lady was not good enough for River Bend. Because Vir was going to be there. So far I'd only run into him by accident, but this time I knew I'd see him.

Get a grip, I told myself, *it's no big deal*.

I had the henna thing going on, so I thought I'd rock the bohemian look. A swingy summery sundress, dangle earrings, a stack of bright bangles, strappy sandals, a dash of lip gloss, and I was set.

Chapter Thirteen

We were an hour early for our meeting at River Bend, because I wanted Vinnie to see the Italian Garden while it was lit up with the afternoon sun. The beautiful fountain, the formal flower beds, the Greek goddess sculptures, the brick patio with its carved wood railing—all looked outstanding at that time of day. The old mansion (in bad need of restoration and crumbling on the inside, sadly) made the garden even more regal and Bollywood wedding–ish. I had taken lots of pictures for Vinnie before we booked the place, of course, but it wasn't like being there.

"I love it, Mini!" Vinnie said.

Whew!

We had just gotten back to the Carriage House, where we were to meet everyone, when Vir drove up! In, of all things, an Indian-built hybrid—a Mirchandani Mirage.

He looked incredibly nice in khakis and a linen shirt. I'd only seen him in shorts (or pajamas!) before—and dressed up, he looked, if possible, *more* gorgeous.

"Vinnie, this is Vir," I said with impressive calm. "Vir, my sister, Vinnie."

"Dr. Yashasvini Kapoor, right?" he said with a smile. "I've heard a lot about you!"

"And I'd heard nothing about you before yesterday," Vinnie said. "Strange, huh?" But she smiled at him anyway.

I really should have given her a heads-up about Vir before she landed, I guess. I nearly did the day I called to tell her about my SAT score, but then I ended up not.

"So how did Mini find you?"

"I just, um...ran into him," I said.

"Literally!" Vir said. The memory seemed to amuse him.

"And where did you *run* into him?" Vinnie raised an eyebrow.

"Near Lake Waban," I said, answering with geographical precision.

"The first time, Yogi was chasing Roshan, my mum's cat," Vir said. "And then another time, Mini lost her k—"

"Way!" I said hurriedly. "I lost my way! While walking Yogi!" I'd kept the losing-my-keys episode under wraps so far. I'd never hear the end of it if it all came out. "And Vir showed me how to get back to the lake trail," I finished.

"Exactly!" Vir said, covering for me. "The trails can be really confusing."

"How do you know the trails so well?" Vinnie said. "Do you live around here? Doesn't sound like it by your accent!"

Wow, Vinnie was totally grilling the guy! I turned my back on Vir and gave her the Look. Vinnie ignored me.

"It's British, I'm afraid," Vir said. "I lived there until seventh grade, and I think it's permanent."

"His mom is the dean of Fellsway," I said. "She's amazing!"

"Oh, nice!" Vinnie said. "Have you met her?"

"No," I said, at the same time as Vir said, "Not yet!"

"Uh-huh!" Vinnie said thoughtfully. "Funny what you miss when you don't live in the same state anymore!"

"Cool ride, by the way," I said, changing the subject. "I didn't even know you could get these things in the US."

"It's my mum's car," Vir explained. "She's pretty committed to being green."

"But how did you even import an Indian model here?" I asked. "Mirchandani Motors is Indian, isn't it?"

Vir waved a hand vaguely. "It was a gift from—the Indian embassy, I think? She didn't have to deal with bringing it over."

"That's awesome!" I said. "Bet Dad would love to take a look at it!"

"I'll bring it around if you like," Vir said immediately. "I'd like to meet him again anyway."

"Again?" Vinnie asked, eyebrow hitched to her hairline once more.

"Yeah, we met at the British car show," Vir said.

"Really?" Vinnie said.

"There's Shoma Moorty!" I spotted a four-wheel-drive in the distance.

"I'll go look at the power outlets in the hall," Vir said. "And measure the walls and stuff."

"Hello, beta!" Shoma Moorty leapt out of her Jeep, exuding energy. "I had forgotten what a beautiful venue this was! Only last year we had two weddings here."

"Hi, Shoma!" Jen Courtney, the event manager, opened the door to the Carriage House. "It's great to see you again!"

I guess those two did know each other. What a small world this wedding business was!

Meanwhile, Vinnie was still looking at me with a how-could-you-not-tell-me-everything-about-that-guy stare.

"Mini," she said, arms crossed. "We need to talk!"

"No we don't," I said. "And don't jump to conclusions!"

"Yeah, right!" Vinnie said.

Three o'clock, and we were still waiting.

Jen Courtney, Vinnie, Shoma Moorty, and even poor Vir had gone over the tables, the chairs, the dance floor, the restrooms, the rain plan (we'd use the tent attached to the Carriage House—it could seat 180 people), the mandap, the aisle design, the fire extinguishers that had to be on hand before the ceremonial fire could be lit.

But no discussions about the food, the kitchens, or the serving staff could happen because there was still no sign of Mr. Sunny Sondhi of Curry Cuisine.

I called his main office and his son at least three times. They promised me he was on his way, but I was beginning to have my doubts.

"He'll be here!" I smiled manically at the assembled group. "He will!"

"Why are you booking this guy?" Vir asked quietly when no one was looking. "He seems flaky."

"Vinnie wants him to cater," I whispered back. "He did Manish's sister's wedding too, and the Iyers really liked him. Manish is Vinnie's fiancé," I added, since Vir was looking lost.

My cell phone rang.

"This is Sunny Sondhi," said an irritated-sounding voice.

It's him, I mimed to Vinnie. "Mr. Sondhi! How far away are you? We're all waiting for you to arrive!" A car turned the corner as I spoke. That had to be him!

"I think I see you," he said. "I'll park and be there in a minute. Just wait."

Sunny Sondhi was tall and dapperly dressed. We'd been waiting around for him for hours, but he showed up with an annoyed expression as if we had kept *him* waiting. No apology either.

I knew he was busy—of the five or so Indian caterers to pick from in the Boston area, Curry Cuisine was the biggest name—but this was ridiculous.

"Hello, Mr. Sondhi." At least one of us seemed to know the Curry Cuisine guy well. He actually cracked a smile at Shoma Moorty.

"Hello, hello!" he said. "I didn't think we had catered here before, but I remember this kitchen. So, do the catering vans have to pull up here? And where are the tables?" We went over the table and dance floor setup, where we would put the buffet table, where the dosa chef could set up his dosa station—outdoors only, as per the fire marshal. "That's all I need to see," Mr. Sondhi said. "Thank you, I have another appointment."

And we were done!

"I'll call about the music selection," Vir said. "It was nice meeting you, Vinnie."

"Likewise," said Vinnie.

The questions started before we'd pulled out of the rambling wooded drive.

"Why didn't you tell me about that guy?" Vinnie asked.

"Vir?" I asked. "No reason. Just because he's cute, you don't have to jump to conclusions."

"You're so cute and awkward around each other," Vinnie said. "Something has to be up!"

"Wait!" I lifted a finger because my cell phone was ringing. "Can you grab that?"

"Sure." Vinnie pulled my phone out of my satchel. It was Shayla. Her car was in the shop and I was supposed to give her a ride home from River Bend. Only, what with all the waiting around, I had forgotten.

"We'll be there in a minute, Shayla," Vinnie said. "Sorry we forgot you!"

When we picked Shayla up, Vinnie started interrogating *her* about Vir instead.

Shayla, being Shayla, was only too happy to spill.

"He went to school in the UK," she said. "Then he moved here with his mom and went to school in Cambridge. Then he went to boarding school in India. He's going to MIT in the fall. And his parents are divorced. I don't think he has any siblings."

"Thank you!" Vinnie was suddenly grinning. "Smart too, huh? Did we pay him a deposit yet?"

"No!" We hadn't as yet officially signed up with Vir. "He doesn't have any references! I don't know how we can trust him to do a good job. This could be a disaster!"

"Nah," Vinnie said. "DJ'ing isn't rocket science. He can handle it."

"Hey, Rachel needs a DJ too!" Shayla said. "For Jason's Bar Mitzvah. Didn't you hear about that?"

"Rachel is back?" I asked. "I thought she was still in Israel!"

"She's been back for ten days," Shayla said. "And you'd know this if you weren't so busy with this whole wedding thing—sorry, Vinnie, but it's true. Everyone's been talking about Jason's Bar Mitzvah disaster!"

Yikes! I really hadn't been to Turnabout for two whole weekends? Amy would be well within her rights to revoke my staff discount! And I hadn't even heard what Rachel had gotten up to in Israel. I guess they'd been busy grappling with Jason's Bar Mitzvah situation.

"What happened?" I asked, feeling horrible for not having known.

"Amy had hired a band, like, last year or something," Shayla said. "But half of them just got the flu—in the middle of summer—and they can't perform. They've been calling around, but all the good DJs already have gigs for this weekend."

"This weekend!" I said.

"Yeah, they're kind of desperate," Shayla said. "Do you think Vir is free?"

"We could ask...," I said. "But how would he know anything about Bar Mitzvahs? He's been in India for the past four years."

Chapter Fourteen

So, apparently, during the two years of middle school Vir spent in the US, he went to no fewer than *nine* Bar and Bat Mitzvahs.

"My mom graduated from Brandeis," Vir said. "What can I say? All her friends in the US have kids my age, and we moved here when I was thirteen. And a lot of my friends at Nobles and in Newton were Jewish too. I'm kind of an expert on Bar Mitzvahs."

He went to Noble and Greenough while he was here. Figures that he'd be at a prep school instead of Newton North.

"I thought she went to Fellsway," I said. "Isn't she an alumna or something?"

"She went to Brandeis for grad school," Vir said. "Dude, she has a lot of degrees."

"So, you'll do it?" I asked.

"That depends," Vir said. "Are you going?"

Now, what did that have to do with it?

"Of course," I said. "Rachel is one of my oldest friends, and Jason's practically like my little brother!"

"Sign me up, then," Vir said. "That way you can see if I'm good enough for Vinnie's wedding."

"You'll have to get the kids to do party games and teach them dance moves," I warned. "The limbo, the Chicken Dance, 'YMCA,' and the—"

"Electric Slide?" Vir said. "Sure, no problem. Whatever gets them moving, right?"

"Right," I said. I had a feeling he was laughing at me again.

Rachel and I had caught up before the party. She looked great—natural tan, cool new cut from Tel Aviv, and she'd brought back enough Dead Sea mineral creams and potions to last a decade. Shayla must have briefed her about Vinnie's wedding and about Vir, because she was up to speed with everything.

She was up on the bimah now, radiant in a retro fit-and-flare dress, reading in fluent Hebrew. I smoothed down my dress nervously—it was a periwinkle lace frock.

Throughout the temple service I had had butterflies thinking about Vir setting up at the sports club where the party was scheduled. Amy had hired him on my recommendation. What if he wasn't good?

"Dad, I'm going to go ahead in case Amy needs help," I said.

Dad looked cute with a yarmulke tilting precariously on his graying head.

"I'm not going to the party, Mini," he said, pushing his glasses up. "I have a conference call set up in an hour. I'll see you back home."

The sports club was a great venue for the party. The kids would have their choice of activities—swimming in the pool, climbing on the indoor rock wall, playing mini-golf, or shooting hoops on the basketball court. The staff directed me to where the dinner tables and dance floor had been set up—the indoor tennis courts, which had been transformed with decorations, balloons, and lights.

Vir was already there, setting up his DJ gear. It seemed to consist of a MacBook, a complicated-looking deck with tons of dials and buttons, and a pen drive. He was deep in conversation with Amy, going over the music, games, and announcements, but they stopped when they caught sight of me.

"Mini, thanks for telling us about Vir," Amy said. "He's been amazing. It was so nice of him to step in on such short notice."

"Just good luck, I guess," I said. "Vir, is that everything you need?"

"Yes," Vir said. "I've set up the speakers and done a sound check. And the lights too—do you like them?"

The roof of the tennis court was lit up in blue and pink pastels—it looked awesome. I was impressed.

"I have to go make sure the appetizers are being served, honey," Amy said, "but stay and chat with Vir. Rachel and Shayla will be down here soon!" She had the happy glow of a mom who has made it through half of a long-planned Bar Mitzvah and has full confidence that the second half will go off without a hitch.

"You look nice," Vir said after she left. "Nice hat."

I put my hand up to my twenties-style beaded fascinator in the same periwinkle as my dress. "You think? I made it, you know."

There was that amused look again. "You did not!"

"Did too! And it's a fascinator, actually," I said, "not a hat."

"Fascinating!" he said. "Though it does look a bit like a cat toy—my mum's cat would love it."

No one had ever compared my handiwork to a kitty toy before. Though I had to admit that Bobbin had swatted one around at Turnabout once or twice.

"He has nice taste, then," I said. "And how can you have lived in England and not know about fascinators?"

"Very easily, it seems. There are a lot of them here today, aren't there?" Vir said, looking around. Other guests had started filtering in, holding drinks and snacking on appetizers.

"Uh-huh," I said, surveying the headbands, cocktail hats, and fascinators bobbing around on the dance floor with quiet pride. "I made most of them."

"No way!" he said.

"It was for a fundraiser," I explained, "for the American Cancer Society. I have an online Etsy store that I sell stuff on. The money goes to my favorite charities—the American Cancer Society, the Jimmy Fund, the MSPCA. And the royal wedding was a great time for a fascinator sale. I sold everything I had in five days. Lots of local people bought some."

"I think my mum might like one," he said. "How do I find the store?"

"Just Google 'Megha & Me'—that's the name of my Etsy store," I said. "There isn't much left right now, but I could make her a custom one!"

"Thanks," Vir said. "You'd better go—I think they're serving dinner. I'll see you after the party."

"Listen, Vir," I said, suddenly panicking about his upcoming performance. I mean, Vir wasn't really the loud, high-energy emcee type, was he? He was more kind of…laid-back. "Please do your best? It's not like I don't trust you, but this is a BIG deal for Jason."

"Don't worry," he said, completely unfazed. "I've got this."

"How're you guys doing?" Vir said, mike in hand. "I don't know about you, but I've got a feeling that tonight's gonna be a good night!"

It's all in the attitude, I guess. He made even something as over-played as the Black Eyed Peas—Jason's pick, if I had to guess—feel fresh.

In the end I felt really stupid for worrying—because, honestly, he was outstanding. You couldn't have asked for a better emcee. Limbo, twist, conga line, hora, he made that group of kids do everything, Brit accent and all. And the candle-lighting ceremony was so incredibly touching—Jason spoke about his grandparents, aunts, uncles, cousins, and friends, and his parents and Rachel, of course—and they all came up to help him around his spectacular Bar Mitzvah cake. I swear I cried. And I wasn't the only one.

"You can't just stand there!" Rachel grabbed me from the edge of the dance floor. "You've got to dance!"

"Okay, okay," I said. Dancing wasn't really my thing, actually. "I'm doing it, aren't I?" Even I had a silly grin on my face, just like everyone else on the dance floor.

The music had changed to a slow, sweet song. Perfect for shy middle school kids—including our new Bar Mitzvah, Jason Siegel—to muddle through their first slow dance.

Vir left the console and came over to where I was standing.

He held out a hand. "Would you like to dance?"

"Sure," I said. I was glad the lights were low because I'm pretty sure I looked horribly self-conscious—is it actually possible to have a whole-body blush? Then both his hands were around my waist, and both mine were on his shoulders. Breathe, Mini, I told myself.

"Do you have grandparents?" Vir asked as a sweet old couple— Jason's grandparents—swept by on the dance floor looking bliss-fully happy. He was a good dancer; I looked like I knew what I was doing just by following his lead.

"I have three grandparents," I said. "My Nanaji is an old army man. He retired back in the eighties, around the time Mom and Dad got married. He's off traveling half the time, visiting old friends, doing his own thing, though he's based in Delhi…Gurgaon, actu-ally. So I don't see him that often, but when he does surface—he's awesome. But my Nani passed away when I was four."

I was aware that I was babbling, but I couldn't stop—sheer nerves, I guess.

"Who else?" Vir asked.

"Dad's parents, Beeji and Bauji," I said. "They moved here when Dad was two."

"Do they still live here?" he asked.

"They moved back to India four years ago," I said. "To help Bade Bauji, my great-grandfather, with his business. Have you heard of KDH Spices?"

"Kake Di Hatti, right?" Vir asked. "KDH Spices—Homemade Is from the Heart! Don't tell me your great-grandfather is Kake!"

Kake is Punjabi for a little boy—like "buddy," or "laddie." *Kake Di Hatti* would translate to Buddy's Shop, I guess.

"No, he's not Kake." The idea of my tall, refined, white-haired great-grandfather being Kake made me laugh. "He named it after his son!"

"Your grandfather is Kake, then?" Vir asked.

"No, Kake Tauji is," I said. It was kind of funny that the name had stuck to my dad's uncle. I guess people do have buddy uncles too, don't they? "Will you stop laughing at my family?"

"I'm not laughing!" Vir said. "I think very highly of KDH Spices! Sprinkling some on my food made my boarding school meals almost edible! And I've been to the restaurant they have in New Delhi in … what's that market …"

"Karol Bagh," I said. I had happy memories of the place where Bauji grew up. Mom had grown up there too, but her family—Nanaji was minor Rajput nobility—lived in the huge old houses around the park, far from the bustle of the main market where the Punjabi refugees got their start. But things reversed over the years—the old houses crumbled, and the Punjabi entrepreneurs made fortunes and moved to South Delhi. "I haven't been there since I was seven."

"You should go back," Vir said. "It's changed a lot in ten years."

The music had stopped, but there was a crazy beat pounding in my ears—Vir still had his arms around me. For a minute we just stood there as people milled around us in the dim light.

"Duty calls," Vir eventually said, and let me go.

Chapter Fifteen

Yogi's barking broke through my concentration as I carefully took apart a vintage Chanel trench coat. It had no commercial value, since it was torn beyond repair. The Turnabout Shop stock that could not be resold or donated went to me. If I saw something that had a cool cut or silhouette, I pulled out my seam ripper and tried to learn its secrets, the way my dad took apart radios and computers when he was a kid.

"What is it, boy?"

I should have known even before I looked out the window. The DHL van was parked at the curb.

Yes! I tore downstairs. The delivery guy was waiting at the door with a humongous parcel. I scanned the box as I signed for the package. A familiar handwriting stared back at me.

OMG, it was from Masi—it *had* to be Vinnie's lehenga!

The box was nearly as big as I was, and heavy too. I got it in the door, tottered upstairs with it, and laid it carefully on Vinnie's old bed. Yogi sniffed it thoroughly—it must have had some really interesting smells.

"Wait," I told the dog. "This has to be opened *very* carefully."

I sliced through the packing tape and opened the box— scrunched-up tissue paper hid the contents from view. The crisp smell of packaging paper and...sandalwood filled the room. It smelled like India. It smelled like Masi's office.

Casting off the tissue paper, I got my first glimpse of the lehenga. Wow! The gold organza fabric was beyond *anything*! And the exquisite handstitched embroidery made it look so rich, and yet so understated, if it's even possible for spun gold to look understated. It was stunning!

I lifted it—the weight of it was surprising. Beneath it was the dupatta—a light-as-air red silk, edged with the same old-gold embroidery as the lehenga. It looked like something royalty would have worn two centuries ago, not something Vinnie would wear in a few weeks!

A sense of calm washed over me. It was going to be all right. Whatever else happened with the wedding planning now, Vinnie would be a gorgeous bride. And the dress was made to showcase Mom's jewelry. Vinnie was really, actually getting married, and things were going to turn out fine. Thanks to Mallu Masi.

Just to be sure, I held the lehenga up to me. Way too short, but I'd worn enough of Vinnie's hand-me-downs to know that it would fit her. The top was loose for me too. Not much at the waist and bust, but a lot on the shoulders. It would *totally* fit Vinnie.

I did a twirl, swinging the heavy edge of the lehenga out slightly, and threw some packing peanuts in the air in celebration.

I folded the lehenga and put it back into the box. That's when I noticed the blue silk in the box—there was another lehenga beneath.

It was firoza blue—the color of turquoise, late summer evenings, and sea glass washed up on the beaches of Cape Cod. It had once been my favorite color, and though I had several other favorites now I still loved it. Masi remembered.

The lehenga was an ankle-length circle skirt lavishly embroidered in gold and silver dabka and semiprecious gemstones. It reminded me of the first time I had ever seen a lehenga being embroidered. It was in Mallu Masi's workshop in Rajasthan. A circle of blue silk fabric had been stretched into a massive embroidery frame, and four of Masi's best embroiderers were working on it simultaneously with spools of golden thread.

"See the pattern, Mini?" Masi had said, showing me the intricate lines stamped lightly on the fabric. "That's my design."

I'd watched as the men painstakingly brought Masi's design to life—one stitch at a time. It would take months to finish that one piece. That's when I fell in love with fabric.

But something was wrong. This lehenga was too short, for one. I quickly checked the hem, and there was enough fabric turned in that I could unpick the edge of the fabric and lengthen it by several inches. Big whew! And it was too wide in the waist. Mallu Masi had gotten my size backward and hadn't bothered clarifying.

The drawstring waist meant I could tighten it to fit, but that would make the fabric bunch up. And that's the thing with a circle dress design—once it's been cut and stitched, you can't size it down without ruining it. There was no way I could wear it without it looking extra bulky around the middle.

I smiled ruefully.

Masi still thought of me as the gawky thirteen-year-old I'd been when she saw me last. Partly my fault, I suppose. After she ditched me that winter, I had stopped communicating with her. And things had changed a lot since then. I'd had a late growth spurt and shot up several inches, for one, and my cross-country running in high school had made sure it was all muscle. Mallu Masi thought Vinnie was the only sporty one, clearly.

The year I got fit started with my Beeji and Bauji packing up and going to India. Bade Bauji was undertaking a major expansion at KDH Spices—he wanted our Bauji's help to set up the automated plants. Also, both my grandparents were sick of the snow. Other snowbirds go to Florida—my grandparents went all the way around the world instead.

Also, my dad turned into a health fanatic, started cooking all our meals, and sucked at it. I'm not saying he didn't try to cook well. He tried very, very hard. But most of his efforts were aimed at making sure there were enough nutrients, antioxidants, and vitamins in our food, and minimal amounts of trans fats, free radicals, and other nasty stuff—with cancer in our genes, he wasn't taking any chances with my health or Vinnie's. We didn't eat any fast food. The meals he made were always perfectly balanced as per the food pyramid. But even after I flung liberal amounts of KDH spices on them, they stubbornly tasted like cardboard.

How he could be related to the founder of KDH Spices, I have no clue.

About the same time, I finally discovered a sport that did not involve hitting a ball with any degree of precision—cross-country running. All I needed to do was put one foot in front of the other, over and over and over, and some ingrained tenacity made me good at it.

So between Dad's healthy food and cross-country practice, I gained a new lifestyle.

Masi still hadn't gotten the memo, I guess.

On the positive side, Vinnie literally had tears in her eyes when I showed her the lehenga via video chat.

"It looks so *filmy*," she said. Which was what Mom called things that could be right out of a Hindi movie.

"It is right out of a Bollywood film," I told Vinnie. "Look!" I held up a poster of *Meri Bollywood Wedding* with Koyal Khanna wearing the same gold lehenga as Vinnie's. I got it from the notice-board at Ace, where someone had pinned it a few weeks ago. I had recognized it instantly.

"Wow, it was in a movie?"

"The same style was," I said. "It's kind of famous, I guess. And sold out everywhere!"

"That's hilarious," Vinnie said. "Guess it helps to have relatives in the business. But what about *your* lehenga?"

"It's really, really beautiful," I said. "But it doesn't fit. Way too short."

"That's tragic!" Vinnie said.

"Hey, I'm not the one getting married. And I'll fix it, if I have time," I said. "But I've been thinking, Vinnie—what about getting saris for all your bridesmaids—including me?"

"We can't possibly pull that off as well," Vinnie said. She looked very comfortable today in loose-fitting blue scrubs. But she'd just come off a night shift and also looked completely exhausted.

"We can," I said. "Saris are one size fits all, so we don't have to worry about fittings."

"What about the blouses?" Vinnie asked.

"I can stitch them," I said. "I'll just buy an extra sari and use the silk for the blouses. That way they'll match perfectly."

"I'll ask the girls if they'll wear saris," Vinnie said. "But won't it be a lot of work to stitch the blouses?"

"Yeah, but it's doable," I said. "And imagine how great it'll look in the pictures. Do you think they'll wear red silk saris with a gold border? It'll make such a nice contrast to your gold lehenga. I found a place online where you can order ten of them!"

"I'll email everyone, Mini, and cc you," Vinnie said. "Can you make sure they're okay with it?" She yawned and stretched. "I'm sooo sleepy. Such a long day at the hospital, but we had some really interesting cases. You see a bit of everything in the ER and it's go time all the time. It's really satisfying to finally get to help people, though. Sometimes I can't believe I'm actually a doctor."

"You are going to be an amazing doctor." I was so fiercely proud of her.

"Not yet." She shook her head tiredly. "But I'm getting there."

"Go to bed!" I ordered. "I'll email them!"

"No, Mini, you're already doing so much!" Vinnie said. "I'll email them tomorrow. I'm sorry the lehenga Masi sent didn't fit you. Why didn't you send measurements?"

"Because I thought she was sending me a sari when she didn't ask for more measurements!" I said. "I've been thinking, though.... I can let down the hem to fix the length and change it from a full-circle skirt to a three-quarter-circle skirt. I'll just have to see if Amy can let me use the sewing machine at the store—mine can't sew such thick fabric."

"Maybe you should send it back," Vinnie said. "What if you ruin it?"

I folded my arms and tilted my head at her. "I won't."

"Okay, I believe you."

"You should."

"How's Vir?" Vinnie asked. "Did he end up DJ'ing Jason's Bar Mitzvah?"

"Uh-huh." My heart did a backflip, and I'm pretty sure a "YMCA" as well. "He did great. But you do need to go over the schedule and the songs and the announcements with him, now that he's definitely doing your wedding. That way it will be just how you want, okay?"

I spread out the lehenga fabric into a perfect circle on the living room floor. I had already unpicked the hem, and thankfully even the fabric that had been turned in was embroidered, so it lengthened seamlessly. It looked like a pool of blue silk spangled with gold and silver.

Then I raised my best pair of scissors.

Normally I'd be petrified to cut through one-of-a-kind hand-embroidered silk of this quality, but I was mad. Mad enough not to care how it would turn out, if I did end up ruining it. In fact, I was sure that cutting the lehenga up was going to be positively therapeutic.

With steady hands, I cut out a quarter slice of firoza-blue silk like a piece of a giant pie chart.

There, done.

Amy had said I could stitch the skirt on the Turnabout Shop sewing machine—the store's machine is industrial-strength, and they have an overlocker and serger and everything. Even though I usually prefer using my twenty-year-old low-end Singer that used to belong to Mom for my personal alterations, I was taking NO more risks with this fabric.

It would work, I knew it would.

In a bid to shake off the blues (no pun intended), I packed my watercolors, bottle of water, and brushes into my French easel and headed to Fellsway with the dog. Painting *en plein air* always helped me slay whatever was bothering me. Besides, I had to add to the portfolio that I'd been neglecting for weeks. Now that I wasn't retaking the SAT and Vinnie's wedding planning was off to a good start, it was time to focus on college app stuff. My portfolio was exactly where it had been when junior year wound down and I finished submitting everything for AP Studio Art. It would be good to paint something that wasn't going to be graded and evaluated!

I set up the easel by the small stone bridge at the far end of the lake. The water lilies were blooming in the creek below, and if I was lucky a few of the lake's resident swans would visit to inspire me. Yogi flopped down on the ground and watched the ducks sailing by, resigned to his fate. He knew what to expect after I set up the easel—hours of sitting around for him, while I messed around with paint and ignored him.

An hour later I stepped back and surveyed my work.

Not bad! I always did my best work when I had something to get out of my system. My low spirits were gone too. I wiped my hands on a rag and decided to let the paint dry before doing more with the scene.

"Hey, that's awesome!" Vir had somehow materialized next to me and was examining the painting with interest. "Is that for your art supplement?"

"It is," I said, trying to play it cool. "Do you like it?"

"You had better not give this up when you go to uni, that's all," he said. "Did you decide which design schools you're applying to?"

I smiled. Was he a college counselor too, as well as a DJ? He pushed back the damp strands of hair that had flopped onto his forehead and fixed me with a stern look. Something about it made me forget to inhale.

Through strategic breathing—short, shallow breaths worked

well, I found—I was able to get enough oxygen to my brain to actually function.

"No," I said. "I don't want to go out of state."

"But you're selling yourself short," he said. "Seriously!"

"My dad won't even consider it. Do you want me to move away or something?" I meant it as a light comment, but his eyes warmed in a way that sent a shiver tingling down my spine.

"No," he said. "I don't want you to move, actually." Before he could say more, Yogi started a low warning growl that made me jump.

"NO!" A bolt of black fur dashed toward Yogi. It was that danged black poodle again.

I moved to block the poodle's path and she swerved to get around me, with a laser focus on Yogi, who had his fighting face on—hackles up, lips drawn back in a snarl. Then it happened so fast I could do nothing to stop it—the dog slammed into my easel and sent it flying.

"Whoa!" Vir had stepped on the dog's trailing leash, bringing her to an abrupt halt, more by accident than design, and grabbed my canvas with his other hand.

How fabulous was he?

"Good save!" I said.

"Shadow!" The owner came into view at a flying run. "Oh, I'm so sorry."

Vir handed her the leash, adding a firm request to keep that "blasted beast" under control in future.

She had dragged Shadow out of sight before I saw the damage to my easel. One of the legs was completely destroyed!

"No!" I crumpled to the ground where the splintered wood from the easel's leg lay, looking totally and irreparably smashed.

"Is it expensive?" Vir asked. "That woman should pay for it, you know."

I spread my fingers helplessly, at a loss for words.

"Are you okay?" he asked.

It was all too much! I wrapped my arms around myself and burst into tears.

"Hey, hey." Vir put a heavy arm around me. "It's okay, it's just a...stand or whatever. You can replace it, can't you?"

"No," I said fiercely. "I CAN'T."

"Okay," Vir said. "Then...we'll fix it."

"You can't fix that!" The tears came fast and furious and I couldn't talk at all. Yogi's whining brought me back. "It's okay, Yogi, the bad dog's gone."

"It's special somehow, isn't it?" Vir asked. "Your stand?"

"I got it on my thirteenth birthday," I said. "From my mother." The tears started up again.

To his credit, Vir thought it through before speaking.

"You said your mother died when you were ten," he said. "Do I have it wrong?"

"No," I said, wiping my nose on my sleeve. "She bought it before she died and asked Dad to give it to me on my thirteenth birthday."

"Wow," Vir said, putting an arm around me. "That's definitely irreplaceable."

"She did that a lot," I said. "She even bought a doctor's-bag-style handbag for Vinnie's med school graduation. Dad kept it locked up all these years and we gave it to her in May. It looks cool even now—in a vintage kind of way."

I stopped on a hiccup, aware that I was babbling.

"Wow!" Vir said, as if handbags were the kind of thing that wowed him normally.

"And she designed some amazing gold jewelry for Vinnie's wedding," I said. "That's why I want the wedding to be perfect. She's not around to do it, but *someone* should, right?"

"Right," Vir said. "She loved you both a lot, clearly."

"Uh-huh," I said. And then I didn't speak for a while, just sat there on the grass with Vir and Yogi next to me.

"I can fix it, you know," Vir said. "Bit of wood glue, and some screws and splints—piece of cake."

"Really?" I said.

"Yeah," he said. We picked up the pieces together and put them into my easel carry case. "It won't look exactly the same, but it'll stand, I promise."

I kind of believed it would.

Chapter Sixteen

Vinnie never sent the email to her bridesmaids about the saris.

She had a whole week of double shifts—what were they trying to do? Turn her into a physician, or kill her?—but I had the names and addresses from the guest list so I called and emailed until they were all on board. Except for Nahid, one of Vinnie's medical school friends who was a resident at MGH now, who didn't love it but said she'd wear it anyway, they all approved of the sari we liked—a wine-red silk with a thin gold border—and they insisted on paying for them. In a week, the saris had arrived, and most of them came over to be fitted for blouses.

The good thing about custom blouses was each girl could pick a design that suited her. Someone wanted spaghetti straps, others cap sleeves or a simple sleeveless blouse. I was happy to give them the cut they wanted—but it took a big chunk of time out of my summer, even if I did one or two a week.

I was especially psyched when Nahid, the one who didn't like the sari at first, said she liked how she looked in it.

"I was just afraid of all that material, you know," she said. "Ammi tried to teach me how to drape it but I've never gotten the hang of it. Just don't expect me to wear it on my own!"

"It's easy," I said. "If we pin the pleats at the right spot for each of you, and you practice a bit—you'll get it. But you don't have to. I'll help you the day of the wedding."

"I'll give it a try…," Nahid said. "I'm turning, I'm tucking, I'm flinging—okay—how does it look?"

Success! With some practice, they were all getting the sari on themselves. Whew! For a minute I thought we'd have to buy these Eazy Pleats magnetic clips they kept advertising on the bridesmaids' sari websites I'd been frequenting! Can you believe such a thing exists? Honestly, you should be able to make a pleat on your own—especially if you actually own a sari to practice on. They teach you to fanfold in kindergarten, for heaven's sake. Still, I admit, I had to send Vinnie a link. Let's face it—she never got the fanfold thing in kindergarten either.

The caller ID said *Private* but it was Vir.

"Hey," he said. "You haven't been to the lake lately. What's up?"

His voice sounded so close, so deep. "I've been busy with the bridesmaids' outfits—for the wedding."

"You're making them yourself?" he asked.

"Just the blouses," I said. "I'm nearly done. Just two left to complete, but the girls they are for are out of state, so it'll have to wait. When they get here I can do an in-person fitting and finish up."

"Have you been painting at all?" he asked.

"No," I said. "No time!"

"Come over to the lake and finish that painting," Vir said. "I promise I'll keep a watch out for the poodle. I'll even walk Yogi while you're working so he isn't bored."

"Really?" I asked.

"Really," he said. "Your easel is nearly done—the glue still needs to dry, though, and I don't want to rush it."

I felt a warm rush of gratitude for him for taking the trouble to fix it.

"Okay," I said. "I'll see you in a bit!"

All my good clothes were in the laundry—but I didn't want to be dressed up today. I was too tired to make the effort and it was hot, hot, HOT. It was time I stopped worrying about what I wore around Vir, anyway.

I dragged on a paint-covered T-shirt and a pair of Vinnie's old volleyball shorts and turned over the waistband so they wouldn't slide off—which made them even shorter. They said WESTBURY across the butt, but it was ninety degrees out—at least I'd be cool.

I didn't have my easel back yet anyway, so I left the paints behind. I wanted to get in a sketch of the Fellsway campus from across the lake—charcoals would do. Vir had said he'd meet us by the topiary garden, so I found a shady spot where a low stone ledge ran along the edge of the water. If I sat on the ledge I was practically invisible to anyone walking along the path, and I could take off my shoes and dangle my bare feet in the cool, clean water of the lake. I planted myself there and opened my sketchpad.

After a peaceful half hour getting some stellar sketches done, I heard footsteps coming my way. Vir! I peered over the edge of the wall just as he walked up to me. But why was he carrying a towel?

"Hey!" he said. "Nice spot!"

My heart rate escalated to the point of being audible, or so it seemed. I took a deep breath.

"It's cooler here," I said, and held up my hands to frame the scene I was trying to capture. "And the perfect vantage point."

"Yes, it is," he said, and pulled off his shirt to reveal an impressively firm and muscled torso—and caused my heart rate to go from highly escalated to practically flatline.

What was he *doing*?

He climbed down to the ledge and took off his shoes. Then he sat down next to me and dangled his feet in the water—while I concentrated on not being asphyxiated from the proximity to his extremely attractive and also half-naked self.

"Not bad," he said, talking about the water temperature, apparently, and waded into the lake, leaving the towel and a pile of his clothes and shoes next to me. "I'm going for a swim."

I took a gulp of air. "Are you sure the water's clean?" I asked.

He just laughed and dived deep. He came up ten feet out and clawed away from the edge of the lake with long, muscled arms. The water rippled away from him in circles.

Yogi waded in after him. The water at the edge only came up to his chest. That was as far as he usually went.

Vir treaded water and waved at Yogi. "Come on, Yogi!"

I jumped up. "Vir—no!"

"No?" he asked. "Why not?"

All the nerves I'd felt earlier vanished. "He doesn't swim. I mean, only if his *life* depends on it. He fell in once where it was deep and sank out of sight! I thought he was going to drown, but he managed to paddle back. But it kind of put him off the whole thing."

Vir had swum back while I'd been talking.

"Hey, chill!" he said, wading out of the lake, his wet hair plastered to his neck. "He just needs someone to swim with him. That way he'll feel safe."

"Well, I can't take him to the pool," I said. "Most beaches on the Cape don't allow dogs in the summer. And I refuse to get into this water. It's probably full of germs . . . and fish poop."

He laughed. "I swam in the Ganga a few months ago," he said. "In Haridwar." He said *Ganga*, not *Ganges*, and he pronounced it right. "This looks like drinking water after that. Let Yogi try. . . . Maybe he'll swim with me."

I wasn't sure a dog as old as Yogi could learn to swim.

"Come on, Yogi," Vir said. He grabbed a stick floating a little way out and threw it farther. "See the stick? Go get it!"

"No." I dumped my notepad and pulled off my shoes. "What if he's forgotten how to swim?"

I waded out until I was next to Vir, fish poop be damned, but he grabbed my hand to stop me from going farther. "He's doing fine," he said quietly, "see?"

Yogi was paddling back with the stick clamped between his teeth, looking pleased with himself.

"Yogi! Good dog!" I was so proud I was skipping around in the water. "Good, good dog!" He climbed onto the ledge, dropped the stick, and shook himself—spraying us with lake water.

Vir handed me the stick. "You throw it," he said.

I flung the stick out and Yogi went right after it again. He really had lost his fear of swimming.

"This is great!" I said. Then promptly lost my footing and slid sideways in sickening slow motion until I slammed into Vir. "Ooops," I said, grabbing his arm to steady myself, "I'm so sorry."

"Can *you* swim, by the way?" he said. "Or do you need instruction? Because I'm kind of good at this, I think."

He had his arm around my waist and I was inches from his chest. "I can stay afloat," I said with dignity.

He set me on my feet at arm's length and looked me over with a silly grin on his face.

"Excuse me," I said, outraged. "Are you, like, checking me out?"

"Of course!" He grinned wider. "You're pretty."

"That's"—I grasped for words—"that's just messed up. How can you be so obvious? What would your mom say?" I waved an arm toward the house in the background.

"She'd be fine with it," he said. "See, the thing is, you can check me out too."

He struck a pose with both biceps flexed for a second and looked at me challengingly. "Well?"

The whole thing was stupid enough to make me laugh.

"You know," I said suddenly, "I thought Vinnie would marry someone like you"—I flexed my own arm—"all ripped, and buff, and sarcastic."

"Careful." He steadied me as I started to slip. "And do I detect some disapproval of Manish? He isn't perfect like me, I take it?"

"You're not perfect!" I said. "And he's great, he really is. I just thought you're the type she'd go for, but instead she fell for him. I mean, he's really, really nice, and he is so funny as well, but he's also…not a big dog person, and musical, and not into soccer, and…"

"So…what's your type?" From his tone I could tell he wasn't kidding around anymore.

"I don't know," I said. The sun had gone behind a cloud, and a drizzle had started. The waist-deep water around us was dancing with raindrops.

He still had both hands on my arms. Which were goose-bumping, and not exactly from the rain.

"How about ripped, and buff, and sarcastic?" he suggested softly.

It felt like my heart was pounding in my ears. I was dimly aware that he was waiting for an answer, but I just stared at him. Behind him, Yogi was sitting on the ledge and chewing on his stick.

"I like you, Mini," Vir said. "A lot."

He looked so vulnerable. Something inside me melted, like a marshmallow in hot chocolate.

"I..." I could feel a shy smile coming over my face. "I like you too, Vir."

He took a step toward me and put an arm around my shoulders, which I'm really positive would have felt great, probably, but the momentum of it pitched us both into the lake.

"Oh, no!" I tried to get up, but the rocks were slippery beneath my bare feet. He fell too, and when we helped each other up we were both laughing like idiots.

We got out and sat on the stone bench, the towel around us both and Yogi next to me, damp and reeking of wet dog fur. There was no need for the towel, really, since the summer sun was beating down again by then, but it felt nice to cuddle. We made plans to see a movie on Thursday after my Ace shift. And we didn't talk about Vinnie's wedding again. Not even once.

Chapter Seventeen

"You're looking sharp today, Mini," Sonal said. "What's going on?"

I smoothed down my dress nervously. "Really?" I asked. "It's not too much?"

It had taken some dedicated sorting through the racks at the Turnabout Shop—which I had to do anyway to catch up my hours—plus my entire staff quota for August to pay off the dress. It was a cute-as-a-button navy-blue dress, and it looked great with the red ballet flats I scored last month. It had also taken Rachel an hour—I *so* owed that girl—to work my hair into long, loose waves.

"No, no, your dress is very pretty," Preet said, before asking pointedly, "Are you going out with...friends?"

Honestly, I was having Vir pick me up at work so Dad wouldn't cross-examine me, but the Ace moms were even worse than him.

"Yeah," I said.

"What's his name?" asked Sonal.

"Vir..." I stopped because (a) she had tricked me into admitting I was going out with a guy, and (b) I wasn't sure what Vir's last name was. It had to be Chabra, right? "Vir Chabra."

"Nice name," Preet said. "Punjabi too."

"Really?" I said. "I didn't know Chabra was Punjabi."

"Yes," Sonal said. "Are you going to see a movie?"

"Uh-huh," I said.

"Is that him?" Kaveri's mom peered out of the storefront. A Mirchandani Mirage was pulling up to the curb.

"That's him!" I said. "I better go!"

"No," Sonal said. "Let him come in. Here, do some paperwork, so you look busy."

I stared at her as if she had two heads. "Why?"

"So we can see him," Sonal said. "Do it!"

"Okay," I said, and sat down at the desk and stared blankly at a fractions work sheet. This was nuts!

Vir got out of the car and scanned the shop fronts, looking for me. He knew I worked at Ace. He spotted the sign and walked to the door.

"Yes?" Sonal said, sounding completely normal. "Can I help you?"

"I was looking for Mini," Vir said. "Mini Kapoor. She works here?"

"Mini," Sonal said, deadpan, "there's someone for you." I looked up to see Vir standing in the waiting area, knee-high in little kids, with every mom's eyes on him with unanimous approval. My heart swelled with pride.

He looked awesome in dark-wash jeans, a polo shirt, and leather lace-ups. He had dressed up too.

"Hi, Vir," I said. "Sorry I wasn't outside. I had to finish up here...."

"Take your time," Vir said.

"Are you and Mini Kapoor going on a date?" Rahul asked. The room erupted in muffled giggling. I was mortified!

"Um...yes," Vir said. "Are you Rahul?" I had only mentioned Rahul once, but Vir remembered.

"Yes, I am Rahul Singh," Rahul said solemnly. "Are you good at math?"

"I think so," Vir said. "I'm starting at engineering school this fall, so I'll be doing a lot more math. But I love it, so that's not a problem."

"What school?" Sonal asked.

"Um...MIT," Vir said, and there was a murmur of approval from the room.

My face turned red and I widened my eyes at Sonal to back off.

"Mini is very good at math too. She had a perfect score in her SAT math section."

"I know," Vir said. "She's great at a lot of things."

"What movie are you watching?"

"We haven't decided yet," I said.

"You should see *Meri Bollywood Wedding*, it's playing in Westborough," Preet said.

"No!" I said, remembering the Mallu Masi cameo in the

movie—I did not want to think about her tonight—and at the same time Vir said, "God, no!"

"Kids these days don't like Hindi movies, huh?" Preet said.

"I like Koyal Khanna," Rahul said. "She's pretty."

I had to smile at that!

Sonal nodded crisply. "Well, we shouldn't keep you kids."

Rahul walked over and opened the door for us.

"Have a good date, Vir and Mini."

"Thanks, Rahul," Vir said. "Bye, Sonal, Preet."

He remembered their names too!

"That kid's cute," Vir said as we walked to the car. "So did I pass?"

"What do you mean?" I said, feigning ignorance.

"They were making sure I was worthy," he said, "of you!"

"Nonsense!" I said, smiling.

It was a good thing he didn't turn around to see the aunties giving me winks and thumbs-ups through the window.

"Hey, the driver's seat is on the left!" I said. "Shouldn't it be on the right in an Indian car?"

"It was for an American trade show," Vir said. "I think." He held the door to the passenger seat open for me, and I climbed in.

"That's so cool," I said. "I bet my dad would like to look at it!"

"I'd be happy to show it to him," Vir said.

"What does your father do, Vir?" I asked as we pulled onto Route 9.

"He...um, he's into farm equipment," Vir said.

"Farm equipment?" I asked. What was that—tractors and harvesters and stuff? "In India?"

"Yeah," Vir said. "The agricultural sector is huge. So, is this movie hall your local hangout or something?" Okay, I got it. He clearly didn't want to talk about his dad. "You must have gone there all your life."

"Yeah, I saw my first movie in it when I was…three," I said. "I had a little booster chair that the movie hall provides for toddlers and an extra-long straw to drink my apple juice with. Vinnie was ten, and she made Mom take us. I don't really remember it, but Vinnie does. I wish I could remember it, though…."

"I have something for you," Vir said. "It's in the boot. Don't let me forget to give it to you when I drop you home."

By *boot* he meant the trunk, I assume. "What is it?" I asked.

"The easel," Vir said. "I fixed it."

He fixed it in a week—seriously? Was there anyone like him in the world?

"Thank you," I said.

He took his eyes off the road for a second to look into mine. "You're welcome," he said.

The movie was awesome, and the ending was sweet. But I was glad of Vir's shoulder and the wad of tissues I'd brought in my handbag because there were some really sad bits too.

"Thanks for that," I said. "Hey, maybe next time we should see a Bollywood movie? I know a theater in Westborough that screens all the new releases. Not the one the moms were recommending, something else."

"Maybe," he said, but he sounded doubtful. "Some of them are great, but you need to pick carefully. Would you care for some candy floss?"

"Cotton candy?" I said. "Sure!"

I guess I could add Bollywood movies to the list of things Vir didn't want to talk about.

When we pulled up to the house, Dad was outside walking Yogi. That was *so* an excuse to talk to Vir—he never takes the dog out after ten at night. May as well get it over with! OMG, did Dad have to wear his high-waisted dad jeans and those horrible shiny white sneakers?

"Dad, this is Vir," I said.

"We met at the car show!" Dad said.

"Nice to see you again, sir," Vir said.

"Nice car," Dad said.

"Thanks," Vir said. "I love your vintage Esprit too."

"Not vintage, exactly," Dad said. "It's too old to be new and too young to be vintage. Want to take it for a drive?"

"Sure," Vir said. And with that, they both vanished into the garage, which Dad had STILL not cleaned despite his promises. Way to go, Dad. Show Vir the messiest part of our house the first time he visits. I stomped into the house with the (also abandoned) dog. Ten minutes later I heard the vroom of the Lotus backing out.

It was another ten minutes before they were back, and though

Dad parked the car and went into the house immediately, to his credit, it still felt like he was around.

"Thanks, Vir. I had a great time!" I took a page from Vir's playbook and gave him a firm handshake.

"Me too," he said, and gave me a rueful grin and a cheery wave before driving off.

Chapter Eighteen

Three weeks to the wedding and my checklist was looking excellent!

Vinnie and Manish had managed to get their license while they were in the state, and Vinnie had hired the bartenders, gone over the wine list, paid for an alcohol license from the town of Fellsway, and organized a bus to transport the out-of-state guests from the hotel to River Bend.

She got it all done online or by phone while getting through her first month of residency—my sister is a champion. And the RSVPs were piling up. There were a few people who hadn't responded, but the majority had checked in.

Work was fine. I had my AP Studio Art and original artwork back and I scored a 5! I'd even added a few pieces to my portfolio—and I'd made progress on my personal essay for college apps (it's never too early to start, as per Dad, Vinnie, and Vir).

Speaking of Vir...things were going really, really well! Dad and he hit it off, apparently. Why was I surprised? Vir was just the *Nova*-watching, technology-loving MIT geek type Dad would approve of. And he knew an astounding amount of stuff about cars. When I stressed about Dad working late and paying no attention to the wedding preparations, Vir defended him and went on about Dad's start-up, and how close they were to getting Intel Capital in the bag as far as funding was concerned. It was a little weird how they had clicked.

"In fact, I might intern with them next summer," Vir said. "If they haven't crashed and burned by then."

"That's reassuring," I said.

"I think they'll be fine," Vir said. "That's my assessment. If the economy doesn't tank and no competing technologies emerge, they'll do all right."

"He's so tightfisted about the wedding," I fretted.

"He doesn't want to jeopardize your college fund—it took him a decade as a corporate drone to build it up."

"So, you're defending him?" I asked.

"I'm explaining his point of view," Vir said.

"Hey, what's your dad like?" I asked.

"He's...fine," Vir said.

"Uh-huh," I said.

"Actually, he's a genius in his field."

"Really?" I said, trying and failing to imagine a genius in the field of farm equipment. "How?"

"It's too boring to talk about," Vir said. "Wanna get lunch?"

I saw him nearly every day while walking Yogi—and that dog was such a strong swimmer now, he was fetching sticks with the Labradors!

We hung out with Shayla, and Rachel, and everyone at Panera Bread (half my AP class was working there that summer). I took him to Westbury High School even though school was out. WHS was brand-new—well, nearly four years old. We were the lucky class that got to start freshman year in the new building.

"It's awesome," Vir said. "I can't get over how this is a government school, and it's so amazing. It's at least as nice as Nobles."

Government school? That was funny!

"It's called a public school," I said.

"*Public school* in England means an exclusive private school," Vir said. "Like Eton, where my mum wanted me to go."

"Why didn't you go there, then?"

"Dad went to Mayo in India, so I did too," he said. "That way we will always have that connection, see?"

"I get it," I said. "I like that Mom had a role in the new Westbury High even though she never saw it finished."

"What do you mean?" he asked.

I glanced around the familiar campus. It looked so deserted and peaceful in summer, not teeming with people as it usually was.

"I'll show you," I said, and grabbed his hand. "Follow me."

The front doors to the school were open because of the summer camp—I steered Vir through the lobby into the quad, the heart of the school. It was surrounded on three sides by the main building, and the back was open to the town lake.

"Okay, we're here," I said, and took a deep breath and pointed. "Look down there."

The brick pathway was made up of carved bricks with names, dates, and messages. "What is this?" Vir asked.

"Commemorative bricks," I said. "When they were building the school, you could buy a brick for a hundred bucks and put a message on it. Dad bought five bricks, one for each decade of her life, even though the last decade wasn't finished."

"For your mom?" Vir asked.

"Yes," I said. Usually, I walked the other way during school and only came here alone—when I stayed late at school for something, or on the weekend—never when crowds of people were stomping all over the path. "Look—it's these five bricks," I said. "So this entire section of the pathway is in memory of my mom."

"This one is yours." Vir knelt down and touched it with his fingers. "How come it says *Mini* and not *Padmini?*"

"Because I was ten, and no one called me Padmini." I sat down cross-legged on the grass by the pathway. "It didn't feel right to Dad, it didn't feel right to me—so we stuck with Mini. And I insisted we put Yogi on my brick too."

"That's cool," Vir said. "And it's such a beautiful spot too." He looked over to the town lake.

"Yeah," I said. "We don't have a gravestone to lay flowers on, like other families, so I put them here sometimes. Just a single flower, but it makes me feel close to her."

"Let me guess—she spent a lot of time helping out at the school?"

"She did—even volunteered while she was ill," I said. "Lots of people didn't want to raise taxes to build a new school, but the old one was totally falling apart, and it would have cost nearly as much to fix it. Mom was really into spreading the word, convincing people, getting the vote out—you know."

"Did she know how it would look when it was done?" Vir asked.

"Yes," I said. "She saw the plans. She knew what it would be like, and that even though Vinnie would have graduated, it would be finished in time for my class."

Vir slung an arm around my shoulders and pulled me in for a long hug.

"What was your school like?" I asked him. "The one in India?"

"Mayo College?" he asked. "It was really regimented— uniforms, strict rules, divided into houses—very old-school. But I loved the campus. It's full of historic buildings—the first students were maharajahs, you know, and they each built their own house just for them and lived there with a whole bunch of servants. That's why the architecture is so interesting and each schoolhouse is named for a princely state... Jaipur, Jodhpur, Ajmer... But what I liked best was the horses."

"You had horses on campus?" I asked.

"Yeah, fifty horses," Vir said. "We had a great polo team—I was captain, actually. I still miss my horse, Sultan. He was the best."

"You know, I think my grandfather went to school there," I said, an old memory surfacing. "My Nanaji, Mom's dad. It's in Ajmer, right? We're Rajput on my mother's side."

"He's a Mayoite?" he said. "That's a random connection! Hey, my mom wants to meet you—tomorrow, if that's okay?"

"What!" I said, totally panicking. "I mean, yes, of course, I'd like to meet her. But what if she doesn't like me, or something?"

Vir smiled. "She'll love you."

Behind him I could see a bunch of kids canoeing in the lake—and pointing at us. I went red.

"I'm not comfortable with public displays of affection, Vir Chabra," I said, pulling away.

He frowned slightly. "What did you call me?"

"Vir Chabra," I said. "That's your name, isn't it?"

"It sounds nice," he said, grinning. "But I use my dad's last name."

"Oh, that explains why nothing showed up on Google," I said. "Only some pediatrician in Texas and a guy in Jabalpur who collects pool tables."

"You Googled me?" Vir raised an eyebrow. The warmth died slowly out of his eyes—weird. In fact, he looked kind of worried.

"Standard procedure according to my friend Shayla," I said. Why was he so surprised that I'd Googled him? "So, what's your Facebook handle?"

Vir ran his hand through his hair. "You know what? This might sound weird, but if you don't mind, I'm going to Google myself to see what's out there before I tell you," he said. "Who knows what crap's up on Facebook? I hate all these social networking sites."

Okay, maybe he thought I was coming on too strong? Being all sneaky and stalkerish or something? This was awkward!

"Look, whatever-your-name-is," I said, trying to sound casual. "I'm on Facebook as Padmini Lata Kapoor. Feel free to friend me whenever you want. I won't Google you or anything until you do."

"Promise?" He smiled.

"Totally!"

Chapter Nineteen

When Vir called and asked if it was okay to meet his mom today, I was covered in mud, sweat, and hot wax.

There's a perfectly reasonable explanation.

Vinnie and Shoma Aunty had put their heads together and come up with some complicated floral centerpiece. It was a tall glass column vase filled with water, with colored pebbles at the bottom, submerged orchids in the middle, and floating candles on top. Given a choice, Vinnie always preferred the simplest of floral arrangements, so I was dumbstruck that she wanted this thing, but she'd seen it at a friend's wedding and had fallen in love with the look.

Arrgh! Thanks for the inspiration, Mark and Hannah Richelt! I bet you had a big extended family and/or a well-paid florist to put these things together, but sadly for us, it was going to be me and my dad fussing around with candles and orchids the day of Vinnie's wedding!

What, I ask you, was wrong with those gorgeous Moroccan lanterns that Shoma Aunty had offered to loan us?

Anyway, back to the centerpieces. I was nervous about meeting Vir's mom, so I decided to try the arrangements that morning, just to stay busy. I didn't have anything as exotic as orchids on hand, but I got some hydrangeas from the garden and dug up some regular pebbles (literally, hence the mud) and some Yankee Candle tea lights.

Surprise! It only took ten minutes to fill up our biggest vase with water, throw in the rinsed pebbles and the cut flowers, and float some lighted tea lights on top. I did get some hot wax on me trying to position the tea lights, but OMG, it looked fabulous! No wonder Vinnie was going on about it. I took a bunch of pictures and emailed them off to her. I might still need her girlfriends' help, but it wouldn't take long to put them together—whew.

The phone rang. "Vinnie, did you see the pictures?" I said. I might have looked like a hot mess, but the pictures were excellent!

"No," said Vir. "It's not Vinnie—sorry!"

"Hey." I tucked a sweaty hank of hair behind one ear. "What's up?"

"You free now?" he said. "Mom wants to meet you. I can come get you in an hour if it's okay."

"In an hour?" I cast a panicked look at myself in the mirror across the hall. "How about an hour and a half? I've been in the garden, and it was crazy hot. Let me get showered and changed!"

"Okay," he said. "I'll be there."

"She won't eat you!" Vir said bracingly. "Stop hyperventilating!"

We drove up the long drive to the Georgian-style building at the top of the hill—the dean's residence.

"She sounds so intimidating," I said. "What if she hates me!"

"My mom? Intimidating?" Vir looked genuinely puzzled. "No way. Wait till you meet the rest of my family!"

I didn't point out that he still hadn't said anything about his dad or the rest of his family. But taking the high road was killing me.

Vir's mom was waiting outside, with an incredibly fat and fluffy cat by her side. I recognized him as the creature Yogi had chased up the hill the day I first met Vir.

"Mom, this is Mini," Vir said. "And this lazy thing is Roshan." Vir's mother didn't look intimidating, actually. She had a curly mop of salt-and-pepper hair, and a sweet smile, and a rather stylish dress, in an academic sort of way. She held out both her hands to me. "It's great to meet you, Mini!" she said.

"It's great to meet you too," I said.

"Let's go on the terrace and we'll have some tea," she said, and opened the door for me, her pearl earrings swinging prettily. Roshan the cat followed us, rubbing up against Vir's sandal-clad ankles.

"You're so pretty," Mrs. Chabra said. Or was that Ms. Chabra? I was wearing something resembling my math tutor outfits. Skinny jeans, white cotton top with pretty eyelet lace—basic but cute. "I told Vir you were, the first time I saw you."

"When was that?" I asked. I didn't recall meeting her before.

"When your dog had the run-in with Roshan here," she said.

"I'm *so* sorry about that," I said. "Yogi hasn't been around too many cats and—"

"Don't be sorry," she said. "You did us a favor!"

"How d'you mean?" I asked, mystified.

"Vir had just gotten here from India, and he was so jet-lagged he was sleeping till noon every day," she explained. "But after he saw you that morning, he started getting up and shaving and jogging around the lake at the crack of dawn."

"He did?" I gasped. "He did *not*!"

"*Mum*," Vir said, red in the face. So it was true? I'd never in a million years have guessed! And he had played it so cool, just smiling briefly if I did run into him.

"Yes he did," she said. "And then he'd say 'I saw the girl with the dog today'—and smile till evening."

"I'm not sure I believe it," I said, stunned.

"And I love your dog," she said. "He has such an ancient silhouette, like he stepped out of an Egyptian frieze!"

"Doesn't he?" I said. "Like Anubis! The Romans had dogs like him too. I went to the Pompeii exhibit last year at the Museum of Science and saw a picture of the *Cave Canem* mosaic. It's a sign with a picture of a dog just like Yogi and it means—"

"Beware of Dog," she finished. "I know it. He's very classical."

I was starting to like Vir's mom more and more. And yet, I was still nervous.

"Roshan is adorable," I said. "Can I pick him up?"

"Please! He loves attention!" she said.

It's absolutely impossible to be nervous with a purring cat in your lap, so I managed to relax after that—I *so* owe that cat.

We talked about school, university, and politics in India and the US. Thanks to having to share a TV remote with my dad, I was pretty well informed.

"I heard your older sister is getting married. Congratulations!" Vir's mom said. "How's the wedding planning going?"

"It's going," I said. "We have a tight budget, but I think we've managed to plan things the way Vinnie would want. She wants a small and pretty outdoor wedding, so that's what we've organized. Except for the janvasam, which is going to be in the temple, we're sticking to a Punjabi-style wedding."

"Your mother would like that, right?" she said.

"Yes," I said. "I think she would."

"It's not important to have a flashy wedding," she said. "It's important to make sure the people getting married are well matched." She smiled ruefully. "I should know!"

"Well, we're trusting Vinnie on that one," I said. "But they seem happy!"

"That's great!" she said. "Vir says you have real artistic talent, and that you like design, but you're not applying to any design programs—why's that?" That was completely out of left field.

"Er...I'm not really that good," I said.

"I've seen your Etsy shop—you're good," she said. "What else?"

I shut my mouth and gulped. She had seen my Etsy shop? Not even my Masi had seen that!

"Okay," I said. "My dad wants me to get a"—I made air quotes—"'proper college education.'"

"What's improper about art?" she asked. "If that's your career of choice?"

"He wants me to have a more comprehensive education," I said. "Something that will ensure I'm gainfully employed. And to be honest, I'd rather stay close to home. My older sister is already going to be in Chicago for another four years. I don't want to leave Dad and Yogi and go off to New York!"

"I'm sure they'll be fine," she said. "But have you thought about RISD?"

"I have! And that's the best option, close to home," I said. "But even if I get in—which is super hard—Dad will say design isn't enough. That I should expand my horizons, learn from the accumulated wisdom of humankind, get some marketable skills so I can actually support myself. Like RISD doesn't have a stellar placement record for their design grads!"

"They also have a dual-degree program with Brown," she said thoughtfully. "Did you know?"

"No!" I said. "Really? How do you apply to that?"

"I think you have to apply individually to Brown and RISD," she said. "And if you get in to both, you can apply for the dual-degree program."

"That sounds great!" I said. "I mean, it's really, really tough to get into either of those schools, but I could try!"

"There are the Tufts SMFA programs too. They offer a combined five-year BFA and BA degree, and a four-year BFA," she said.

"I love the Museum of Fine Arts," I said. "I didn't know their school was part of Tufts."

"And it's only a couple of miles from MIT," Vir said. "Both the Medford and MFA campus."

"That should not weigh on her decision, Vir," his mom said.

"Thanks for all the advice," I said. "It's really helpful."

"You're welcome." She smiled. "Remember that closest to home there's always Fellsway."

"Fellsway is definitely on my list," I said. "I love it here."

"We don't have a design curriculum," she said. "But we've had a fashion design club since 1999, and they manage to pack in a great deal within the liberal arts framework. Vir will be happy if you do choose Fellsway, though. And I might see more of him if you go here too!"

"Thanks. I'll think about it," I said. "You must be so proud that Vir got accepted into MIT."

"Yes, I am," she said. "And so is his father. He went there too, you know."

"So you're legacy?" I asked Vir.

"That's not why I got in." Vir sounded a little defensive. "It's the reason I'm going, though, instead of to the other colleges I was accepted at, like Stanford, Columbia..."

"Okay, I believe you!" I said.

"I wanted him to go to Oxford," his mom said. "But he's kind of set on following in his father's footsteps."

"Only where school is concerned, Mum!"

I tried to keep a straight face while they bickered about Vir's father, but she must have seen something in my expression that made her add, "Vir, I think you should tell her"—she waved a hand around vaguely—"about Dad."

"Fine," Vir said shortly.

"Before the August fifteenth thing," she insisted.

"What August fifteenth thing?" I asked, feeling a bit lost.

"There's an event for India Day in Boston," Vir said. "It's sponsored by my dad's company. I want you to come, but Mum wants me to give you a heads-up about the family before then." He had a sheepish grin on his face. "They're a bit much."

Bit much how?

"Your dad's in farm equipment, you said, right?" I said, totally confused by now. "Why are they sponsoring stuff here?"

"He told you his father is in farm equipment?" Vir's mom sounded like she was choking on something.

"Yes," I said. "And that he was a genius in his field but it's too boring to talk about."

"That's not entirely accurate, is it, Vir?" she said. "Well, I have to finish up some work in the office, so I'll say bye now. It was wonderful meeting you, Mini. I'll see you again, I'm sure! Vir, you can't spring the whole circus on Mini without telling her what to expect. You need to talk to her—now!"

Well, that was direct!

She laid a hand on my shoulder. "I'm so happy Vir found you!"

"Me too," I said, and she vanished into the house, leaving Roshan to keep us company.

The sun was setting over the lake, but it was still warm on the stone terrace.

"So, what's the big mystery about your dad?" I asked Vir.

"It's just that—I can't stand my stepmother," Vir said. "I really don't like her. And I was stuck in Mumbai living with them for ten months. I loved working with my dad, and I learned a lot—but I was sick of her. She's one of those socialites, you know, and she dragged me around to parties like I was some kind of lapdog, and dangled me before her friends' daughters. So I left without telling them, and for a few hours they even thought I was missing. They got mad, and I got madder. It was ridiculous. Anyway, my dad and I have made up, and they are coming to Boston in a couple weeks, and it'll be nice if you could meet him—so, will you?"

"Fine," I said. "But who is your dad?"

"Ramesh Mirchandani," he said. He looked braced for impact like he had just launched a nuclear missile or something.

"Like the..." Why did the name sound familiar? "Like the...car?"

"Yeah," Vir said. "Mirchandani Motors is the family company. My dad and his brother run it."

I was too astounded to speak. My boyfriend's dad was one of the Mirchandani brothers who owned Mirchandani Motors. *What?*

"FARM EQUIPMENT?" I said at last. "Vir!"

"Hey, we're big in tractors too," Vir said. "That's how the company started. In fact, tractors are still sixty percent of the business."

"So that's why your mom has a Mirage?" I asked.

"It was an exhibition car," Vir said. "Mom liked it, so Dad arranged for her to have it. They still, you know, communicate."

"So, are you rich or something?" I asked.

"Rich is relative, but yeah," Vir said. "My dad's side of the family is well off, by any standards."

"Okay," I said. "Does that mean you don't really want to set up a DJ business?"

"That was just so I could see more of you," Vir said. "But I'll do Vinnie's wedding, of course. I promise!"

"You had better!" I said. I sat still, trying to take it in. "Vir, it might take me a while to process this!"

"Can I hold you while you do?" he asked.

"Please!" I said, and laid my spinning head on his shoulder. "You know, I may owe my Ernie Uncle an apology. I think he tried to, like, set us up, and I *totally* doubted his judgment."

The surprise was that Dad knew.

"Yes, he told me that day he brought you home from the movies," Dad said.

"When you were driving around in the Lotus?" I asked.

"That's how it came up," Dad said. "We were talking cars. He knows a lot about automobiles, and engineering, and he's going to MIT. I like him. He doesn't act entitled or anything."

"And when exactly were you going to share this with me?" I asked.

"I thought you knew," Dad said. "Anyway, what's the big deal? It doesn't change who he is otherwise."

Chapter Twenty

I was "officially" meeting everyone at the India Day concert.

Vir's dad, uncle, aunt, and two cousins—all the rich, successful Mirchandanis—and also the dreaded stepmum slash socialite. No pressure, right?

Seriously, what do you even wear to something like that—a party dress, an evening gown? Nothing I owned was remotely suitable, and it was too late to order online. The only thing left to do was to (a) check out the Turnabout Shop just in case someone unloaded a stunning dress in mint condition and/or (b) go shopping with my emergency fashion fund clutched in my hand.

I headed for the mall. No luck. The only possibility that I actually considered was a dress that looked like something Audrey Hepburn would have worn back in the day. But would it work for the event? I tried it on for laughs before changing back. It was fantastic! But, alas, it was also $1200! The sticker shock was still with me when I left the mall.

But I knew how to fix that.

Mum always said when you can't buy something because it is very, very expensive, go treat yourself to something happy, and fun, and beautiful that is very, very cheap—a pretty pair of earrings, a bright scarf, or a small cup of Häagen-Dazs ice cream.

So, on the way home I stopped at the little garden shop on Route 27, and bought a gorgeous bright red geranium plant in a plastic pot. For $1.20!

"Enjoy!" the guy at the checkout said to me as I paid up.

"Thanks, I will," I said. He was holding a sign that said HARDY MUMS. "When are the mums coming in?" I asked.

"Another couple of weeks," he said, leaning on a rake. "They're just about ready in the greenhouse."

"I'll come get some when you get them in," I said.

"You always do," he said.

They always came in right before school started in September. Mom used to buy a minivan-load of chrysanthemums around then. A present for the Hardy Mums, she called it, meaning mums as in mothers. And she dedicated the first day of school to transplanting the flowers into window boxes outside our house. I remember coming home from school to see her looking happy and rested and the front windows in our house full of bright blooms.

I was still smiling when I watered my bright red geranium at the kitchen sink and set it in a sunny spot on the windowsill. I could buy a thousand of these plants for the price of that dress.

Imagine! That was the same price tag as that lehenga that Masi sent.

Masi's lehenga! I had forgotten about the fabric I cut out of it. I had one quarter circle of a beautiful firoza-blue hand-embroidered silk. Maybe I could do something with it. I ran into my room and threw open my closet again.

There it was! I spread it out and considered carefully. If I used the bottom half, there would be enough fabric for a skirt—but what about the top? I pulled out my fabric basket filled with remnants from various sewing projects. I'd collected many shades of silk while I was working on the fascinator fundraiser—including a spearmint-green silk. There was quite a bit of it left over, if I remembered right. Now, if only it would work with the lehenga fabric.

I spread out the two fabrics side by side. The blue of the ornate lehenga fabric was the exact same heft and saturation as the plain green silk. The contrast in color really made the pattern of the fabric pop!

Somewhere I had a pattern for a fitted V-neck bodice. It took me ten minutes of rummaging in my pattern drawer to find it. I pulled my dress form to the center of the room and found a box of pins, a rotary cutter, and my heavy scissors. This could work.

"It's genius!" said Rachel. "You've outdone yourself, Mini."

I had FaceTimed Shayla and Rachel to show them the dress. I did a happy twirl and peered over my shoulder at the full-length mirror behind the door to my room. There were threads dangling from the neck, the blue tulle I'd layered lightly beneath the skirt needed to be edged, and the bottom of the concealed zipper had to be tucked and hand-stitched, but I was happy.

The firoza fabric had been transformed into the bias-cut skirt of my new dress, and the top was a fitted spearmint-green bodice with a deep V-neck, front and back. It was a neat little color-block dress that was totally made of awesome.

My room, on the other hand, looked like a disaster. It was covered in beads and sequins (from the lehenga fabric) and snippets of silk and thread too—but it was worth it.

"I agree," Shayla said. "It's epic!"

"It's Masi's fabric that makes it work," I said. The blue fabric really was something special—all jeweled and magical and Arabian Night–ish—god knows how many hours of hand embroidery went into making a yard of it. "The rest of the dress is just a showcase for it."

"It is," Rachel said. "But it's not just the skirt fabric. It has great structure, classic lines, and it fits really well. It's outstanding, Mini. You look fantastic in it!"

"I don't have any shoes to go with it." I sighed.

"I think Mom just got some pumps from a sample sale. They're that exact shade of blue and green—in your size," Rachel said. "I bet she'll let you borrow them."

"You're making my prom dress, Mini!" Shayla said. "I'm booking it now!"

"I will," I said, covering a big yawn with one hand. I was so tired. "I owe you guys!"

"Get in bed!" Rachel said. "Zip the thing off and hang it up. You need your beauty sleep!"

And so I did.

Three days later I got dressed in the new outfit feeling like Cinderella going to the ball. I didn't have glass slippers, but the pumps (Rachel brought them over from Turnabout) were even better.

My bag in spearmint green looked great with the dress too. Pink lips, smoky eyes, smooth hair, and the gold peacock earrings Mom had left for me in the safe-deposit box completed the look.

I was ready, or so I thought—I had no clue how crazy the evening was going to get.

"Who are you wearing?" the reporter yelled at me from behind the barricade.

This was un-believe-able. I had imagined a quiet cultured evening with slightly intimidating, snooty people. Not so, apparently!

Instead I, Mini Kapoor, was at a red-carpet event, clutching Vir's arm with cold, panicked fingers, barely able to balance on my shoes because of nerves. It was supposed to be a concert of Indian classical music at the MIT campus. People rock up to those things in jeans. I mean, I went to the MIT SPARK and SPLASH programs here years ago.

"Argh!" Vir muttered. "I should have known."

"Should have known what?" I asked.

"That it would be a media circus!" he said. "Anything organized by my stepmother turns into that. Somehow, I thought, since it was in Cambridge, Massachusetts, instead of Mumbai, Maharashtra, that it would be different!"

"But why're they taking pictures of you?" I asked.

"Not me," Vir said. "They're taking pictures of you."

And indeed they were.

"Is that a Mallika Motwani?" a woman's voice said.

I was shocked enough to turn and stare at the questioner.

"It is definitely her signature lehenga fabric." The woman pushed up her no-nonsense eyeglasses and glanced over me critically; she had a camera and a friendly grin—and a notepad. "That scalloped hem is pretty distinctive. It's from her blue collection, isn't it? The one she unveiled at this year's DCW. Could you spin, please?"

I lost the deer-in-headlights stance and spun obediently, even managing a shaky smile—but I was secretly horrified. A fashion blogger who could ID Masi's fabric! What were the odds?

"But the cut is completely different from her line," the woman said. "She didn't make the dress—so who did?"

"An...undiscovered local designer?" I said. It sounded lame even to me. "Thanks, we have to go in!"

"Vir, is it definitely over between you and KK?" someone yelled as we walked away.

My head snapped back. "What did he say?" I asked.

"Didn't catch it," Vir said. "They're talking to someone else."

Vir walked rapidly away from the reporters. "It does look like a Mallika Motwani," he said. "I did see that at DCW. Not her typical style—is it? I like it."

I stared at him in wonder. Did he say "her typical style"? Had the world gone completely mad? How the hell did Vir know about Masi's typical style?

"What the heck is DCW?" I asked.

"Delhi Couture Week." Vir grinned at me.

"Don't you live in Mumbai?" I asked.

"We have a farmhouse in Delhi," he said.

"A farmhouse? In a city?"

"Not a working farmhouse exactly. That's just what they call it," he said.

"Is it, like, a mansion with its own helipad or something?"

"How do you—"

"OMG, I was kidding!"

"Forget that," Vir said. "I like Mallika, though. She's great! She wouldn't sell a lehenga that looked like your skirt to my stepmother—for any price!"

"Really?" I asked. Vir's stepmother bought Masi's clothes?

"It was really funny," he said. "I've never seen my stepmother so upset. She's one of her top clients too. Wait till she sees you in this!"

"Have you met her?" I asked.

"Of course," he answered. "She's such a battle-ax. How did you get that dress off her, anyway? I know she doesn't do anything but Indian-style clothes—lehengas, salwars, saris—that kind of thing."

Battle-ax! A snort of laughter escaped me. He definitely had Masi pegged.

"She sent me the lehenga," I said. "For the wedding. And she had no idea what size I am, of course. So it was huge! I had to alter

186

it to get it to fit—and there was all this leftover fabric. I didn't have anything dressy enough for today so I used the fabric to make this."

"Okay—what?" Vir looked shocked. "How did you get her to 'send' you a dress that's worth lakhs of rupees?" He stared at me critically. "You look amazing in it, but this definitely cost more than your bag from Turnabout—and you've been going on about how expensive that was! Wasn't it a waste of money to buy it if you had to alter it that much?"

"I didn't have to pay for it," I admitted.

"And why's that?" he asked.

I slung my handbag over my shoulder defiantly and raised my chin. In the background I could see cameras flash. "Because Mallika Motwani is my Masi."

"This is just too perfect," Vir said. "They're all set on disliking you, just because I found you on my own, and because Mum likes you...."

"Your mum likes me?" I asked. Yay. That was good to know!

"Hell yeah!" Vir said. "But my mum and my stepmother—they don't ever see eye to eye, so I was a bit worried that things could get ugly. But this is good. It could definitely make everything easier."

"But you said Masi was rude to her," I said. "How is that good?"

"Oh, it's good!" Vir said. "She thinks Masi is an artistic genius. She doesn't get offended when she's rude to her. Okay, here we go...."

A tall, slim woman in a deceptively simple georgette sari stood by a man who was definitely Vir's dad.

"Mummy." I could tell Vir was uncomfortable saying that word. "Meet my friend Mini. And guess what we just found out? She's related to your favorite designer."

"Really!" Vir's stepmother clutched at my arm, but she was staring at my dress, not at me. "Yes! I remember that embroidery! She wouldn't sell me the lehenga, darling. Said it didn't come in my size. I didn't know it came in a dress! How are you related to Mallika, Mini?"

She finally looked at me, and her gaze was friendly and approving.

Vir hadn't even mentioned Masi's name, I realized, but she knew from looking at my dress who he'd meant. Maybe Masi really was her favorite designer.

"She's my Masi," I said.

"Wonderful! But I didn't know Mallika had a sister," she said. "Is your mother older than her, or younger?"

"My mom was older," I said. "But she passed away years ago."

Her eyes opened wide. Her sympathy was genuine. "I'm so sorry!" she said. "I didn't know."

"It's okay," I said. How could she? It's not something people talk about.

She inclined her neck graciously. "Well, any niece of Mallika is a friend of mine," she said, as if that settled everything. "We're even related, I think. Her husband is a Motwani and they're cousins to the Mirchandanis—the Sindhi connection, you know."

All I knew about my Motu Mausa, Masi's husband, was that he had a contracting business that managed huge projects—government buildings and roadwork and whatnot.

"It's amazing that you know Masi and Mausa. I mean, there are one billion people in India," I said. "What are the odds?"

"Yes, but some circles are quite small, you know?" she said. "I'm very glad you and Vir became friends. We were sooo woo-rried about him being soooo far from home. Didn't know what type of friends he'd make here. His father and I just hoped he would steer clear of the wrong type."

It occurred to me that Vir's mom lived here, and yet they had no confidence in her ability to keep him away from the "wrong type." And what was the "wrong type," anyway? I could see why Gulshan Chabra and Vir's stepmother didn't see eye to eye.

"I'm sure he will," I said. I guess I had reason to thank Masi for something. The minute Vir's stepmother knew Mallika Motwani was my aunt, they treated me like—one of *them*!

"Mini," Vir said. "This is my dad."

Mr. Mirchandani was a handsome man. He looked like an older version of Vir, basically. But Vir was browner, taller, and more athletic-looking. His dad was fairer, and his hair was graying at the temples. He had a sharp, intelligent glint in his eye that reminded me of Vir.

"Nice to meet you, Mini," he said. "Your Masi is a big friend of my wife, it seems. Small world, isn't it?"

Chapter Twenty-One

"You were wearing a dress made out of the fabric of the lehenga I sent." Masi was nothing if not direct. Apparently some of the pictures from the event at MIT had somehow made it back to her. Through Vir's family or the fashion blogger who had been there, I don't know. "Please explain."

"I'm sorry, Masi," I said. "It's just that I had nothing to wear...."

"Who made the dress for you?" she said.

"I did! And I didn't ruin the lehenga!" I said. "I had to take it in, so there was all this leftover fabric. I just used it to make a dress."

There was silence at the other end.

"You made that dress?" Masi asked.

"Yeah," I said.

"And 'took in' the lehenga?"

"Yes, and I got compliments from everyone. Shayla and Vinnie and Vir and even Dad—not that he knows anything about it.

But it wasn't a bad use of the fabric. I'd have sent it back to you if I knew you wanted it."

"How did the lehenga turn out?" Masi asked.

I paused, confused. Wasn't that, like, off-topic?

"Great!" I said. "There's a lot less bunching at the waist now, because I changed it from a full-circle skirt to a three-quarter. I could send you a picture, if you like."

"That would be nice," Masi said. "When did you learn to sew?"

"In seventh grade," I said. "And I also did a summer course two years ago at the School of Fashion Design—the one on Newbury Street? I've done alterations for this fashion consignment store I work at for a while now too. And I should probably tell you I've been using your fabric for my Etsy shop. Just in case that's an issue."

"What's an Etsy shop?" Masi asked.

"It's a website where you sell handmade items," I said.

"Can I see it?" Masi asked.

"Sure," I said. "I'll send you a link."

"Just tell me the address," Masi said. "I want to see it now."

I felt a twinge of irritation breaking through my guilt. Did she have to be so demanding?

"If you Google 'Etsy' and 'Megha & Me' it should come up," I said.

There was silence at the other end.

"That's the name of your shop?" she asked softly. "Megha & Me?" She'd lost the combative tone. "That used to be us growing up. Megha and *me*."

"I didn't realize...that," I said. "Did you find it?"

"Wait . . . ," she said. "Yes, I see it."

"I didn't really use a lot of your fabrics," I said. "Just recycled bits and pieces from the clothes I'd outgrown. It seemed such a pity to throw them away. I hope that's okay. . . ."

"It's fine, Mini," Masi said. Her side of the phone fell silent; all I could hear was static crackling.

"Do you still want a picture of the lehenga?" I asked.

"Don't worry about it now," Masi said. "I'll see it at the wedding."

I nearly dropped the phone. "You're coming?" I said.

"I'm invited, aren't I?" Masi said. "I got a card and everything. Nice card, by the way—did you design that too?"

"Yeah," I admitted. "When are you, um, arriving?"

"On Tuesday," Masi said. "And how come you were with Vir?" She knew him, I guess.

"He asked me out," I said. "We've been . . . dating."

"Where did you meet him?" Masi asked.

"He's DJ'ing Vinnie's wedding," I said, not wanting to get into the whole long story.

"You're paying Vir Mirchandani to DJ Vinnie's wedding?" Masi sounded incredulous.

"Yes," I said.

"Mini, do you have any idea how much that kid is worth?"

"Masi, I know his family is wealthy," I said. "But kids take jobs even when their family is well off. It teaches work ethic. What's wrong with that?"

Masi sighed in exasperation. "Nothing at all, Mini. I'll see you on Tuesday."

"She can't come now, Vinnie," I wailed. "She'll spoil everything!"

Vinnie was no help. "It's time you stopped trying to keep her out of everything. And anyway, it's my wedding and I want her here helping."

"What help can she possibly be? And I haven't kept her out!" I said. "She's the one who's always kept herself out. She didn't even come when Mom—"

"Mini," Vinnie said sharply. "That wasn't her fault!"

"How can you say that?" I asked. "She was always flying around the world—she could totally have come. You're the one who ended up doing everything."

"I didn't," Vinnie said.

"You did! You even dressed Mom. God, Vinnie, I don't know how you even..." I fell silent, overcome by memories.

"It wasn't hard," Vinnie said at last. She was always solidly dependable in an emergency. "I wanted to be a doctor, remember?" Funny, we had not talked about any of this—ever. Why it came up just now, I have no clue. But I couldn't stop.

"You put Mom in that long dress she wore when she and Dad first met—I remember. How did you find it? How did it even fit her after all those years...?"

"It fit because Masi made sure it did," Vinnie said quietly. "She sent it."

"Masi sent it?" I asked. "I . . . it was always here."

"Masi went to the old house in Karol Bagh," Vinnie said, "and dug through all the steel trunks in the storeroom. The ones that hadn't been opened since Nani died."

I have a vivid memory of those trunks. Large black-painted iron trunks that had been over the length and breadth of India on Nana's army postings. They said LT. COL. P. S. RAGHAV in crisp white letters. Mom's whole childhood was stored in them. Masi had to dig through them?

Vinnie was still talking. "And she found the outfit and she had it altered so it would fit and she couriered it here a month before it happened."

"She did?"

"Yes," Vinnie said. "Mom told her that's what she wanted to wear at the end. You think Masi didn't do anything—how do you think it feels to mail your sister clothes for her funeral?"

"But she didn't come . . . ," I said.

"Mom didn't want her to," Vinnie said. "She didn't want a big deathbed scene. She just wanted one more normal day at home with us, reading Percy Jackson, training Yogi with you, and talk-ing about plans for college with me. As normal as she could make it. And another. And another. As long as she could. So Masi didn't come. But she talked to her every night after we went to bed."

I was probably fast asleep by then, and no one ever told me.

"And when Mom was so drugged at the end because of the

pain, the doctor said someone should tell her it's okay to let go—
even if it didn't feel like she could hear. Masi did it. She talked to
her all night that last night before she died. Mom could hear her, I
know."

I had tears streaming down my face. "I didn't know," I said.
Masi had just gained a whole lot of respect in my mind.

Shut. Up.

That's why he didn't want me Googling him!

How could he? Really—how *could* he?

I didn't even mean to pry—the trusting lovestruck sap that I
was. I was just curious about how I looked in the picture Masi saw
on that fashion blogger's website. Can you blame me? I've never
been on any kind of fashion blog before, so I had to see if they got
my good side, and how my dress looked in the picture, and if anyone had commented on it, or liked it, or hated on it, or whatever.

So I searched for the event and there it was, a super-flattering
picture of me in my color-block dress alongside Vir—who also
looked gorgeous, though it kills me to admit it. But next to it were
pictures of Vir, my Vir, with Koyal Khanna—the Bollywood
actress Koyal Khanna! That was why he didn't want to watch
that movie I asked him about. SHE was in it. And she was his
girlfriend—at least according to the news reports.

And those pictures! Vir and Koyal on a white-sand beach in
Goa—with her in a tiny bikini that I would never in a million

years have the guts to wear. Vir and Koyal at a movie premiere—the movie premiere of that movie I tried to get him to watch, in fact! Vir and Koyal wearing preppy, sporty outfits at some IPL match (whatever that means).

How does one deal with something like this? I was so angry, because the Vir I thought I knew was not the Vir who would lie about having a girlfriend and actually keep me from finding out about her by pulling the whole "don't Google me yet" tactic.

I should have called him and demanded an explanation, but I just couldn't. I had so much stuff to do for the wedding, and this was all way too much right now. What would I even say? None of it made any sense unless he was really that guy who would actually do something like this. Was he?

I ignored Vir's texts that day. And I didn't walk Yogi around the lake as we'd planned. I cried into Yogi's fur before falling asleep. There was no other explanation. He was that guy and I was a clueless fool.

I was never going to trust Vir again.

Ever.

I carried on planning the wedding.

Now that Masi was coming, I had to make sure that the mehendi—the one event we were having at home—was perfect. I threw myself into planning it, which also helped keep my mind off Vir. We'd booked the mehendi lady already—so the next-most-important thing was food.

That meant a trip to Sher-e-Punjab.

"I'm so sorry I can't give you the contract for the wedding," I said. "Ladkewale Tamil hein…" He smiled at my accent as I tried to explain that we had to have some South Indian dishes at the wedding—rasam, sambar, payasam, etc.

"No problem, ji," he said. "We'll cater your mehendi. Anything else we can do to help? Have a lassi and samosa before you go. No payment needed."

I sat down in the pink vinyl booth with the plastic flowers and ate the best samosa I had had in a long, long time. In fact, I finished everything they put before me. They didn't have a lot of stuff on their menu, but what they made, they made well.

My mad-at-Vir energy (as well as lassi and samosas) fueled my mehendi-planning efforts. Next stop, Talbot Rental. They rent everything—tents, tables, chairs, linens, china, stemware, silver-ware, heaters, air conditioners, carpets, lights—anything you can think of.

I was sure we couldn't fit everyone in the house, so we needed tables and chairs. I had a look at the linens as well—just to see—even though it was smarter to get disposable paper and plastic from the party store instead.

But you know what I found? Curry Cuisine was overcharging for the linens! We'd picked the simplest linens and china and silverware—white floor-length table covers, burgundy napkins, simple gold-rimmed china—and he was charging double what Talbot Rental advertised. What was up with that?

There wasn't much I could do—we had accepted his quote and put down a deposit. We were stuck with him, I guess. I felt deflated. Not only was that Sunny Sondhi a pompous ass who gave us the runaround, but he inflated his prices as well.

I'd call Ragini Aunty and ask about the rates he gave them last year, I decided. And check with Shoma Moorty too. Good thing I had her number on speed dial.

"The rates are fine, beta," Shoma Moorty said. I could hear loud music in the background—no surprise, she was at a wedding. "But don't be late paying him, okay? Did I tell you what he pulled at Mishra Ji's son's wedding last year?"

"No—what?" I asked.

"The balance was due the day of the wedding. The parents were sitting in some ceremony with their older son, and the younger son didn't have his checkbook—so he threatened to take all the food away!"

"What?" I asked. "Did he?"

"No, the younger son went to the ATM and took out cash. I thought he was going to knock Sunny Sondhi down, he was so angry."

"That's not good," I said.

"And I *told* him! I said: Mr. Sondhi, it's a small world and it's their son's wedding. How can you do this and shame them in front of their in-laws? I said I would give him a check myself, and that he knew my credit was good. But did he listen? No!"

"I'll pay him on time, Aunty," I said. "Thanks for telling me!"

"And, beta, I never knew that Megha's sister was Mallika Motwani!" she said. "So many of my brides want her lehengas for their trousseau. Tell me she's making Vinnie's wedding dress!"

Could she sound any more worshipful?

"She is, Aunty," I said. "She definitely is."

Ragini Aunty had nothing but praise for Curry Cuisine, though.

"He was on time, and the waitstaff was excellent, and the food was delicious," Ragini Aunty said. "It was buffet style, most practical, you know, with our kind of food. But we didn't have to worry about annnything."

She spoke really fast. My brain could barely keep up with decoding her accent in time to hear her next sentence.

"Everything else going well, yes, kanna?" Ragini Aunty said. "I was just telling Uncle, Vinnie is sooo lucky to have a sister like you. You're doing so much for her wedding, managing everrrything. Is your grandmother coming from India soon? And your aunty?"

"Beeji and Bauji are coming on Thursday, and Masi is coming tomorrow," I said. "Actually, I better go, Aunty, I have to clean and stock up before they get here. Beeji and Bauji's house has not been opened in ten months—it must be covered in dust!"

"You'll go clean it, and stock it?" Ragni Aunty said. "Such a good granddaughter! I tell you, they're very very lucky to have you!"

"Thanks, Aunty," I said.

"Wait, wait, Padmini, there's one thing I want to ask you," she said. "It's about the date!"

"What about the date?" I asked warily.

"I talked to the priest, you know our priest Sundaraman,"

she said. "It turns out that the twenty-eighth of August is an Amavasya."

"Okay," I said, "Amavasya is a no-moon night, right? Like Diwali."

"Yes, but it's not a good day to have a marriage," she said. "It's too late to move it, no?"

Too late to *move* the date? Hell to the yes, it was!

"Aunty," I said, "it's too late to do anything now. The invitations have been sent. People have made travel plans. It's set in stone."

"I talked to your father before, but he didn't listen at all," Ragini Aunty said sorrowfully. "I didn't want to tell Yashasvini and Manish because they would think it was too old-fashioned to care about astrological dates. But if you talk to the priest, he may be able to fix a better *time* on the same day. Just talk to him, kanna."

"I have to get a list of what he needs for the wedding anyway," I said. "I'll call him."

"Here's his number," she said.

Did I feel up to calling him? NO. But Vir's number flashing on my cell phone was enough to make me punch in the priest's number anyway. Anything for a distraction. I grabbed the calendar on my study desk to check out the moon phase for August 28. Aha! The new moon was actually on August 29, so we were good.

"Hello, Sundaraman here." I recognized his voice, now that I heard it.

I think I saw him shoot hoops with Vinnie and a bunch of boys after a pooja once. I could see why Manish might want him to officiate.

So, the way the new moon is calculated in Hindu astrology is not scientifically accurate. Even though the actual new moon was on the twenty-ninth, it showed the new moon phase starting at noon on the twenty-eighth!

"Look, there's no way we can change the date," I said. "What can we say to Ragini Aunty to make her feel better about it?"

"Just what I said to her before," Sundaraman said. "These are old things, and this is a new time. If it is convenient, then yes, use the good date and time. Otherwise don't."

Not bad, Sundaraman, not bad.

Chapter Twenty-Two

Vir called—again.

And this time he called the landline instead of my cell phone. And when Dad handed me the phone without explaining who it was, I got tricked into speaking to him.

"Mini!" Vir said. Hearing him say my name was a physical shock. I'd been deleting his messages without listening to them because I couldn't deal with hearing that voice. I should have hung up—but I didn't.

"Where have you been?" he said. "I've been calling every day. Can you just tell me what's going *on*?"

"I don't want to talk," I said. Dad took one look at me, picked up his drink, and vanished into his office.

"Okay," Vir said. "Okay, fine. But can you tell me why you don't want to talk?"

"I'm really busy planning for the wedding. And Masi and my

grandparents are arriving soon. I don't have time for distractions," I said. True. All of this was true. But a tear slipped down my cheek. Odd—I hadn't even realized I was crying.

"I understand. But we're good, right? When I saw you last time everything was fine," he said. "What happened since then, Mini?"

Why did he have to sound so sweet? It just wasn't fair. But I couldn't even think with those images swimming before my eyes. The ones of him and the perfectly beautiful Koyal Khanna. I swallowed the hurt resolutely.

"What happened, Vir Mirchandani, is that I *Googled* you," I said, and hung up.

Manish was supposed to talk to Vir about the music this week. I told him instead that we didn't have a DJ anymore. To avoid actual contact, I'd dropped Vir a note in the mail—yes, in the actual USPS mailbox, stamp and envelope and everything. Manish took it well—in fact, he sounded pretty excited about arranging all the music himself. And now, thanks to his musical talent and that of his friends—he played in two bands, apparently—it was all going to be live.

Yay, I guess.

"Thanks for picking such a kick-ass venue, Mini," Manish said. "It rocks. And the acoustics in that Carriage House are great."

He was even having a piano trucked in so he could serenade Vinnie with a song he wrote especially for her. No wonder Vinnie loved the guy. I bet he never even looked at a Bollywood star with Vinnie around.

"Did I tell you I booked the horse?" Manish said.

"You did?" I asked. I had sent the link with the wedding horses to him. He had to okay it, obviously, since he had to ride the thing.

"Yeah," he said. "It's a surprise for Vinnie. I told her that Tamils don't do a baraat, so she isn't expecting it."

"That is *so* sweet," I said.

"I was nervous at first, but Vir was great!" he said.

"Vir?" I asked.

"He went with me to the farm," Manish said. "And walked me through the whole thing. Even brought Benadryl, because of course I was allergic to the horse, or maybe it was the hay."

Talk about dedication—this guy really loved my sister, didn't he?

"Vinnie will love it!" I said. "Is there anything you need as far as equipment?"

"I've talked to Jen at River Bend," Manish said. "What they have is pretty basic, but with that vaulted ceiling, everything will be fine."

"We just won't have the lighting we planned on," I said. "But if you want, we can rent the stuff from Talbot Rental. I have Vir's notes on where to put the lighting so it looks best."

"He's a great guy," Manish said. "I mean, I've only properly spent time with him once when we went to the farm, but he's cool. Why isn't he doing the lighting, again?"

"Because I fired him," I said.

"Oooh—that's harsh," Manish said. "Bad breakup?"

"Yeah," I said.

Okay, I wasn't even seeing him anymore, and now my *grandparents* knew about Vir! Could it possibly get any worse?

Mallu Masi was not the only one who saw the pictures of Vir and me. Beeji, my grandmother, had turned into a gossip-column follower ever since she had moved to India. But she hardly expected her granddaughter back in the US to feature in them.

Needless to say, she told Bauji. And Bauji gave me a long, stern lecture, via telephone, and now they were both coming a few days early for the wedding—with Bade Bauji, her father, in tow! Don't get me wrong—I love my Baba and Beeji.

"Mini, you have to be careful who you're friendly with," Beeji said on the phone. "That boy is not like you. He's very wild and he's had so many girlfriends. Actresses and all. I've read in the magazines."

"Look," I said, "I'm not seeing him anymore. So can we forget about this?"

"Okay, okay," she said. "Just be careful, bache, that's all."

"Beeji, why is Bade Bauji coming?" I asked. "Isn't it too much for him? He's ninety-two, and he's never even left India before."

"I told him there's no need," Beeji said. "But he wants to come."

"How did he even get a visa?" I asked. "Isn't it really hard to get a tourist visa for the US if you haven't been here before?"

"Of course he got a visa," Beeji said. "They know he has a big business in India."

So that was three more confirmed guests to add to the guest list—180 guests invited, 150 confirmed.

As Nanaji says when he's overwhelmed, baap re! Though neither his father nor mine was going to be any help to me now.

Mallu Masi was the first overseas visitor to arrive.

Dad and I took the minivan to the airport—nothing else could transport the luggage Masi was sure to bring. We waited at the customs gate for her to come into view. After a long stream of British tourists (the flight was from London), she appeared—and she had not changed a bit! Same artfully highlighted shoulder-length hair, same bouncy striding step and smooth olive skin. How could she step off a plane after a daylong journey looking that fresh and unwrinkled?

"Mini!" she said, and grabbed me in a long hug. "Look at you! You're tall like your dad, but you look just like Megha!"

"Er... thanks," I said, extricating myself. "It's good to see you, Masi."

It actually felt true.

"Mallika," Dad said, grinning boyishly. Wow, I couldn't remember seeing Dad smile like that in years. He and Masi had always gotten along well.

"Vinod," she said. "So good to see you, ya!"

"Wish you'd brought the boys with you," Dad said. By which he meant Motu Mausa (Mohan Motwani, Masi's husband) and their twelve-year-old twin boys, Arvind and Avinash.

"Ari and Avi are at school," she said. "Their school reopened on July first, Mini, otherwise I would have definitely brought them. But they'll come in time for the wedding, and Nana is coming too! Mohan can't get away from work, though."

"Oh, that's too bad. I haven't seen Motu in years!" Dad said.

"Nanaji is coming too!" I squealed. "That's awesome!"

Nanaji, my other grandfather—Mom and Masi's dad—doesn't travel overseas as much as he used to. Last time I saw him was two years ago when he spent the whole summer with us. And he's hard to contact because he's usually off visiting his army buddies, who have retired to every remote corner to be found in India—none of them have internet access. I hadn't even known he got the wedding invitation I'd mailed to his Delhi address.

"Of course he is," Masi said. "Your Bade Bauji can make it, when he's, what—ninety-two? So why can't Nanaji?"

The atmosphere at home was suddenly festive. Masi breezed into the house, threw her stuff all over the master bedroom (Dad had lived in his study for the last seven years), put on loud Bollywood music, and forbade poor Yogi to "shed all over my pashminas."

We ordered takeout and Dad went off to pick it up.

"Show me how you altered the lehenga, Mini," she demanded. "I just have to see what you did with it!"

"It's in my closet," I said. "I'll get it!"

Before I could get over to my room, she was already there and, having flung my closet door open, was oohing and aahing over various items in it.

"Where did you get that?" she asked.

"Careful," I said. "It's vintage."

"I can see that!" she said.

"And here's the lehenga!" she said. She pulled it out and examined it with interest. "Nice work, Mini. Clean sewing too. You have a machine that can handle fabric this thick?"

"I don't," I said. "But my friend's mom's consignment store has everything because they offer alterations, and she let me use their sewing machine. I just have this…"

"Megha's old machine?" she said, taking in my sewing corner in the far end of the room. "I remember it."

"I love the lehenga, Masi," I said. "Thanks for sending it to me. I didn't realize it was your signature piece, otherwise I would never have taken it apart."

"Is this the dress you wore when you went out with Vir?" she asked.

A shard of hurt stabbed at me when she said his name.

"Yes," I said. "Yes, it is."

"It's excellent." Masi turned the dress inside out and examined the stitching. Thankfully, I had sewed it cleanly. "I'm proud of you."

It shouldn't have meant so much, but it did.

"Thanks," I said.

208

"Do you know I've had a ton of orders for this design already?" she asked. "They all want the dress that the Boston girl was wearing."

"Get out of here!" I said, shocked. "Really?"

"Really," she said. "Mini, what's this?" She held up a child's firoza-blue double-breasted pea coat. "This can't be yours."

Oh, no! I snatched it back. "It used to be," I said. "But I never wore it. Here's Dad now, Masi. Let's go eat."

So here's the downlow on why I'm still upset with my Masi. The September Vinnie left for college was probably the hardest time in my life. Worse even than when Mom died, because right after it happened I was so numb it didn't even feel real. And Vinnie was there that spring and summer to cushion me from it. But when she left for college, it really hit hard—and the only thing that kept me going was the promise Masi made me.

She said she would come to visit in December and I would go to India with her. I believed her. Because she had *promised*—more than once! She was going to New York for work—it was an exciting collaboration with Saks Fifth Avenue. She was finally going to launch a ready-to-wear collection in India and overseas. And after her meetings she would come to Boston and take me back to Delhi for three weeks. I'd miss a week of school, sure, but that was hardly a big deal in sixth grade.

I was so excited about that trip. It was my Golden Ticket. When

Vinnie came home for Thanksgiving, she took me shopping for it. I hadn't had a birthday party that November—Dad and Vinnie took me to see *Penguins of Madagascar* instead. But Vinnie bought me a double-breasted pea coat—in my favorite firoza blue with bright brass buttons—just for my trip to Delhi. Mom had told us how cold it could be there in winter, and how the houses were not built for the cold weather, and how no one had central heating. I didn't remember being there in winter, but Vinnie did.

Vinnie went back to college after Thanksgiving, but I looked at my new clothes, and my suitcase, and packed and unpacked them. Then held the jacket to my face and dreamt of India. It felt soft and smelled of pure wool, excitement, and adventure. I just knew that my trip would be incredible! I'd drink ThumsUp in Masi's office, and visit her sewing units, and babysit my cute twin cousins—it would be epic.

But a week before Mallu Masi was supposed to come to New York she canceled her trip—just like that. No explanation. Nothing.

It was a little bit like that morning I found Mom, all over again. The light went out, and I had to cope.

I finally wore the new clothes to school in January. But I never wore the beautiful blue pea coat. That's why it still hung in my closet as a warning—never trust Mallu Masi.

Chapter Twenty-Three

I went over to air out Beeji and Bauji's house and stock up their fridge—it's no fun food shopping while jet-lagged. Masi offered to help—I had no clue how much help she would actually be. I mean, when was the last time she used a vacuum cleaner— if ever? But she was determined to come along, so I was stuck with her.

"I like your car," she said. "Your favorite firoza blue with a white roof and racing stripes, huh? It's cute."

"Thanks," I said. A good word about my car or my dog was always welcome—even from Masi.

"I still remember when your Nanaji taught Megha how to drive! He made her use that tank of a car he had—the Ambassador. Did you ever see it?"

"I've seen photos," I said. The Ambassador was the first car to be manufactured in India.

"Yeah," she said. "He set up *gharas*, you know, the terra-cotta water pots? Arranged an obstacle course in a field at our farmhouse and made her drive around them. By the end of her first try she had flattened them all!"

"Wow, did she blow a tire?" I asked. It was good to hear something about Mom I didn't already know.

"No, but she scared a herd of buffaloes!" Masi said. "Nanaji's farmhand swore they wouldn't give any milk that day because of it." Tears of laughter streamed down her cheeks. When she was like that, it was hard not to like her.

Beeji and Bauji's place looked dusty and smelled stale—it had been sitting in the baking summer sun for months. They should really rent it out—just so it would be looked after. It took three hours of vigorous vacuuming and throwing open of windows and doors just to freshen the musty air inside.

"What's down there?" Masi asked as I flipped on the light in the basement and walked downstairs.

"Just storage," I said.

I stared at a stack of suitcases—vintage hardcase American Touristers—and was struck by an idea. Beeji stored her old saris in them. Maybe Mom's wedding lehenga was here instead of at home? Dad and I had been through every box in our attic and found nothing.

"I'm just going to look in these, Masi," I said. "If they're open."

I took down the first one, snapped the clasps, and lifted the lid. Beeji's old saris, dupattas, and salwar kameezes, neatly packed. But no bulky silk lehenga. I shut it and opened another one. This one had old linens hand-embroidered by Beeji half a century ago.

I passed a hand over them—the tiny stitches looked bright and felt crisp and new, even now—why had she never used them to set a table? Or displayed them in her china cabinet? What a waste!

"Look!" Masi had been opening suitcases too. "That's Megha's lehenga."

Brilliant pink silk spilled from Masi's hands—Mom's lehenga. I knew it right away even though I'd only seen it in pictures. The pink was an unusual crushed raspberry spangled with silver tilla work—hand embroidery done with metallic thread, a specialty of Punjab.

"We've been looking for this everywhere!" I said. "In the garage, in the attic, in all the storage boxes at home. I didn't realize she left it here!"

"They lived with Vinod's parents the year they got married, right?" Masi said. "Before they bought a house. I guess she must have given it to Beeji for safekeeping."

"Do you think it'll fit Vinnie?" I asked.

"Yeah," Masi said. "If it needs any fixing, I can do it. I designed it, after all. I was so proud of it! You're looking at the very first Mallika Motwani, Mini. And I wasn't even a Motwani then!"

"You made Mom's wedding lehenga?" I asked.

"With input from her, of course," Masi said. "Megha was great at it, but Nanaji didn't let her study design. There was no future in it, he said. But when I finished class twelve, NIFT had just opened in Delhi a few years earlier."

"National Institute of Fashion Technology?" I asked.

"Yeah," Masi said. "It opened in 1986, and Megha talked them into letting me apply. If it hadn't been for her, I'd have been doing a Bachelor of Commerce at Shri Ram College of Commerce, Delhi University, like your Mausa! Hey, will Vinnie wear this for the reception if we fix it?"

"Yes!" I said. "That's why I was looking for it! I'll have it dry-cleaned and then we can fix it. She'll be so surprised and thrilled!"

"Speaking of surprises," Masi said, "I wanted to ask you about a wedding present for her."

"She has a wedding registry, Masi," I said.

She waved a dismissive hand. "Not anything from there! No, I had the recordings I have of Megha reading books out loud made into an audiobook for you two."

She what?

"How do you have recordings of Mom reading?"

"Arre, she used to call and put the phone on speaker and just let me listen too. You know in the last months…I recorded them and I've been playing it to the boys. Ari and Avi are just the right age for Percy Jackson, and I thought you girls would like it too."

"Yes." I gulped. "That would be just perfect."

"Okay, let's finish up here!" Masi said, clearly done with housework.

It was still light as we drove home.

"So, I'm thinking of the ready-to-wear line again, Mini," she said over the music station I'd turned on to discourage conversation. In spite of the thaw that had definitely set in since she told me about Mom's audio recording, I was still wary of warming up to her completely. "I haven't thought about it for a while, but after six years, the time seems to be right again."

"What happened last time?" I asked. "Why did you pull out?"

"You remember that?" she asked. "You were so little!"

"Remember?" I asked—she thought I'd *forgotten*? "Of course I remember. I was really excited about going to India, you know." That had to be the understatement of the decade. "Vinnie helped me shop when she came home for Thanksgiving. I bought gifts for Ari and Avi with my allowance. And then you canceled...."

I could feel her eyes on me but kept mine firmly on the road.

"Vinod said you took it well," she said finally.

"What does Dad know?" I said. "The pea coat you saw in my closet—Vinnie bought it for me as a birthday present, for that trip."

"It looks brand-new," she said.

I shrugged. "I was so disappointed about the trip that I never wore it."

"Okay," she said. "*That's* just tragic. You would have looked so cute in it, Mini."

"It's too late now," I said, keeping my eyes firmly on the road.

"I don't think I ever saw you for more than a day after that," Masi said. "You were always off to summer camp or something when I visited."

"I didn't..." There were tears glinting at the ends of my lashes but I didn't brush them away. Maybe it was time to have it all out. "I didn't *want* to see you. Before that, I thought you were the only person who got me. Dad and Vinnie were always on about engineering and medicine and stuff. You were the one creative person in my life, and you clearly wanted nothing to do with me."

"But I did!" Masi said. "I came the next summer, but you weren't there."

"I just couldn't...," I said, "...you know, get excited about doing stuff with you only to have you bail on me—again. That's why I signed up for summer camp. And it was great!"

"I was disappointed about that trip as well, Mini," Masi said.

"Then why didn't you come?" I flung at her.

She said nothing.

I waited in bitter silence. What possible reason could she have?

"You want to know?" she said. "Okay, I'll tell you!"

Oh, this ought to be good!

"That November—they found a cyst in my mammogram," she said. "A large one, and it was irregular so they were afraid it could be something more."

No! The word screamed in my head. My knuckles were white, I was gripping the steering wheel so hard. Of course! The hushed phone conversations with Dad that I tried so hard to overhear— that's what they had been about. How bad had it been?

Meanwhile Masi was going on explaining—how it changed her priorities, how she put her business on the back burner, let her nanny go, started packing lunch for Ari and Avi with her own hands, how she made sure she picked them up after school, spending every moment she could with her family, and how she made sure she had checkups every few months for years.

"The first time, they put me through a bunch of tests, including a biopsy. It looked like it might be cancer..."

My heart was pounding. Please, not that!

"They removed it, but it turned out not to be malignant. But that's why I canceled the trip, the deals, and your holiday. It wasn't even a year from the time Megha passed. I didn't want you to know—it would have scared you. Vinod agreed."

Oh, crap, was there any danger of a recurrence? The car behind me changed into the next lane because I was going way too slow. I'd better pull over before I drove into a tree. An exit was coming up and I took it and parked at the first gas station off the road.

Masi was looking worriedly at me.

"What's wrong? Do you need gas?" she asked.

I climbed out of the driver's seat and walked over to her side. She had gotten out, looking puzzled and concerned. I probably confused her even more by wrapping my arms around her in a tight hug.

She hugged me back, and then I was sobbing all over her pashmina wrap. She felt so tiny and fragile.

"You're okay now, right?" I asked her. "It never came back?"

"I'm fine, beta," she said. "I'm fine—really!"

I let her go and stood there awkwardly trying to explain.

"Masi, I never thought...," I said. All these years I had blamed her and refused to communicate with her—and she had just been trying to protect me, while dealing with way more crap than anyone deserved. I may be taller than her but right then I felt about two inches high.

"Silly kid," she said—her eyes wet with tears too. "It was just a scare. There's no need for you to worry—I promise."

217

Apparently I'm not great at figuring things out. I jump to stupid conclusions and clam up and stop communicating. I had been so wrong about Masi and lost so much time because of it. Could I have been wrong about Vir too?

So this time I called him.

"Mini?" he said. "Is that you?"

"Yeah," I said. I looked down at the notes I'd made to get me through the call.

"I know I've been acting strange, but I saw the pictures of you with Koyal and other, um . . . girls—and I freaked."

"Understood," he said. "I should have told you."

"It was a total shock," I said. My voice kind of broke at that point. Hold it together, Mini, I told myself.

"I understand," he said. "But Mini," and here his voice took on an aggrieved tone, "you should hear me out, instead of just *assuming* . . ."

Really?

After all the things he kept from me, this was all *my* fault? I hung up the phone, my hands shaking.

I could kill that guy!

This was much, much harder than I thought it would be.

The phone rang.

"What?" I snapped.

"Look, I know this is not the best time!" Vir said.

Too right, it wasn't.

"It isn't," I said. "I'm really busy right now, Vir. I want to get through the wedding, we're having all kinds of problems with the—"

"Weather, I know," Vir said. "I've seen the news reports. And I'd like to help—please. If there's anything I can do, just let me know."

Wait up. What problem with the weather? But if he was offering to help, I wasn't going to say no.

"Fine," I said.

"And when this is over, let's sit down and talk about this rationally," he said. "It's not how it looks—I promise."

"Sure," I said.

Could there *be* a rational explanation?

I hoped so.

For now, I had more important things to deal with. Like looking up the weather forecast.

"It can't get all the way here, can it?" I swiveled from the Weather Channel reporter on the television screen to look at my dad and back again. "It'll break up and just turn into rain, right?"

"I expect so." Dad didn't seem worried. "What are they predicting?"

"Shhh, listen!" I said.

The reporter was wearing a rain slicker and leaning into the wind, his wet hair sticking to his face. He had to yell to be heard over the storm. "Hurricane Indra has hit Puerto Rico, knocking out power lines and ripping up trees. Computer forecast models showed Indra moving northwest over the Dominican Republic and then heading toward the Florida peninsula, possibly arriving there on Thursday."

The screen changed to a map showing several possible storm tracks over the mainland. Most of them went over Florida, then took a left overland, heading toward Texas.

"It's not tracking north." I exhaled. "We'll be fine if it keeps going west. But just think about all the people who have weddings planned along its path!"

"I'm sure they'll manage," Dad said, wiping his glasses before looking closely at the storm track. "Just relieved it isn't heading here. I think we're safe."

"Not yet," I said, and made a mental note to review the rain plans for the wedding, just in case. "The storm track could still change."

Chapter Twenty-Four

"Hurricane Bob!" Dad said. "That's the one I'm thinking of!"

We were driving to the airport to pick up Beeji, Bauji, and Bade Bauji. The weatherman on the radio was recapping the hurricanes that had brushed New England in the past—a total of four in the last half century—Hurricanes Donna, Bob, Irene, and Ingrid.

So there *had* been hurricanes in New England in my lifetime—who knew! I guess you just don't pay attention when you're younger. According to radio guy, there was some possibility that the hurricane in the Caribbean could hit New York and even make it all the way to Massachusetts.

As if!

This was the first hurricane of the season and they were all just panicking for nothing. Weren't they?

"Was the last one bad?" I asked Dad.

"Don't remember," Dad said. "It did a lot of damage but on the Cape mostly, not inland. We just got rain and wind. I don't even think I took the day off work."

Which isn't saying much—Dad never takes a day off work for anything.

"So is Bade Bauji going to be wearing jeans and a jacket instead of his khadi kurta?" I asked. It had been ages since I'd seen him.

"He said he didn't want to risk being frisked by security because of his clothes, so he bought a special outfit for the plane trip," Dad said.

I couldn't imagine anyone frisking Bade Bauji. He commanded respect. Granted, the last time I saw him I was only seven—but I'd been very impressed. And I knew his life story, of course—the story of how he founded KDH Spices.

He left West Punjab with nothing after the partition of India. All their family property was lost after West Punjab became part of Pakistan. He started from scratch in the refugee camps in Delhi, setting up a business that sold preground spices to housewives. And then his Punjabi spices became famous! He pioneered the selling of boxed spices, basically. People could use them at home to make their own dishes taste amazing because, as the KDH tag line says, *Homemade Is from the Heart.* He expanded their line to all kinds of Indian dishes—chana masala, rajma, muttar paneer, sambar, tandoori, and so on. And through it all, Bade Bauji always wore the simple homespun Gandhian fabric—khadi—that he had put on as a symbol of the independence movement in the 1940s. Except now he was wearing Levi's to avoid getting stopped and searched in an American airport. I bet he looked adorable, though.

"There he is," Dad said, smiling. Bauji was wheeling the cart with Beeji and Bade Bauji—who looked elegant in khakis and a bomber jacket.

Beeji was in a starched salwar kameez, ambling along like a ship in sail. No concessions made there—and I wouldn't want to be in the shoes of any security person who decided to frisk her!

"Peri pona, Bauji." Dad swiped a hand in the direction of Bade Bauji's feet. I made a halfhearted attempt to follow suit, feeling kind of ridiculous. I meant well, but it just didn't look or feel right if I did it.

"No, no, beta," Beeji said. "No need. How are you, Mini? You are looking fine!"

Beeji was an odd mixture of very traditional and very American. She'd lived here for forty years until Bauji decided he wanted to help modernize the KDH Spices grinding operations and also help launch the new Ayurvedic spices line.

Bade Bauji examined me carefully. "You look like your mother," he pronounced at last in his slow, deep voice and careful English. "You have your father's height, but you are Megha through and through."

"Thanks!" I said. I knew I always liked him.

"Minnni!" Bauji said. Bauji had not changed. Same lantern jaw, same big grin—he looked like the builder he was, even though he had now decided to dedicate his life to researching and bringing Ayurvedic spices to the world. A strange thing for an engineer and builder to be into, but, hey, whatever works, right? "How's the house looking?"

"It could do with some work!" I said. This was our old joke. Dad couldn't be bothered fixing anything around the house, so Bauji always sent his old subcontractors over to help out whenever anything was seriously in need of fixing. When the boiler died, when the water pipes froze, when the toilet made a weird whistling sound as it flushed, when the door stuck, when the roof tiles blew off—it was Bauji's trade friends who showed up and fixed the plumbing, retiled the roof, and hammered open the door.

Bauji and I had also convinced Dad to replace the windows, finish the three-season porch, expand the deck, and take care of various other home improvement projects. It was his way of being there for us even after moving away. I missed having him around.

"I'm here now," he said. "If there's anything you want done before the wedding, we still have time!"

Vinnie was here!

Manish picked her up at the airport and brought her home after a visit with his parents in Newton. He even came into the house and gingerly petted Yogi with latex gloves on. Even though Vinnie said it was stupid to risk breaking out in hives five days before the wedding, he scored major points with me and Dad. He was trying, I had to give him that—he was definitely trying.

As soon as he left, we went upstairs with Masi and looked at the dress. Vinnie hadn't even seen it yet, except in pictures and video.

"Masi, what if it doesn't fit?" Vinnie said.

"*Arre!*" Masi said. "We're here, no? We'll make it fit!"

"Okay, but what if I hate it?" Vinnie said.

"*That* we can't change now," Masi said.

"But you won't," I added. "I promise, Vinnie!"

"Okay," she said. "Here goes!" She opened the box and lifted the tissue.

Silence.

"Well?" Masi said.

"Say something!" I said, dying of suspense.

"Masi!" Vinnie looked stunned. She opened her arms, at a loss for words, and squeezed Masi. "It's so much more beautiful in real life. Thank you, Masi! Thank you!"

"Put it on first," Masi said, all smiles, "before you start thanking me!"

"But it's so, so beautiful," Vinnie said, cradling the dress.

"Yes, we all agree it's beautiful," I said. "But put it on, Vinnie. Now. We want to see—does it even fit or what? Okay, go!"

"Okay, okay!" Vinnie grabbed the box and vanished into her room. Masi grabbed my hand and squeezed. "I've dressed so many brides, beta, that it's all old to me now. All this fitting-shitting." How I kept a straight face while she rhymed *fitting* with *shitting*, I don't know, but she was obviously sincere, so I did. "But this is Vinnie, and I'm nervous. I'm actually *nervous* about this. What if she hates it, huh? Haven't been this nervous since I made Megha's lehenga all those years ago."

I patted her hand, but I was a wreck myself. Masi might have designed it, but I'd picked it out and convinced Vinnie it was the one. What if she did hate it? The door opened.

A vision in gold and red stood in the doorway, looking like she'd stepped out of a Bollywood movie. Kajol in *Dilwale Dulhania Le Jayenge*, Alia Bhatt in *Humpty Sharma Ki Dulhania*, or Koyal Khanna in *Meri Bollywood Wedding* ... all nothing to my sister, Dr. Vinnie Kapoor! I'm biased, clearly, but she looked fantastic.

The choli fitted her perfectly, setting off her curves; the old gold glowed against her tanned, toned arms. There was a small amount of bare midriff before the lehenga hugged her at the waist and flared out in a froth of gold. The heavy embroidery at the hem made the skirt swing at the slightest movement. Oh, shoot! She had thrown the pretty red scarf in a horrible bunch over one shoulder, but we could fix that.

"Vinnie!" I literally had tears in my eyes. "Have you *seen* yourself?"

"No," Vinnie said. "But it feels good," she added, and gingerly walked a step or two in the not-too-high heels I had put out for her. "But how does it look?"

"Okay, wait, first let me fix this. Turn around!" Masi ordered, then laced up the back of the choli properly and started to drape the red scarf over Vinnie's head.

"Wait! Put this on first!" I set a blue velvet jewelry box down on the bed.

"Oh, right." Masi put down the scarf and snapped open the jewelry case. "I had forgotten about this. Oh, look at this! It's Megha's design!" She lifted the gold necklace reverently. The gold glittered in the light. "Just look at this!" She clasped it gently around Vinnie's neck as I held up my sister's glossy black hair (shoulder-length now, thankfully). Masi held out the earrings and Vinnie put them in. I pinned the maangtika into place so it dangled high on her forehead, and Masi arranged the cranberry-red scarf over her hair.

"Remember, with your hair and makeup styled, you'll look even better," Masi said.

"Just look, Vinnie," I said, and turned her around so she was facing the full-length mirror on the back of my door.

"Wow, that's me?" Vinnie gasped.

"Sure is!" I said.

She turned this way and that. "Manish is not going to believe this," she said. "I look amazing!"

"Okay, let's show Dad!" I said, steering her out of the door and downstairs. "Dad, get a load of this!"

"What?" Dad said. He was wandering around with an open plastic cup of low-fat yogurt in one hand and a spoon in the other, oblivious to the excitement upstairs.

"Put that down first!" I said, taking the yogurt from his hand and dumping it in the trash. "It might get on the dress. Okay, Vinnie, come through!" I opened the door to the kitchen. "Ta-da!"

Vinnie floated in, smiling happily.

"Vinnie!" Dad was suddenly all smiles. "You look like a million bucks!"

"Doesn't she?" Masi said. She pulled out a fifty-dollar bill and waved it around Vinnie's head before putting it in the slot of my MSPCA collection box. "Nazar na lage!"

"What are you doing?" I asked. "All that waving thing?"

"Warding off the evil eye!" Masi said. "Vinnie, come! We have one more outfit for you to try!"

"I don't need another outfit!" Vinnie said.

"It's for the reception!" Masi said. "Mini, go get it!"

I knew what it was, of course—but we had not told Vinnie about finding Mom's lehenga. I followed them upstairs and grabbed it out of my closet, where it was hanging shrouded in a plastic dry-cleaning covering.

Vinnie pulled the plastic off. "No way!" She had tears in her eyes this time.

"Way!" I said. "Masi fixed that too. Go try it on!"

We waited for her to get into it, and then she was back, encased in the raspberry-pink-and-silver outfit.

"How does it look?" she asked.

"Brilliant!" I said.

It was very vintage—like something Madhuri Dixit would have worn—but Vinnie's fresh young face updated it immediately. There was a lump in my throat. It wasn't that she looked like Mom exactly, but there were flashes of Mom in the way she moved and smiled and sounded, even. And with that lehenga on, there was no mistaking it.

"Do that thing with the evil eye, Masi," I said. "Do it immediately!"

If we were lucky, it might turn the storm that was coming into a bit of light rain.

"It's very grand!" Ragini Aunty said. "It will be beauuutiful, Padmini. Beauuutiful."

"I didn't even know this was here," Manish said. "Vinnie played field hockey and soccer here, Amma."

It wasn't time for the wedding rehearsal—that was on Friday— but most of the immediate family was here now, so we brought them to River Bend anyway. Vinnie and Manish, Masi, Beeji, Bauji, Bade Bauji, Dad, Ragini Aunty, Venkat Uncle—and me.

"The mandap will go here," Vinnie said. "Shoma Aunty will be draping it in rust and dark red sheer fabric, and there will be flowers above the mandap on all four sides."

"Will there be banana trees, and a kalash with mango leaves and a coconut on top?" Ragini Aunty asked. That was the traditional configuration—Vinnie didn't love it, so we had nixed it— but how to tell Ragini Aunty that? Vinnie looked uncertain, so I stepped in.

"Of course there will, Aunty," I said. It wasn't a lie, precisely. There would be mango leaves and coconuts and a stack of shiny brass pots—just not front and center. We'd bury it behind the orchids that Vinnie liked so much. That would keep them all happy.

"Group photo!" Manish said. And everyone arranged themselves into two lines in front of the graceful marble fountain—they finally had it working, thankfully—and smiled dutifully for the camera. Ragini Aunty in her bright red Kanjivaram sari, Beeji in a very Punjabi lace salwar kameez, Bade Bauji in his homespun cotton kurta, and the rest of us in jeans.

"Let me," Jen Courtney said. Manish explained the way the camera worked and then took his place in the family lineup, his arm around Vinnie in spite of the presence of all the parents and grandparents and a great-grandparent. To their credit, they took it in stride.

Everything looked perfect, even the clear blue sky.

"Say cheese!" said Jen.

We were invited to Beeji's for dinner. I was on the phone the whole way, trying to get hold of the remaining two bridesmaids who did not have sari blouses as yet. With less than four days to go! I left messages on the phone, via email, on their FB pages, and with their mothers. "Please call today!" I said into the phone. "Otherwise you won't have a blouse to go with your sari for the wedding!"

"We're here!" Dad announced, and we spilled out of the mini-van onto Beeji's driveway. Dad, Masi, Vinnie, me, and Yogi, of course. "Something smells good!"

My grandparents' house is in the neighborhood my dad grew up in. Bauji builds huge mansions in wealthy suburbs—the kind with four-car garages and floating walkways and two-story atriums with crystal chandeliers. Once in a while when he has one sitting on the market he contemplates selling off the split-level and moving into it. But it's so not him. This house, where Dad planted the now-towering pine trees on either side, and helped Bauji put in the garage, and filmed sci-fi pictures with a Super 8 camera in the backyard—this is them. That's why they're holding on to the house, even though they live in India most of the year now.

Bauji did gut the interior and remove a few walls and put in granite, hardwood, and marble to upgrade the place whenever his building crew had downtime. The new granite-and-rosewood kitchen with the recessed lights and slide-out pantry wasn't really Beeji's cup of tea. But she could make magic in any kitchen anywhere.

Knowing Beeji, I was expecting an extravagant spread with the newest KDH spices showcased in every dish. She didn't disappoint.

Chana masala, with fresh bhatooras, okra, kadhi, pulao— no meat dishes because the Iyers, who were also invited, were vegetarian.

"They don't eat this and don't eat that," Beeji muttered. "Har tarah ki allergy pal rakhi hai. Hamari kuddi inni lambi chaudi, aur unka munda..."

"Beeji!" I warned.

"Ki hoya?" Beeji said. "Sehat nai banti vegetarian khane se. Vinnie, you make sure you feed your kids proper Punjabi food, okay?"

"Beeji!" Vinnie said. "Don't you dare say anything like that when they come!"

"And I'm making laddoos," Beeji said, uncovering a couple of platters with the flourish of a sorcerer. "For the wedding!"

"*Laddoos,*" I said, gazing incredulously at the hundreds of fist-sized golden-yellow balls that had magically appeared on trays all over Beeji's kitchen. It was clearly a work in progress. There was a giant pot full of fresh golden-brown boondis soaked in syrup on the countertop that were yet to be rolled into proper fist-sized laddoo balls. "You're making laddoos for the wedding? What are we paying that Sunny Sondhi for, then?"

I mean, the woman had just gotten here—how did she even make this much food in such a short time?

"But there should be some homemade sweets from the home, no?" Beeji said. "This is Vinnie's favorite."

"It is good hospitality," Bade Bauji put in unexpectedly. "Anyone can buy sweets, but..."

"We know!" I said. "Homemade Is from the Heart!"

But poor Beeji looked winded. It was completely unnecessary for her to have cooked dessert for an entire wedding party before she was even over her jet lag.

"Beeji, no one makes sweets at home anymore," I said. "Even in India they get a halwai to make it if they really want it fresh. And anyway we've ordered a massive wedding cake."

"Those South Indians," Beeji said. "Some of them don't eat eggs, you know. And Manish is allergic to nuts, and with that kind of thing it's better to have homemade—always. These caterers put nuts in everything. In sweets more than anything."

For all her complaining about their dietary restrictions, she had the needs of the "South Indians" in mind—typical Beeji.

"And that's why Curry Cuisine is bringing gulabjamuns for

them," I said. "They catered for Manish's sister's wedding, remember, and Manish ate their dessert and survived. Let's just put this away for now, okay?"

Beeji looked mightily offended, so I added, "I'll help you squeeze the rest of them after they've left. Just please go get dressed, and Vinnie and I will set the table and everything."

When we were full of Beeji's, in Ragini Aunty's words, "excccellent cooking," we turned on the Weather Channel and watched the forecast. Yeah, the storm was definitely headed our way. The Massachusetts Emergency Management Agency bunker in Framingham was being prepped in case the governor had to head there to coordinate the response. All the New England states were bracing for impact. If we were lucky, it would swing west and inland and miss Westbury, or it would swing east and out to sea, but right now it looked a lot like it was beating a path to Vinnie's wedding mandap. Yikes!

"We have a rain plan," Vinnie said. "Right, Mini?"

"Yes, they have a tent that we can set up for the ceremony. It's semiattached to the Carriage House, where the reception is going to be held. We'll just have to put the dance floor in the tent and put the mandap on top of it and the white chairs for the guests grouped around it. And when it's done we'll have to skip cocktail hour and go straight to the reception."

"The rehearsal is on Friday at River Bend," Vinnie said. "We'll talk about it then."

Dad's cell phone rang and he walked out of the room, only to return two minutes later grinning from ear to ear.

"Great news," he said. "Intel Capital finally called, and... they're giving us all the funding we asked for!"

"That's awesome, Dad." I hugged him. "That's epic!"

"You can spend anything you want for the wedding now," he said. "And I won't say a thing!"

Maybe the tide was turning for our family after all.

I ran upstairs and fetched a platter from Beeji's kitchen.

"Laddoos for everyone!" I said.

Chapter Twenty-Five

I. CAN'T. EVEN.

I can't even *begin* to explain what it was like when we found out that the dang hurricane was headed straight at us at the exact place and time of Vinnie's wedding. Just like that. *BAM*.

The only hope left was for it to weaken into a big rainstorm instead.

If I were the praying type, I would have been praying, but what was the use? Miracles had stopped working for the likes of us a long time ago.

All we could do was wait. We'd know within hours, definitely. Until then there was nothing to be done except wring our hands, write place cards, and go on as if a storm the size of Texas wasn't barreling down on us at 120 miles an hour.

So when we headed to the wedding rehearsal at River Bend on Friday there was a lot weighing on our minds.

Instead of just the event manager, there was a group of people waiting for us at River Bend.

"This is my boss, Karen Cummings, the general manager of the Massachusetts Botanical Society," Jen said. "I thought we should have her in on the discussion in case we need to get her approval for anything. We've been monitoring the weather too."

"It looks like the storm will hit on Sunday for sure," Karen said. "We will do everything we can to make sure your event still runs smoothly, but as of now the outdoor part of the event has to be canceled."

Vinnie and Manish held hands tightly—they were so adorable. "Of course," Manish said. "We want everyone to be safe."

"Can we move to the rain plan?" Vinnie asked. "Move the wedding ceremony under the tent and skip cocktail hour to go right to the reception?"

"That would be the best solution," Jen said. "The only problem is…"

"If the storm is predicted to have winds over fifty miles an hour," Karen said, "then we have to pack up the tent."

"Pack up the tent?" I asked. "But it had a concrete floor, it had metal scaffolding. It's not like a pop-up tent or anything. I've seen it up in the snow!"

"Yes, it's pretty sturdy," Jen admitted. "But fifty-mile-an-hour winds are too much for it to withstand. We can't take the risk of it collapsing on a party of people."

"Of course not," Dad said. "But this is hypothetical, right? If the storm takes a different track, we're good."

"That's correct," Karen said.

"If we do have to take the tent down," I asked, "where can we have the ceremony?"

"Well," Jen said, sounding apologetic, "an open fire is not allowed inside a landmarked building. And all the buildings at River Bend are historical landmarks. They can have candles, yes, but not an actual fire or anything."

"So we can't get married at River Bend at all?" Vinnie asked.

"If you promise that the fire will be very, very small, we could make an exception," Karen said. "It's a very unusual situation, and we want to be as accommodating as we can."

"Am I late?" A tall young man in a business suit walked through the double doors of the Carriage House. He had a pleasant face, but the resemblance to Sunny Sondhi was unmistakable. "I'm Vicky Sondhi, from Curry Cuisine."

"Was Mr. Sondhi too busy to come?" Dad asked.

"My dad's busy, so he sent me," Vicky said. "I guess we have a weather situation on Sunday. Just want to make sure we're on the same page as everyone."

I'd been thinking about the timing of the wedding—maybe that was the solution. We had scheduled it for three PM with the reception at seven PM. It was traditional in the North to have weddings in the evening.

"How about we reschedule the wedding to nine AM?" I asked. "We can have the reception at noon and serve lunch instead of dinner? We have the grounds and buildings booked for the day, right?"

"That may not be a bad idea," Jen said. "The storm is supposed to hit hardest late afternoon and evening. By then your guests could be on their way home if you're lucky."

"Can you serve lunch instead of dinner?" I asked Vicky Sondhi. It was great that he was here after all. "It's just a six-hour difference, but it would solve everything. We'd have to call the bus transportation company, and all the guests, and the bartender, and the priest, and Shoma Moorty. She said there was a big wedding in Boston on Saturday. Remember, the horse was booked for it too?"

"The Bernstein-Patel wedding." Vicky Sondhi nodded knowledgeably. "Everyone's talking about it. All the wedding horses nearby are booked for it. They're going to have a ten-horse parade—the groom is an equestrian, and his whole family rides."

I tried not to laugh at the thought of a whole bunch of guys riding up on white horses, doubtless wearing red turbans too. What had stopped them from hiring the elephant? "Good for them," I said. "We have to call Shoma Aunty, but if she's good with coming out early and getting the decorations done, we'll handle everything else. How does that sound?"

"Excellent," said Vinnie.

"I don't know," Manish said. "I have some friends coming in from California on Sunday afternoon. They won't be able to make it."

"How many friends?" I asked.

"Six or seven," Manish said.

"They'll have to miss it, then," I said. "Odds are that their flight will be canceled anyway, so there's no point waiting for them."

"Not so fast," Manish said. "Let me think about it."

"Okay," I said. "I do think they're closing Logan Airport for the storm, though, Manish. Can they take an earlier flight?"

"Maybe…I don't know," Manish said.

Leave him alone, Vinnie mouthed at me. *Fine*, I mouthed back at her.

"How about you guys continue discussing this?" I said. "I still have a lot of work to do at home for the mehendi."

The mehendi was still tomorrow, and I didn't have Shoma Moorty to help decorate the house. Masi was at home, busy stitching the blouses for the remaining two bridesmaids. Beeji was making laddoos for absolutely no reason except that it made her feel like she was doing something.

I ordered five gorgeous umbrellas via Dad's Amazon Prime account. Thanks to their free next-day delivery, at least we'd have some umbrellas that wouldn't clash with our Mallika Motwani couture. Then I snapped shut my laptop. I had had enough. First I was going to walk my dog. Then I was going to get my hair done. They had my cell phone number. If something went wrong, they could always find me.

I had booked Katrina, my regular hairdresser, to come to the house to get Vinnie ready—but she wasn't coming until 4:30 PM. I wanted to be done before then so I could help get Vinnie dressed without worrying about myself. So I went to the mall, walked into

Mane Event, and got an appointment with a random hairdresser. Not the smartest of moves, usually, but for some reason it paid off. The hairdresser was an excellent listener.

I hadn't even known how stressed I was until I started to talk to her about Vinnie's wedding and the storm, and Mom's jewelry, and my family, and Vir, and so on.

"Don't you worry, it'll all come together," she said.

"So many of the guests are stranded in airports all over the country," I said. "My grandfather and my two little cousins are in London—their flight has been delayed too. I don't want them to miss the wedding." I leaned my head back so she could shampoo my hair.

"Whoever is meant to be there will get there," she said, rinsing out my hair in warm water. "Don't you fret. It's better that everyone's safe on the ground somewhere, isn't it?"

"Absolutely," I said. "There are a *lot* of people who were coming to the wedding who have had flights canceled: from Miami, Dallas, San Francisco, and Chicago. Airlines don't want to take a chance."

"But your ninety-two-year-old great-grandfather got here from India," she said.

"Right, because he came early," I said.

"Just take it one step at a time," she said, wrapping my head in a towel and pointing me to a chair. "What's next?"

"The janvasam at the temple—that's tonight," I said.

"That's the engagement sort of thing," she said. "And then?"

"Then the mehendi tomorrow," I said.

"At your house?" she asked.

"Yeah, but we're prepared for that. They're delivering the tables and chairs tonight and we're setting everything up in the morning."

"And the wedding is on Sunday," she said.

"Sunday morning now," I said.

"So three events in three days," she said as she clipped the last rollers into place. "Just take it one step at a time."

"Okay," I said.

"You have half an hour under the dryer," she said, turning on the domelike dryer over my head. "Read a magazine, and I'll get you some tea."

I had five minutes of peace—the calm before the storm—before my phone rang. It was Vinnie. Vinnie sounding strangely calm and clinical as she broke the horrible news. Massachusetts had declared a state of emergency and all state parks were to be closed on Sunday—including River Bend. There was no venue anymore.

The wedding was off.

"I'll get home as soon as I can, okay?" I said. "We'll think of something, Vinnie, I promise."

"What's wrong?" the hairdresser asked.

I told her.

"My grandparents got married in a hurricane, you know," she said. "There was no one there but ten people and a preacher—it can be done."

"Even if we find another venue," I said, "how are we going to let everyone know and change all the arrangements?"

"You can't do it without help," she said. "So anyone who's ever said *let us know if we can do anything*—call them. Tell them what you need. They will feel better if they can help."

"Okay," I said. "I will."

"Attagirl," she said. "Now let's make your hair look gorgeous."

An hour later I emerged rested, determined, and ready to do battle with that storm. When I turned on the radio in the car, the WBUR news team was reporting live from MEMA headquarters, confirming that the governor had declared a state of emergency ahead of Indra. They were expecting it to hit by Saturday night. I shook my newly styled hair in disbelief. It didn't seem real that a Category 2 storm with hundred-mile-an-hour winds could potentially arrive in Westbury the weekend of Vinnie's wedding. But that's exactly what it looked like right now.

Chapter Twenty-Six

"They don't have a choice," Vinnie said. "The State of Massachusetts has ordered them shut."

"So we'll find an alternative venue," I said. I didn't even believe it. We both knew how far in advance places got booked.

"We tried," Vinnie said. "Dad's been on the phone ever since we left River Bend. Everything outdoor is canceled and everything indoor is booked."

We had to think outside the box. "How about here?" A wild idea was taking hold of me. "At our house! Tomorrow—before the storm hits hard!"

"Are you crazy?" Vinnie said. "We can't fit over a hundred people in here. Even with the people canceling, we'll have at least that many people."

"Maybe not inside," I said, and grabbed my car keys. "But we have the yard—at least until it starts raining. I'll be back, Vinnie!"

"But where are you going?" Vinnie wailed.

"Just get ready for the janvasam," I said, and gave her a kiss. "And try not to worry."

I hopped into the car and pushed a button on my cell phone—it's a good thing I had Talbot Rental on speed dial. The ringtone buzzed at the other end. Pick up, pick up, pick up—dang it! Someone rapped on my car window as I backed slowly out into the street.

Vir!

I had nearly run him over—if you can run anyone over at two miles an hour.

You can't do it without help. The hairdresser's stern voice sounded in my head. *Tell them what you need.*

I stopped the car and jumped out.

"Vir, drive the car!" I said. "I have to make a phone call."

"You trust me with your car?" he said, looking warily at me.

"Are you kidding me?" I said. "My dad let you drive his Lotus!"

"Fine, fine, I'll drive," he said.

There was a charged silence as he eased the Mini up the hill. The bitter words we had exchanged crackled between us, demanding resolution, but this was not the time.

"Er . . . where exactly are we going?" Vir asked.

"The Westbury Town Hall," I said. "If they're still open!"

He was an excellent driver—even I sometimes stall at the top of the hill, but not Vir. Meanwhile someone at Talbot Rental answered the phone. "Hi," I said. "I'd like to book a tent for tomorrow, please."

"What kind of tent?" the girl asked.

"A twenty-foot-by-forty-foot tent," I said after consulting my notepad. Yeah, that was the largest size I could fit on the front lawn. The backyard had trees, and the side lawn was sharply slanted—so they were both out.

"Okay," she said. "Do you want side walls for the tent?"

"Yes," I said. "The ones with clear windows."

"What date is this for?" she asked. "Wait, you said tomorrow, right?"

"Yes," I said. "Saturday the twenty-seventh of August."

"What town?" she asked.

"Westbury," I said. We had made it to the town center and Vir was parking by the library. I jumped out of the car and sprinted for the town hall. They usually closed at four-thirty. I still had five or ten minutes—if they hadn't changed their schedule for the summer. If they had shorter summer hours we were toast.

"And do you have a dig-safe permit?" the girl at Talbot Rental asked. That was the question I'd been dreading.

"No," I said. "But I am trying to get to the town hall. With any luck, they'll still be open and..."

There were no lights on in the town hall. The door was bolted. Shoot! Of all the days for the town hall to close early!

My crazy idea to save the day had just crashed and burned.

"I'm here, but they're closed," I said. Then I added hopefully, "Can we still get a tent?"

"We can't put up a tent without a dig-safe permit, ma'am," she said. "I'm sorry."

"It's my sister's wedding," I explained dejectedly. "It was supposed to be at River Bend on Sunday but they've canceled because of the hurricane. So we're trying to move it to our house. But we can't do it without a t-tent." My voice broke. I so didn't want to cry—not with Vir watching. But what on earth were we going to do *now*?

"Your sister's wedding got canceled? That's terrible!" the girl said. "Look, hold on a minute, let me talk to someone."

"Okay," I said. "I'll hold." Vir had caught up with me. He took one look at my face and pulled me into a hug. I was too surprised to even resist—and I had to admit, it felt good.

"You there?" the girl said. "Okay, I checked with my boss and he did say that we can't put up a tent without a permit...."

I rested my head on Vir's shoulder for a minute before regaining my sanity and pushing away. Vir let go.

"Thanks for trying," I said. "It's really nice of you."

"No, wait," she said. "We can't put up a tent, but YOU can."

"What?" I asked. Maybe my brain had stopped functioning due to all the impossible things it had had to process lately. Did she just say we could put up a tent?

"We can give you a tent. We just can't put it up," she said. "Do you still want it?"

My heart was racing. "YES!" I said. "Yes, and there are other things...I need to get more tables and chairs than we had booked before...ten tables, a hundred chairs, floor-length tablecloths, napkins, china, silverware, stemware...."

"One at a time," she said. "I have to take this down. How many table covers and what kind?"

"Ten round, white, floor-length for the eight-foot round tables," I said. "I'll need a buffet table too...."

Vir was looking at me as if I'd lost my mind. But he waited to question me until after I got off the phone with her.

"What was that about?" he said.

"Getting a big tent," I said. "So we can have the reception at home."

"But who's going to put up a forty-foot tent?" he asked.

"That's not a problem, trust me," I said. "But food, I need food."

"What about Curry Cuisine?" he asked.

"That Sunny Sondhi cashed the ten-thousand-dollar check my dad gave him," I said. "And he's not answering phone calls."

"WHAT? He gave him a check?" Vir asked. "For the full amount?"

"It's my fault," I said. "I insisted that he pay the guy in advance because Shoma Aunty told us that he threatened to take away food at this other wedding because he *wasn't* paid in advance. We never imagined this!"

"I don't blame you," Vir said. "NO one expected this!"

A brilliant idea seized me.

"I should call Sher-e-Punjab," I said. "Right now!"

I scrolled through the contacts on my phone and found the number. "Sher-e-Punjab? Rajinder Singh Ji?" I said. "Thank God! Badi problem aa gai hai—aapki help chahiye. Can you double our order?" I counted on my hands to get a grasp of the numbers. "Triple our order? Forty nahin, one hundred twenty logon ka khana chahiye. Haan ji, hurricane ki vajah se cancel karna pada. Kal shadi hamare ghar se hogi. Haan ji. Thank you, ji."

"What did he say?" Vir asked after I hung up.

"He said it's an honor to help in a daughter's wedding," I said. "He's going to start cooking right now."

"That's great!" Vir said. But I was already dialing another number.

"Bauji!" I said when Bauji picked up at the other end. "You heard, no?"

"Yes," Bauji said. "What can be done now, I don't know...."

"I do," I said. "But Bauji—We. Need. Help. Do you have the old utilities map of our house that shows where the gas lines are and everything? You do? Great! And can you get ahold of your old construction crew?"

Vir and I drove back in silence. I knew what to do as far as the wedding went—but I was lost when it came to Vir. The way he hugged me, the way he sounded so concerned...I had to believe he cared. But there was all that other stuff. I couldn't even *think* about it now.

"Can I do anything else?" he asked quietly when we got home.

"I'll let you know," I said. "And thanks, Vir."

"I mean it," he said.

"I know," I said, and then paused. "Actually, I just thought of something...."

"Anything," he said.

"Can you pick up some chrysanthemums in the morning?" I asked. "From the garden center on Route Twenty-Seven? They call them hardy mums."

"Okay," Vir said. "What time do they open?"

"Eight AM," I said. "I need at least a dozen large pots. Two dozen if they have them. Any and all colors you can find."

"I'll be there!" he said.

At home, Masi and Katrina had worked their magic to make Vinnie look outstanding. Everything might be falling apart, but our bride was going to look perfect in every way.

"Mini!" Masi said. "Go get changed, beta. We're late! We'll have to go ahead, and your dad and you can catch up later."

"Okay," I said. "I'm going! But I have to tell you..."

"Not now!" Masi said. "We'll talk at the temple."

So even though everything about the wedding and the mehendi—the date and time and venue—was up in the air, we still had to get to the one event that was going off without a hitch—the janvasam. They all piled into cars and headed for the temple.

Dad and I would have to catch up, like Masi said.

I wore the gorgeous sari that Ragini Aunty had given me. It was a luscious double weave—pink from one angle, purple from the other—and shot all over with sprays of gold. I had a basic pink blouse that went well with it, as did Nani's anklet necklace.

The Sri Balaji temple in Sherwood is the hub of the Indian community in New England. I hadn't been to it since my mother's death. None of us had. Because that's when my dad decided that the idea of a concerned and compassionate deity was laughable in the light of recent family history. And in case we'd ever doubted it, there was (drumroll) the uninvited hurricane at Vinnie's wedding.

Still we went. And as we turned off Route 128 and the white-washed spires of the temple came into view, I felt stirrings of childhood nostalgia. This was where I had my first dance performance at the age of five. It must have been even more powerful for Dad—I could almost hear him freeze as we stopped at the temple.

I cast around for an icebreaker.

"Look, Dad!" I said. "The car blessing spot!"

That was where the priest would come out and perform a prayer for an automobile, sprinkle holy water on its hood, and break a coconut in front of it for good luck. I remember coming there after we bought the minivan. Mom had insisted.

Needless to say, my Mini Cooper had not had the treatment, and neither had Dad's Lotus Esprit.

There was a sign in the car blessing spot that said THE TEMPLE IS CLOSED TOMORROW AUGUST 27 DUE TO THE HURRICANE.

"Want to update the minivan's blessing?" I joked.

"It's cheaper than insurance!" Dad said—a Mom quote—and he even cracked a smile. It had been a good day when the minivan was blessed. We had lunch at the Dosa Temple afterward and felt safe driving home in our newly blessed car.

"Come on," Masi said. They had been waiting in the parking lot for us to arrive so we could make our entry together.

A whole contingent of Iyers was waiting for us at the front of the temple. I laughed at Vinnie's face because Manish had decided to go topless after all.

"Hey, Manish has some decent abs under the scrubs and lab coat! Who knew?"

"Will you stop it?" Vinnie said, red in the face.

I guess on the right guy the outfit does look nice. Vir, for example, with his swimmer's physique. He'd look like a model wrapped in a bedsheet. Why could I not get him out of my head?

"Vanakkam, vanakkam," Venkat Uncle said. Which is a Tamil greeting that we were now getting familiar with.

They walked us to the long room that ran along the length of the temple. It had been set up with rows of chairs.

"Mini," Bauji said. "I called Alan Brown and Richie. They'll be at your house at six-thirty in the morning. What time did you say Talbot Rental opens?"

"Seven," I said. "Do they have something big enough to carry everything back with them?"

"Yes," Bauji said. "They have a pickup truck, and I'll bring mine."

"When can they have the tent up?" I asked. "I've asked Sher-e-Punjab to bring lunch at noon."

"They'll be done by noon," Bauji said.

I relaxed enough to finally look around. Bade Bauji was sitting in the front row, the red turban on his head adding a few inches to his tall frame. Beeji, Dad, and Masi were sitting next to him.

Ragini Aunty was holding Vinnie's arm and chatting with a priest. It was Krishna Ji, the head temple priest, the one she said was an Iyengar. He had really gone gray in the last seven years, but otherwise his face was the same—kind, wrinkled, smiling, with a white V on his forehead like the Hare Krishnas. I guess they stole it from the Iyengars. Except Krishna Ji's V also had a single yellow line down the center.

"I didn't know the girl Manish was marrying was Vinnie," he said. "Ragini Amma, I've known this family for a long, long time."

I was smiling without meaning to. He was always so sweet to both of us. "How is Rama Ji?" I asked. "Very good," he said. "Okay, the mahoorat is now, kutti, let's start the Nichayathartham."

They had set up for the ceremony with a red carpet, gold chairs, a gold-and-white brocade backdrop, and stacked pots with mango leaves and coconuts atop—definitely Shoma Moorty's handiwork! It was traditional, but it had a bright and happy wedding vibe.

Manish and his family sat to one side of the priest and Vinnie and Dad to the other. In the center was the small fire pit for the homum. "Amma, please," Krishna Ji said to Masi. "You come and sit and complete the rituals for the girl's mother."

"Sure," Masi said. "Vinnie is my daughter too."

"Pssssst," someone said in my ear.

"Yes?" I turned around to see an imposing woman in a dazzlingly bright yellow sari. "Come with me."

Her tone was pretty authoritative, so I followed her out. She pulled me into the main temple hall. "I'm Radhika, Manish's mom's friend. You are Mini?"

"Yes," I said. "It's nice to meet you."

"We were thinking...." An older man with ash stripes across his forehead materialized next to us. "Natarajan and I think the wedding can be at the temple."

"Isn't the temple closed tomorrow?" I asked.

"Yes, yes." Radhika shook her head, but it was unclear if she meant yes or no. "But it is open in the morning."

I looked at the sign behind her, and this one said: DUE TO THE STORM, THE TEMPLE CLOSES TOMORROW AUGUST 27, AT NOON.

"If they start early, they can be done by noon," Radhika Aunty said. Yes, Radhika *Aunty*—I was definitely adopting her after her genius idea. "We could have the reception another day."

"We could go to our house for the reception!" I said. Yes, that would work. "But will they let us have the wedding here?"

"Not normally," Radhika Aunty said. "But my husband, Natarajan, is on the board of the temple. He can talk to them."

Manish's family and their friends made up half the board, apparently. We were in luck!

Natarajan was smiling encouragingly over her shoulder. "You come with me and we fill out the forms."

"But shouldn't I ask Vinnie or Dad?" I asked. "Or Manish!"

"No time," Natarajan said. "Ragini and Venkat are fine with

it. If Manish and Vinnie don't like it, we can cancel, but we should book it just so we have something."

There was a small office window, behind which sat a plump lady with a bunch of jasmine flowers in her hair.

"Yes?" she asked sharply.

"Now ask for the wedding booking form," Natarajan instructed from behind me. "In English, okay? Not Hindi or Punjabi."

"Okay," I said. "Er...could I please have the form to book weddings?"

Suddenly the woman was all smiles. "You are Ragini's son Manish's fiancée's sister!" she said.

It took me a minute to figure out that this was correct. "Yes!" I confirmed. Natarajan Uncle was doing nothing but smiling and nodding in the background, but clearly his presence had changed the woman's attitude and helped her identify who the hell I was.

"Tomorrow morning," she said. "Yes, we are open!"

Something about the way she said it made me think that the open-till-noon thing had to do with various strings being pulled on the temple board as well.

I concentrated on the simple paper form in my hand. Bride's name, groom's name, temple member making the booking's name—that would be Dad, right? I didn't know if he technically was still a member of this congregation.

I looked back at the form. Temple donation: $500. Was that ALL? Dang, it was cheap to book a temple hall! But I didn't think I had that much money on me. "Er...I'm not sure I have...," I started.

"Make the payment tomorrow," the lady said obligingly.

"Sure, if that's okay with you," I said, handing back the completed form. "So, are we booked for tomorrow?"

"Yes," she said. "Krishna Ji will perform the ceremony."

I smiled. Those simple words made the whole crazy thing feel better—*Krishna Ji will perform the ceremony.* Maybe this was also meant to be.

"Do we have a time?" Radhika Aunty asked.

"Yes, nine AM tomorrow, here," I said, clutching the booking form to me. "Followed by the reception at Twenty-One Andrea Road, Westbury, at noon."

"Write it down quickly," she instructed. I jotted down the details and handed it to her. She walked briskly to the front and handed it to Dad. Dad looked at it, looked up at me, and mouthed: *ARE YOU SURE?*

I nodded vigorously, and he stood up, cleared his throat, and proceeded to read: "We, the families of Vinod Kapoor and Venkat and Ragini Iyer, declare the intention of our daughter Yashasvini Kapoor and our son Manish Iyer to marry at nine AM tomorrow, the twenty-seventh of August, at Sri Balaji Temple, Sherwood. The ceremony will be performed by Krishna Iyengar Ji, the head priest. A reception will follow at noon at the Kapoor residence at Twenty-One Andrea Road, Westbury."

I suppose the announcement is usually a formality at these

things because everyone already knows the details. But this was no formality—everyone was hanging on Dad's words, including the bride and groom.

He looked up. "You may be aware that there has been a slight change in the plan due to the hurricane. We need to let everyone know the new date and venue so they can get here. Please help us spread the word."

With that, Dad handed a platter of gifts to the Iyers, who in turn presented gifts to him. Manish grabbed the box containing the nice Punjabi sherwani we had bought him and went off to change.

"Mini!" I looked up to see Vinnie pass by surrounded by a flock of smiling Tamil ladies. I guess they were going to help her get changed. I got up and Masi put a hand on mine—"Let them," she said.

So I took a deep breath and waited for Vinnie to emerge after they helped her dress.

Vinnie! OMG, Vinnie in a Kanji-freaking-varam! They had even put strings of jasmine flowers in her hair, and some gold temple jewelry too. She looked amazing!

Dad, meanwhile, looked on the verge of tears and ready to bolt.

Luckily I needed him to do something, which always calmed him down.

"Dad, you know the Indian grocery store in Framingham?" I said. "Go there and get this!"

"Now?" he asked.

"Yeah, now," I said. "We're just going to be eating now; they'll understand."

256

"Where's Dad?" Vinnie asked.

"Dude, you look awesome!" I said. She looked stunning. "Manish, you too!" Manish looked even more transformed in the buttoned-up Nehru-collar jacket and pants than Vinnie did in her sari.

"So the wedding is here and the reception is at home?" Vinnie asked. "Will that work?"

"Yeah," I said flippantly, trying not to let her guess the general state of panic under my smiling veneer. "Absolutely!"

"We need to let everyone know!" Vinnie said. "As soon as we get home, I have to call everyone!"

"Vinnie, what about the mehendi?" I asked.

"Well, we have to cancel that, of course." Vinnie looked puzzled.

"But you have to have mehendi on your hands before you get married," I said. "It's tradition. Just look at them!" I turned her hands palms up.

Her palms were bare and tan and decidedly unbridelike. "Ohhh!" Vinnie said. "Do you think I could go to the mehendi lady?"

"I've called and canceled, and she said not to worry and that she'll stay up late and do it for you whenever you can get to her," I said.

"But she's all the way over in Lexington, right?" Vinnie said.

"That's an hour and a half just to get there and back, and how long to put it on?"

"One hour," I said. "If she does a rush job."

Vinnie looked resigned. "Guess I'm getting married without the mehendi, then. No way I can spend two to three hours on just that tonight. We won't even be out of here before ten-thirty—it's more important to get the word out."

"Or," I said, "we can put it on you—Masi and me. It won't be great but at least it will be mehendi."

"You're forgetting that we don't *have* any mehendi," Vinnie said.

"We will," I said. "Dad's on it. This is delicious, by the way!" The vadas and rasam and curd rice they served up after the ceremony were to die for.

"There is so much food left," Ragini Aunty said. "Maybe you can take it home? It might come in handy tomorrow."

"Sure," I said. Good thing I had cleaned out the entire fridge last weekend. We had plenty of room to store stuff.

"Where's your father?" Venkat Uncle asked. "I want to introduce him to my brother-in-law."

"He had to run out on an errand, Uncle," I said. "He'll be back soon!"

"Oh, yes, there he is now," Venkat Uncle said. So soon! Either Dad had floored it all the way to Framingham or the store was closed. I must have looked worried because Dad held up a grocery bag in one hand and gave me a lopsided grin and a cheerful thumbs-up.

Yeah, he had floored it.

"Vinod, I have to ask you for a favor," Venkat Uncle said. "I heard what happened with that fellow Sondhi you hired to cater for the wedding on our recommendation. Please accept this check for what you paid him from our side. Please."

The check was made out for the full amount Sondhi had cashed. Dad looked from it to Venkat Uncle and shook his head.

"No need for that. I will make the guy refund it!" Dad said. "And even if he doesn't, it's fine."

"He may not give back the full amount," Venkat Uncle said. "And you still have so many expenses. It's not right that the bride's side pay for everything. I don't understand why we have so many functions anyway."

"I don't either," Dad said. "But my wife, she would have loved..." His voice cracked for a second as he glanced over at Vinnie and Manish—smiling, happy, surrounded by people—and I reached over to grab his hand. "Look, please don't worry, we don't need the help."

"I am sure," Venkat Uncle said. "But it's not if you need it; it's the principle, you see. It's *both* our children's wedding. We should help."

He was not going to take no for an answer.

"Okay," Dad said, smiling. "If you insist."

"Thank you, Uncle," I said.

"No thanks required," Venkat Uncle said. "We're all family now."

Late Friday night, Masi and I were with Vinnie in her hotel room. She had a room at the Newton Grand, where the wedding stylist was supposed to come in the morning to do her makeup and hair and to drape her chunni. We had forced Dad to go home to bed, since there wasn't much he could do. Vinnie was typing, texting, and calling with one hand while I held a tube of henna over the other.

"Hold still, dammit!" I said. "I'm falling asleep here!"

"Okay, okay," she said. I was attempting to execute one of the designs she had picked off the internet. Thankfully for all of us, her tastes ran to simple symmetrical florals and paisleys. Masi had recused herself from the task of actually putting on the mehendi on the grounds of having bad eyesight and shaky hands. As if! She confined herself to critiquing my efforts, not that I wasn't already nervous enough or anything, and also helping Vinnie type and take her calls—which was actually very handy.

"So, why did we have to cancel the horse?" Masi asked.

"What horse?" Vinnie asked.

"It was going to be a surprise," I said. "Manish was such a sport about it!"

"Aww, that's so sweet," Vinnie said. "What happened to it?"

"The Patel-Bernstein wedding," I explained. "They've had to reschedule too." They must be dealing with the same crazy weather scenario we were.

"Oh, the poor things," Vinnie said. "How long it must have taken them to plan that wedding. I really, really hope it doesn't rain on their parade!"

"I'm just glad Shoma Moorty is willing to do our decorations before rushing off to do theirs," I said. When Vinnie had called her and explained the situation, she had asked for an hour before confirming she could do the decorations at the temple in time for a nine o'clock wedding. Then she had called back and said she would—in spite of the Patel-Bernstein wedding. She would have to be there at what, five o'clock? Pure steel, our Shoma Aunty.

"Turn over your hand," I said, and continued the design over the back of Vinnie's hand. "Ooops! Masi—toothpick!" Masi handed me one and I carefully wiped off the blooper.

"Okay, done. There, now hold your palm outstretched, don't smudge it while it's wet, and don't wash it off for at least two hours," I said.

Vinnie held up her hands and scanned my work. "That looks totally legit, Mini," she said. "You're a pro."

"Yeah, yeah," I said. "You're only saying that because you're stuck with it. Do you want some on your feet too?"

"Just a little...," Vinnie said. I worked a trail of vines and flowers from her big toe across the top of her foot to her heel and wrapped around her ankle. "How's that?"

Vinnie nodded, so I finished the other side before putting down the cone and yawning and stretching. "I gotta get home and crash."

Luckily Vinnie had already gotten into her pj's before starting the whole henna thing, so she just had to roll into bed. I had to drive back.

"You go home," Masi said. "I'll stay here and help Vinnie get ready in the morning. And all the bridesmaids." They were all either staying in the hotel or coming in the morning to get help putting on their saris. I was supposed to have helped them, but now...

"What about your clothes?" I asked.

"Send them with Vinod in the morning," Masi said. "I know you have a lot to do, with the house. I won't be much help there, but I know how to get a bunch of girls runway-ready."

I gave her a hug. I was actually getting used to randomly giving her hugs. I think she even enjoyed them. Yes, she totally did.

And then I went home. I wasn't going to bed anytime soon!

Chapter Twenty-Seven

Saturday morning dawned without a cloud in the sky, though satellite shots showed Indra storming up the Eastern seaboard. It was going to be legendary—or a disaster.

Either way, no one would ever forget it.

Game. On.

I sent off an email to all the gals invited to the mehendi, explaining things. I sent off a more detailed email to Shayla and Rachel. I sent off emails to all the neighbors on the street giving them a heads-up about the traffic mayhem about to descend on Andrea Road—and inviting them all to the reception. There is a saying in Hindi—pittey par doh joot aur—what's two more blows if you're already having your ass kicked? So what were a few neighbors when I'd already invited a whole wedding party?

The doorbell rang. I went downstairs to find Dad opening the door to Bauji. Bauji was holding a big cardboard box that said AMA-ZON PRIME. "This was outside, Vinod," he said.

"Um…Mini, what is this?" Dad asked.

"Umbrellas," I said.

"Don't we *have* umbrellas?" Dad asked.

"Not ones that complement Vinnie's dress," I said. "And the bridesmaids'! These will look great in the pictures."

"Okay." Dad shook his head and turned to Bauji. "Are your guys here?" he asked. Bauji nodded toward the driveway, where two pickup trucks were parked.

"Here's the list of things I've ordered," I said, handing it to him. "It *should* fit in those trucks."

I must have sounded worried because Bauji said, "Don't worry, we'll make it fit."

"I'll go with them," Dad said.

"No, you have to get ready!" I said. "And they'll have more room if you don't go."

And then they were gone. "Go have a shower," I ordered Dad, "and I'll put on the coffee."

I was just going up the stairs when a Mirchandani Mirage screeched to a halt on the curb.

Vir stepped out holding a pot of absolutely brilliant pink chrysanthemums.

What with my late night, I probably resembled something his mom's cat dragged in, but he looked showered and shaved and ready to go.

"I brought your flowers," he said.

"Awesome," I said, tucking a few strands of hair behind my ear in a vain attempt at tidying up. "I thought they opened at eight?"

"They were there at seven AM and let me buy the flowers early," he said, and started bringing in pots and pots of the most glorious vibrant colors of chrysanthemums—pink, yellow, white, red, orange.

I forgot how self-conscious I was for a moment and started hopping around in my flannel pajamas.

"Oh, they're perfect, Vir!" I said. "Thank you!"

"Is there anything else you need?" he asked.

"Will you come to the wedding?" I asked.

"If you want me to," Vir said.

"I do," I said, and smiled warmly at him. Whatever those news articles said, my gut said different. And today, I was going to go with my gut.

"Was someone just here?" Dad asked. That had to be the quickest shower ever.

"Just Vir, bringing some flowers," I said. "Coffee?"

"Vinnie is dressed and ready!" Masi said, giving me the update at the hotel. "We'll go directly to the temple, Mini. Are you dressed?"

"No," I said. I was outside watching Bauji and the guys unpack the gear from Taylor's. "But Dad just left. Bauji and I will get there as soon as we're done."

Bauji and the dudes had a ton of stuff to unload from the pickup trucks. Alan put down a rack of china and the plates clattered alarmingly.

"Careful with that!" I yelled. "Careful!"

"Don't worry." He grinned. "We've got this!"

"The tent goes here, Bauji," I said. "It should fit, I measured it. Did you bring the diagram of the gas lines and electrical lines?"

"Yeah," Bauji said. "I have it right here. There's nothing at all at the front. They all come down the side of the house, down the hill. We can put stakes as deep as we like in the front yard. Alan, Richie, come here."

The guys had gotten everything off the trucks.

"Okay, you know we're short on time," Bauji said. "We need the lawn mowed."

"Do we have time for that?" I asked. The grass wasn't that high, but Bauji was a perfectionist—I had forgotten.

"Yes, we do," Bauji said. "Mow the lawn first and then get the tent up. I want it weather-tight just in case we have rain. Mini, how d'you want the tables and chairs set up?"

"Like this," I said, handing them a layout I'd sketched. "I don't know when we'll have time for the place settings. . . ."

"We can do it," Alan said. "Do you want us to set up the tables and the plates and things? We can do it real nice."

Could they? They had no experience laying place settings for weddings. But they were quick and smart and careful, that much I knew.

"Okay," I said. "I need ten chairs per table, and ten place settings. Tablecloth first, then plates, silverware, wineglasses, napkins..."

"We can do that," Richie said. "Do the flowers go in the middle?"

"Yes!" I said. "Exactly! And if you have time after that, could you get a bunch of fairy lights from the party store and string them on the trees?"

"Like for Christmas?" Alan asked.

"Just like that!" I said. "But only if you have time."

"Go change, beta," Bauji said. "I need to get that list of things the priest wanted to the temple. Your dad forgot it in the garage. You change and come fast, okay?"

"Okay," I said.

I tied on my red bridesmaid sari and secured it with a bunch of safety pins. Apart from Mom's plain gold chain, I didn't put on any jewelry. I didn't want to look more dressed up than the rest of the bridesmaids—I had planned to change into the firoza-blue lehenga for the reception, but now I didn't know if I'd even have time for that.

By the time I finished doing my hair and makeup, it was eight. The guys had already mowed the front lawn and started to raise the tent—which was *huge*!

I rushed to the Mini and started the engine. Tried to start the engine, that is. I had been so tired last night I'd left the headlights on—the battery was toast! And Vinnie's wedding started in an hour!

I called Dad.

"Dad, my car's dead, I need a jump start!" I said.

"What?" Dad said. "Okay, don't panic. Call AAA, they'll get you going!"

"They'll take ages!" I wailed. "I'm not going to miss Vinnie's wedding!"

"Then take an Uber," Dad said.

"That'll take ages too," I said.

"There are jumper cables somewhere in the garage," Dad said. "Maybe the guys can jump-start your car. Or take Alan's pickup truck!"

"They can't stop working—they've got too much to do," I said. "Maybe Vir..."

"Vir is here," Dad said. "It'll take too long for him to get back."

Sounded like everyone was there but me.

"I'll see if Shayla's up. Maybe she can give me a ride."

"Fine," Dad said.

"Pick up, pick up. Pick. Up. The. Damn. Phone!" My pleading was for nothing because Shayla was not doing any picking up of the phone on an early Saturday morning. She had to be up at six for summer camp every weekday—she was sleeping in.

So what were my options?

Only one.

I pushed the button for the other side of the garage, and it rolled open to reveal Dad's car.

Cue the James Bond theme song—I was taking the Lotus Esprit.

I won't lie—it was fun driving the Lotus properly. Dad had only ever allowed me to take it down the street and back. The speed and power of the thing were incredible. I turned into the long wooded driveway that led up to the temple. Vir was standing there with two other guys—was that really Chintu and Mintu Patel? I hadn't seen them since I was twelve years old. All of them had their eyes bugging out at the sight of me in the race car.

"Sweet ride!" Vir was the first one to speak when I rolled down the car window at the temple. "So, are you with the bride's party or the groom's?"

"Vir!" I said. "What are you doing?"

"Directing traffic, of course," he informed me. "I'm helping out, along with these guys—family friends, I gather? We're putting the groom's side in *this* parking lot and the bride's side in *that* parking lot. Of course, some people are just here to pray, and they're completely confused."

"So I have to go to the parking lot at the top of the hill?" I asked.

"Correct," Vir said. "You look gorgeous, Mini." I felt flattered but then he added, "Especially in that car!" Way to destroy a perfectly heartfelt compliment.

I got to the top of the hill, only to be flagged down by a frantic-looking Shoma Moorty.

"Mini, go down to that parking lot!" she said. "Go now!"

"But I thought the bride's side was supposed to go here?" I asked.

"Yes, but that car, Mini," she breathed. "That car is perfect!"

"For what?" I asked. Had she totally lost her mind?

"For the wedding," she said. "We're not getting a horse because it's booked for the Patel-Bernstein wedding, so how can we make an entrance?" She paused for impact. "I thought we could decorate the white Ferrari...."

"Lotus," I corrected.

"Whatever. It's a good-looking car, that's all," she said. "Manish really wanted to surprise Vinnie with a baraat, but it doesn't work unless the guy has a nice ride. We don't have a horse, but once we've decorated it, this will be perfect!"

I could see Dad approaching us from the corner of my eye. "Okay," I said, hurriedly changing gears, and backing out of there before he could get to us.

Because if I told him we were going to sticky-tape rosebuds on his beloved car's impeccable fiberglass exterior, he would lose his mind.

The temple driveway is a circular one-way, so I had to pass by Vir at the entrance again.

"Everything okay?" he asked. Did I mention that he looked strikingly handsome? No? Well, he did.

"Get in," I said.

"Oookay," Vir said. "Carry on without me, guys!" he said to Chintu and Mintu Patel.

"I don't think Manish knows how to drive stick shift," I said.

"Or at least I haven't seen him do it. If my dad's car is going to be in the baraat, I'm putting it in hands I trust—yours."

"I'm happy that you trust me," Vir said. "But I don't know a single person on the groom's side."

"I know," I said. "And please give them these red turbans." I handed him a stack of starched and ironed turban cloths, no pre-tied turbans if Beeji had her way. "Oh, crap!"

"What?" Vir asked.

"They're not tied," I said. "Bade Bauji was supposed to tie the turbans for us so they could just put them on their heads. Do you think those Iyers know how to tie a turban?"

"They may not," Vir said. "But I do!"

"Really?" I asked.

"It was part of our dress uniform at Mayo College," he said. "We had to wear it to temple and all the formal events. So how do you want it tied—Jodhpuri style, or Jaipuri?"

"Vir," I said. "Thank you again."

"You're welcome," he said.

Back in the bride's-side parking lot I finally got a good look at Vinnie. I needn't have worried because of course Masi had done a spectacular job—Vinnie looked ravishing. She didn't look over-done like some brides. Despite all the gold and red, her look was simple and classic—contemporary chic with a hint of traditional. Timeless.

Best of all, her gold lehenga with the cranberry-red veil set off Mom's jewelry to perfection. Masi, Beeji, her bridesmaids, and half the aunties were fussing around her, and for a moment I felt left out. Then Vinnie caught sight of me, and her face lit up.

"Mini, where have you *been?*" she demanded.

"Taking care of stuff," I said. "You look ready to get married, Dr. Vinnie!"

"You better believe I am!" Vinnie said. "Did you get a look at Manish?"

"I did," I said mysteriously. "But I can't tell you anything."

A flash went off next to my face, and I looked over to see an intense young woman behind a huge camera with an extra-large lens attached.

"Sol?" I asked. This had to be Manish's friend Sol, who was to do the photography and videography. What a relief! By the look of her equipment, she was more than qualified.

"You're the sister." Sol had no trouble identifying me. "So can we *finally* take group photographs?" I didn't realize they'd been waiting for me. Sol was already giving directions.

"Vinnie in the center, Dad to the left, Mini to the right, Aunty left, grandparents right," she directed.

All of Vinnie's bridesmaids were picture-perfect in their red saris—and they had twenties-style headbands and fascinators in their hair.

Where on earth did they get those?

"I had some made," Masi said. "With the leftover material from

Vinnie's lehenga. Your designs inspired me, I guess, and the girls thought they were fun so they decided to use them."

"Wow," I said. "Just wow! But where's mine?"

"Right here," Masi said. She produced a hair comb with an antique gold flower mounted on it and pushed it into my hair. Her hands were gentle as she fastened it expertly with a couple of bobby pins.

"Ready?" Sol asked, and Masi nodded. "Okay, perfect. Say 'To hell with the hurricane!'"

We had time for a few more photographs, and then dhol beats announced that the groom's party was advancing up the hill.

"The baraat is coming," Dad said. "Places, everyone!"

Beeji and Masi were going to greet Manish with a lighted lamp and place a ceremonial red tilak on his forehead. And then Vinnie would make her grand entrance flanked by her bridesmaids.

"Is that Dad's car?" Vinnie asked. "He let Manish use it?"

The Lotus was climbing the hill slowly and smoothly without stalling out once. Vir was at the wheel, evidently. Red roses and gold tassels hung festively from the sleek hood of the race car—Shoma Moorty's work. I could hear Dad make a strangled sound in his throat at the sight. Driving was not the only thing Vir had done well—both he and Manish were wearing flamboyant red turbans. Ahead of them came two real Punjabi Dholis with large wooden drums and a bunch of Iyer relatives dancing in a happy, if not very Punjabi, way.

Someone handed Manish his varmala and he turned around to wait for Vinnie's entrance.

"Come on, girls!" I said. "Now!"

Vinnie's bridesmaids and I held the ceremonial red-and-gold canopy high above Vinnie's head. Vinnie walked beneath it holding her varmala garland, Dad beside her, and we started out toward the groom's party.

I could hear gasps of admiration. Vinnie looked every inch the glowing bride, and I think the bright red the rest of us wore added to her splendor.

In the background Sol was clicking away earnestly. Then Vinnie garlanded Manish and the ceremony was underway.

Shoma Moorty had done an outstanding job—the mandap was just the way Vinnie wanted it. Beautifully draped in tasseled silk, with a flower-bedecked welcome arch and a red carpet down the center aisle. I looked back from the mandap and saw row upon row of smiling faces. Beeji, Bauji, Bade Bauji, Dad, Vinnie's friends from high school and med school, old teachers, Beeji's Arya Samaj friends, the Tamils from the Iyers' side. And—it took me a moment to place her—the bank teller from the Westbury Bank of America branch. She had been at the temple to pray and found herself caught up in the wedding. She had been happy to stay.

In the confusion, no one asked Krishna Ji to perform the ceremony the Punjabi way, so he went ahead and followed the Tamil ceremonials instead.

There was a bit when Manish opened an umbrella and pretended to go off to Kashi and stay a bachelor, until he was persuaded to come back. And another when they reenacted the garlanding ceremony but both Vinnie and Manish were lifted up by family members to make the garlanding more difficult for the other person—like a sort of competition. Vinnie didn't get very high with only Dad and Bauji holding her until Vir, Chintu, and Mintu pitched in.

And there was the part when they had Vinnie sit on Dad's lap—not something they do in Punjab, but sweet anyway. They also did some of the more familiar rituals—the seven steps around the fire and so forth.

And before we knew it, they were done!

"You're all invited to our house for the reception," Dad said. "The address is posted on the temple bulletin board."

So it was.

I had been getting texts throughout the ceremony. Shayla and Rachel had gone over to our house soon after they got my messages just to keep an eye on things. Then they promptly called in their moms, so Sue and Amy were there as well. Everything was going well, they reported. The tent was up, the tables set, the flowers arranged. Shayla had walked Yogi—the poor dog had no idea why he had been abandoned since early in the morning and why strangers were swarming over his yard and putting up large, scary things.

But I was still worried about the food! It was to come at noon, and it was already 11:50 and I was nowhere close to getting home. I called Sher-e-Punjab…no one answered. I called Rajinder Singh's cell phone—no response. In desperation, I called Preet.

"Why didn't you call me?" Preet demanded. "All day long I've been worrying about your sister's wedding. Give me your address. I'll go now and talk to my cousin Rajinder."

"Thanks so much, Preet!" I said. "We've not even paid a single cent so far. And if he gets to our house and there's no one there to give him a check—I'm worried he might—"

"Don't worry about anything," Preet said. "But I don't have anywhere to leave Rahul—is it okay if I bring him?"

"Of course!" I said. "And I'll be there as soon as I can!"

After the final group photos, they didn't need me anymore so I hurried home. It had been bright when we took the group pictures and the baraat came up the hill to the temple, but now the sky was getting dark and the wind was picking up. The radio was full of stories of what was happening in New York—none of it good. Over a hundred people were about to descend on our house—I was worried, but there was nothing I could do until we got home.

Chapter Twenty-Eight

The tent was up!

Shayla had told me it was, but it was something else to see it myself. Festive and bright with yellow and white stripes and clear arched windows—it was beautiful to behold. And it was perfectly level, lashed down tight, and looked ready to take on the weather—rain or shine.

The inside was shipshape too—neat, sparkling table settings with their burgundy fanfolded napkins (how *did* Bauji's guys manage that?) and bushels of colorful chrysanthemums in place of centerpieces.

"It's a miracle!" I said faintly as Alan and Richie beamed at me. These guys were clearly in the wrong damn profession.

Also, the buffet table was covered in a floor-length cloth, and arranged on it were sparkling silver chafing dishes filled with mouthwatering curries, rice, and naans—I could smell them even though the lids were shut. Sher-e-Punjab for the win!

This atheist was so going to do kar seva at the local Sikh temple in thanks.

Wahi Guru Ji ki fatheh!

"We put the lights up too," Alan said. "But we haven't turned them on yet."

The trees were festooned with string lights—they looked bright and festive and would be beautiful in all the pictures once Sol got here with her camera. If we still had power.

Bauji had ridden back with me in the minivan, and he looked proud of his crew.

"So, basically we're in good shape, right?" I said to no one in particular, hoping they couldn't sense the panic I was wrestling with.

But Preet, Shayla, Rachel, and Ernie Uncle, who had finally checked his phone messages and, realizing he'd missed the wedding, had headed directly to the house, and even little Rahul—looking adorable in a Nehru-collar kurta—were looking at me with goofy grins, the way people look at adorable babies.

"Awww, check you out!" Shayla said. "The girl in the red sari!"

"There are nine more of those at this wedding," I said, but I was flattered.

"So the tent's up, the food's here." Shayla laid a friendly arm over Preet's shoulders. "Preet here talked to the caterers, and she organized everything. They let her have the chafing dishes and extra serving spoons and stuff to make it easier to serve the food.

And I've walked Yogi. We've pushed back the furniture inside too so there's plenty of room for everyone to move around. Both our moms have vacuumed everything, and cleaned the bathrooms, and put out fresh towels and stuff."

So that was where Amy and Sue had vanished to!

"So, what else do you need?"

"Alcohol!" said Bauji. "We don't have any alcohol!" Other people might say beer, wine, or champagne, but Bauji went straight to the point in his businesslike way. And he was right—we didn't have a drop of alcohol.

"There's a liquor store at the intersection of Routes Nine and Twenty-Seven," I said to Alan. "Do you know it?"

"Sure do," Alan said with a grin.

"We need their best champagne for the toast—lots of it. And beer—any idea what type, Bauji?" I asked.

"We'll get a selection of beer and wine," Alan said. "They'll take back what we don't use if we're buying bulk. What else?"

"Sparkling cider for the people who don't drink," I said. In any Indian group there's bound to be a few of those. "That's all!"

That was when I noticed that my car was parked on the curb instead of blocking the driveway. That had to be Ernie Uncle's work. "Did you jump-start the Mini?" I asked.

"Yeah," he said. "I heard the Lotus got BeDazzled—what did Vinod say to that?"

"It's standing in for the wedding horse," I said, grinning. "It had to have some bling."

He just rolled his eyes—like Dad. "Mini, you have plenty of

room on the street for parking but not if you have over fifty cars," he said. "Do you need people to valet the cars?"

"That would be awesome!" I said. I hadn't even thought of that.

"I'll call a couple of my guys," he said, pulling out his cell phone. "It might cost you, though."

"It's cool." I grinned. "We're good, Ernie Uncle—Dad's start-up just got funded!"

A couple in a Honda Accord pulled into our driveway. The woman in the passenger seat was wearing a sari and carrying a baby—we had our first guests.

"I can greet them for you, but what do I say?" Shayla hissed into my ear.

"Just say 'Welcome and come inside,'" I said, as nervous as her.

"Inside?" Shayla said. "I thought they were eating in the tent?"

"We can put the appetizers in the house and move them out for the lunch after Vinnie and Manish arrive," I said.

Soon the house was full, the samosas were nearly gone, and I was starting to panic. "There's more downstairs!" Preet said. "Go fetch them!"

In the laundry room I found buckets, no, really, *buckets* of extra curry, and platters of samosas and chutneys. And they were heavy and hot—there was no way I could carry them up. I stuck my head out of the laundry but couldn't see Dad, or Vir, or Bauji, or even Chintu or Mintu. "Excuse me!" I said. "Could someone please help carry out some food?"

A tall boy who was clearly related to Manish, given his familiar smile, and one of Vinnie's med school friends took charge and carried steaming-hot samosas out to the hungry hordes.

In the kitchen Preet manned the sink, washing used snack dishes—Amy and Sue dried them. Around them people were eating, chatting, laughing, and mingling. In spite of the tight squeeze, everyone had a smile on their face.

"This is going better than I thought," Amy said with cautious optimism.

"Sweets!" I said. "We don't have them! We canceled the cake!"

Rachel was the one who remembered. "Didn't your Beeji make something—those yellow ball things?" she asked. "They're sweet, aren't they?"

"Laddoos!" I said. "I have hundreds of them and they are nut- and gluten-free—we're saved! Come with me!"

Manish's cousin and Vinnie's friend helped Shayla carry the laddoos from the garage, where they were stacked in the largest, ugliest plastic Tupperware boxes you can imagine—Beeji specialized in them.

In a flash of inspiration, I found Mom's crystal three-tier dessert stand, washed and dried it, and took it out to the tent, ducking through the drizzle that had started up. I set it up on a side table next to the buffet. "Help me stack," I said, and cracked open a Tupperware box. Shayla helped me cover each tier of the dessert stand with golden laddoos.

A little girl in a firoza-blue summer dress, a golden bindi, and blue glass bangles came over to look.

She had tightly curling dark hair, olive skin, and bright, curious eyes. Eyes that looked red from crying.

"Do you want to help?" I asked, and she cheered up immediately.

"Yes," she said, and started to arrange the laddoos even more carefully than us.

We turned the topmost tier into a neat little pyramid and let the girl in blue place the last laddoo at the very top.

It looked impressive.

"What's wrong, honey?" I asked the kid. "You look upset."

"She laughed at my Hindi," she said, pointing at a Punjabi woman—one of Beeji's satsang friends.

"My Hindi sounds funny too sometimes," I said. "It's because we grew up here." She probably got it worse because she was biracial. There was definitely discrimination within our own culture sometimes.

"And I spilled curry on my favorite jacket," she said. "Mom said it's too hot to wear it today but I wanted to. And now it's ruined."

"Oh," I said.

"Do you like blue?" I asked.

She nodded.

"Then I have the perfect jacket for you," I said. "It's exactly that blue, and it has brass buttons, and I bought it for a trip to India, but I never wore it."

"I'm going to India this winter," she said. "I've never been before."

"Then you have to wear it for me," I said. "Deal?"

"Deal!"

"Mini!" It was Masi, newly alighted from Beeji's car along with Dad, Beeji, and Bade Bauji. "Is everything under control?"

"Yes," I said. "The tables and the food are all set. People are having appetizers and drinks. Ernie Uncle's guys are taking care of the cars and parking. We're just waiting for Vinnie and Manish."

"So, why don't you get changed?" Masi said.

I had to admit it—a full morning of driving to the temple and back, of running around, serving samosas, and arranging laddoos had taken their toll. I was a hot mess—my sari was crumpled, my hair damp, and my makeup smudged.

"It's okay, Masi," I said.

"No," she said. "It isn't. Look, Vinnie got changed at the hotel room. You go upstairs and put on your blue lehenga and freshen up. I know the house is packed but I'll make sure no one walks in on you."

She looked pretty determined, so I gave in.

"Fine," I said. "I won't be long."

It only took me fifteen minutes to get changed and comb out my hair, which—thanks to the vast amount of product the nice hairdresser had put in it yesterday—still looked smooth and stylish once I managed to get it dry.

I opened the blue velvet jewelry box with the gold peacock set in it—necklace, bangles, maang tikka, and earrings. They'd look great with what I was wearing.

This is for your wedding, Mini.

No, today was not the time to wear it—at least not *all* of it. I fastened the earrings on and put the rest away—they could wait for the day Mom meant them for.

Then I found a little paper gift bag, folded the firoza pea coat into it, and covered it with tissue paper.

Perfect!

"That's better," Masi said when I reappeared downstairs. "I've been waiting to see you in that dress, Mini. And I'm not disappointed. Now, have you eaten anything?"

"No," I said. "I'll have lunch with everyone."

"Have a vada," Masi said. "Then you can go help again."

"In a minute," I said, looking around for the little girl.

I felt a tug at my skirt and looked down to see her right next to me.

"There you are!" I said. "Here's the jacket I promised you."

She rummaged through the tissue and her face lit up when she saw the jacket.

"It's so beautiful!" she breathed.

"You like that shade of blue?" I asked. "It's called firoza!"

"Thanks," said a woman standing next to her—the girl's mother, I guess. She had a dimpled smile and a Nigerian accent.

"You're welcome," I said.

"It's time *someone* wore that thing," Masi said with an impish grin. "You ready for your vada now, Mini?"

"Yes, I am!"

The samosas had finally finished, and a bunch of Beeji's friends were heating the vadas from the janvasam and serving them up. Masi fixed me a plate with a crisp golden vada and a dollop of chutney next to it. I'd been too busy to eat, so I was super hungry, and it tasted amazing.

Just then there was a commotion outside.

"They're here!" Rachel said, peeking out through a window.

I gulped down the last bite of vada and hurried to the front door.

The Lotus was parked in the driveway—they had arrived!

Vinnie had changed into Mom's old wedding lehenga. She looked so soft and radiant in the vintage pink and silver. Just as she was stepping out of the car, there was a dramatic crack of thunder and it started to rain—again.

"Umbrellas!" I said, and hurried over to the designated umbrella area—I pulled a soft pastel one with Monet's water lilies on it for Vinnie and hurried over to cover her before she got a drop of water on Mom's dress.

"Oh. My. God. Mini," she said, her eyes shining. "Everything looks amazing!"

Sol was in the car with them, still clicking away. I handed Manish another umbrella to hold over Sol. Those pictures had to turn out good!

"Everyone in the tent, please. Vinnie and Manish have arrived!"

A volunteer group of umbrella ushers had sprung up at the garage door, where most of the traffic was making its way to the tent.

"These are the prettiest umbrellas I've ever seen," said a sweet-faced lady in a hot-pink Kanjivaram.

"You're just like Megha—same to same," said Chintu and Mintu Patel's mom, pinching my cheeks rather painfully. "Carbon copy!"

"Mini!" Ernie Uncle strode over in a bright yellow rain poncho—no flowery umbrella for him. "You want to see this!"

"What...," I started to ask, and then gasped at the sight of the rental car with Canadian plates—and my Nanaji and Masi's twin boys, Ari and Avi, wearing matching Camp Halfblood T-shirts, descending from it.

"Nanaji, you made it!"

Masi came tearing out of the tent and wrapped the twins into her arms. She hadn't said a word when we lost contact with Nanaji at Heathrow Airport, but she must have been crazy worried.

"We took a flight to Montreal from London," Nanaji explained. "And drove down from there. What did we miss?"

"The ceremony is over, but everyone is here for the reception!" Masi said.

You should have seen Vinnie's face when Nanaji walked into the tent. You should have seen Nanaji's face when he saw Vinnie all dressed up in Mom's old wedding lehenga. Some things just cannot be expressed in words.

There was a line at the buffet table and people were serving themselves and sitting down at tables and chatting and having a good time.

But there was someone missing still.

"Has anyone seen Vir?" I asked Dad.

"No," he said. "He was there at the temple, though, wasn't he? He was driving my car!" I backed away quickly before Dad said any more on that subject.

There were people to chat with and food to eat and pictures to pose in, but it didn't feel complete without Vir. Where was he?

"Vir?" Chintu said. "I think he said he had to pick up a friend from Logan Airport."

"Is he coming back?" I asked.

"I don't know," Chintu said.

I guessed I'd have to wait and see.

"Mini," said a familiar voice. It was Krishna Ji, the priest. "Congratulations!"

"Thanks," I said. "It was so good of you to perform the ceremony and come for the reception. It's been crazy."

"Not at all," he said. "It is all very auspicious."

"How is that?" I asked.

"Indradev himself is showering blessings from the heavens," he said quietly. "What can be better than that?"

Fair point. Indra, God of rain and thunder, was definitely present at this wedding.

"I was very glad to do Vinnie's wedding," he said. "It's been a long time."

I nodded. "It has."

"Last time I was in this house your Amma was sick," he said. "I remember I sat right here and had tea, and you asked me—you remember what you asked me?"

I knew exactly what I'd asked him.

"I asked for a miracle," I said. "I wanted her to live."

"And I told you that certainly there will be a miracle." He shook his head sadly. "My faith, you know? I did not think anyone could refuse the wish of such a small child, not even God. So many years gone, and I still don't understand it."

I smiled ruefully—for what was there to say?

"But do you know what your mom asked for that same day?" he asked.

"No," I said.

"She had accepted it then—her fate. She was only worried about you all," he said. "Especially you, kutti. Your mom said: 'Krishna Ji, Vinnie is strong and tough, and she's nearly grown-up—she'll be sad, but she'll be okay. But Mini, I just want my Mini to be fine. She's so little, and so sensitive, and she doesn't really understand yet—I don't want her to be damaged by any of this. If only I could know that she will be fine.'"

"What did you say?" I asked.

"I promised her sincerely that you would be," he said. "My faith, you know?"

I stared at him, at a loss for words.

"I can see now that your mom's wish came true," he said. "You are very fine. You are taking care of so many things for your dad, your sister. God may not have heard you, kutti, but he heard your mom. She would be so, so proud of you."

I had tears in my eyes, but I smiled at him through them.

"Thanks for telling me," I said. "It means a lot."

"Hey, Vir, my man!" I could hear Manish from way over in

the garage. The garage had turned into the bar because Alan and Richie were pouring drinks for whoever asked. They had a cooler filled with ice for the drinks, because the electricity had gone with the rainstorm—and they were clearly imbibing as much of the stuff as they were dispensing.

Vir was here!

I headed over to the garage, working my way through the crowd.

"I brought some gear," I heard Vir say. "A generator and amps, an electric guitar, and a PA system. Thought it might come in handy."

"That's awesome," Manish said. "You saved the music, dude. Let's set it up!"

"Hi, Vir," I said, having finally caught up to them.

He had changed into jeans and a button-down shirt.

"Mini, I want you to meet someone," he said to me. "This is Koyal Khanna."

The petite girl with him, in jeans and a T-shirt and four-inch heels, smiled and waved her hand shyly as if unsure of her welcome. But it was her—it really and truly was *the* Koyal Khanna! I have to say, she looked very different in real life. Smaller, somehow, though still extremely pretty.

"Hi," I said.

Vir had gone all the way to Logan in the pouring rain to pick her up?

"You're so pretty!" she said. "Vir said you were!"

This from the person voted Most Beautiful Face in India.

Yes, I had been reading more Bollywood gossip columns than were good for me.

"Thank you," I said. "Would you like to have a drink? Lunch is still warm, and we also have dessert...."

"Later," she said. "I have to talk to you first."

"Ohh-kay," I said.

"I heard that you guys had a big misunderstanding because of me," Koyal said, immediately getting to the meat of the matter. "I've been shooting in New York for my new movie. *Love in New York*, you know. When I got stuck in Boston trying to fly back home, I wanted to tell you in person. There was nothing between Vir and me! It was all fake dating. We're just friends! Vir helped me and Bunty meet up in spite of our parents. That was all."

"Bunty?" I asked. That was a common nickname, but not an actual name.

"Yeah," she said, smiling shyly. "You know how Vir saw you one time only and he was a goner?"

"He was?" I asked.

"Of course he was," she said. "He told me all about it. It was like that when I saw Bunty too. He's from a different community and my parents are very orthodox, even though they let me act and all. They don't like him because he isn't like us."

"Oh," I said. "He isn't?" It wasn't obvious why Bunty didn't fit Koyal's family's idea of a suitable match, as it's hard to place someone when all you have is that they're called Bunty.

"No, he's not," she said. "But he's very handsome, *I* think! And he *gets* me. All of me, not just the Bollywood star part, but the girl I've always been. You know?"

I nodded. You couldn't *not* believe her. She sounded 100 percent sincere.

Koyal was still speaking. "And he's Vir's classmate from Mayo College, so Vir helped us meet up while he was in Mumbai working with his dad and going to all these parties. Because my parents thought I was seeing Vir, they were okay, because, you know, Vir *is* like us, and very rich, so even if he wasn't, they'd probably still approve. But really it was Bunty and me all the time. And then even the media got it wrong. But Vir just thought it was funny and didn't care because he wasn't serious about anyone else, and it kept all the girls off his back if they thought he was serious about me."

"Go on," I said, drinking in this fascinating glimpse into Vir's life.

"But now that I see you, I can tell why he wasn't interested in those stupid girls," she said. "Because you were over here waiting, and he had to come find you."

Koyal Khanna clearly had very romantic notions of love and dating. But talking to her had taken a huge load off me. I might even float off the ground. I knew Vir enough to see that Koyal was not at all his type. She would drive him crazy in no time.

"Koyal really likes homemade laddoos too," Vir said. "And her mom's not here to make sure she sticks to her diet. So, you want to go get some, Koyal? I am, for sure!" He headed to the dessert table.

"Yes," Koyal said, scanning the tent hungrily until she spotted the tiers of laddoos. "I'm so going to get some. Oh, hi, Mallika Aunty!"

"Koyal!" Mallu Masi looked very confused. "What are you doing here?"

"Shooting! Got stuck in Boston because of the storm, but Gulshan Aunty, Vir's mom, said I could stay with them. The rest of the crew is staying at a hotel in Boston."

"That's great! Go eat something. Those laddoos are fantastic. Everything else is too!"

Vir had been talking with Ernie Uncle, who looked smug about the fact that we were friends. He gave me a told-ya look before walking off and leaving me with Vir.

"You talked to Koyal," Vir said. "About..." He waved a hand to encompass us.

"Yes," I said.

Satisfied? his eyes asked.

I smiled back at him happily—because, yes, I was.

"That is Koyal Khanna, Mini?" someone whispered in my ear. One of Beeji's friends with eagle eyes had recognized Koyal even in her jeans and T-shirt. "The one from *Meri Bollywood Wedding*? Wasn't Vinnie wearing the lehenga from the movie for the wedding? The Mallika Motwani?"

"Yes, she was," I said.

"But how?"

"The designer is my Masi, Aunty," I said. "Come, I'll introduce you to both of them. But please don't share photographs of Koyal, or ask for autographs." Koyal was a guest in our house and I wasn't going to let anyone ogle her.

"Good luck with that," Vir said.

The house glowed with the fairy lights strung around our trees.

The last group pictures had been taken, the last gift envelopes stashed safely away, the last autographs signed, and the last picture with Koyal Khanna taken (We won't show anybody the photos, beta, *no one*!). Koyal herself had eaten her fill of Beeji's laddoos, to Beeji's eternal pride.

Outside, Avi and Ari and Rahul floated paper boats in the rainwater overflowing from the gutter.

In the garage Manish and his friends played amazing music. I sat beside Vir, Yogi curled up at my feet, and listened to them play. I'd had no idea that they could sound like that.

And then Manish's friend Samar took center stage. Samar was a Punjabi from Pakistan, and he sang so beautifully that Beeji wept.

"How he sings, that Samar!" Beeji cried. "That's what you call real singing, Mini, real singing!"

"Can we go to sleep, Mummy?" Avi asked Masi. The boys had had enough of the rain and were latched on to Masi from either side, literally dropping where they sat.

"I'll be back," Masi said. "What about you, Rahul? You want to rest too?"

"I'll rest inside with Avi and Ari from Mumbai," Rahul said.

"They can lie down in Vinnie's old room," I said.

Upstairs the kids fell asleep, and outside it still rained. Then Manish sang one last song for Vinnie—the one he had written especially for her. And it was the perfect ending to the day.

Masi and Beeji brought out the rice for Vinnie to fling back over her head as she left the house—a married woman—and Manish and Vinnie drove off. Almost everyone else left then too, Preet and Rahul, Rachel and Amy, Shayla and Sue, even Koyal—Chintu had gallantly offered to drop her at Vir's mom's house at Fellsway College before the storm got worse.

Alan and Richie had taken down the tent and scraped off all the china and rinsed it off with the garden hose and stacked it back into the Talbot Rental containers. Ditto the silverware, the napkins, and the stemware. Everything was counted and stacked and piled, ready to be taken away on Monday. The outdoor lights had been turned off too, though they were still up. We'd take them down tomorrow but there would be no massive cleanup needed after all.

We regrouped inside after Beeji, Bauji, and Bade Bauji left. Vir was still around and didn't show any signs of leaving. Dad went off into the kitchen to make hot chocolate for Masi, Nanaji, and himself—and put on the Weather Channel to check on the hurricane.

"I'm going to get the flowers," I said. "They're still outside!"

"Nothing will happen to them," Masi said. "It's just rain."

"It's just rain now," I said. "Tonight it'll be a hurricane."

"Vir, help her get them, will you?" Masi said. "And Vinod, come sit with me. Now that Vinnie's married, I have to talk to you about the infinite possibilities of a career in design—for Mini."

It was dark outside except for the light spilling from the windows of the house. We didn't even need umbrellas, as the rain had slowed to a drizzle.

"Thanks for getting the flowers," I said as Vir and I gathered up the mums and carted them indoors. They looked brilliant in the living room with the raindrops glistening on them—a living reminder of Mom. "I'm going to plant them in the window boxes when the storm is over—it's kind of a tradition."

"Can I help?" Vir said.

"Sure," I said. "If I can help you move to your dorm at MIT."

"If I can drive you to Providence for an info session at Brown. Deal?"

"Deal," I said.

"Hey, you could write about this for your college essay," Vir said.

We really did think alike.

"I already started a draft."

Three armloads of flowers done, we went back outside to scan the lawn for any remaining mums. There were none. Vir headed back in, but I put a hand on his arm to stop him—I had something to say before the night ended, and I needed to say it now.

"Vir, I'm so, so sorry I didn't even talk to you before assuming that you were—"

"Stop, Mini," he said.

"No, I won't," I insisted. "It really was my fault, and I should have—"

But then I did stop.

Because he pulled me to him and kissed me.

When we came up for air, he smiled down at me.

"Actually," he said, "if anything, it was my fault. I should never have pretended to date Koyal. It was stupid. And then I should have told you, and then—"

He was *totally* ruining the moment.

"Shh, Vir," I said, and kissed him.

The fairy lights in the trees turned on, suddenly sparkling like magical starlight.

Artificial starlight, but pretty nonetheless.

"Look at that," I said in wonder. "That wasn't us, was it?"

"Don't ask me," Vir said. "I've been seeing fairy lights ever since your dog chased my cat up that hill and—"

"Oh, hi!" It was Sol, the photographer. "I just turned them on so I could take some final mood shots of the house and garden before I left."

"What a good idea," I said, trying to extricate myself from Vir's arms—except he didn't seem interested in letting go.

"I don't think I got a picture of you two together," Sol said. "This would make a nice composition too. You *are* together, aren't you?"

"Yes," Vir said, lacing his fingers through mine and giving my hand a squeeze. "Yes, we are."

So we stood there smiling in the gentle rain and posed for the last official picture taken on Vinnie's wedding day.

Acknowledgments

Sometimes books can have second chances.

Sincere thanks to my editor, Nikki Garcia, and my agent, Allison Remcheck, for finding a way to give this one its second chance.

Thanks to the team at Little, Brown for believing in this story, Annie McDonnell for the thorough edits, Jenny Kimura for the gorgeous book design, and Sanno Singh for the lovely cover art.

This book has had another life, and I am grateful to the team at Scholastic India, especially Tina Narang, for believing in it first. I am also thankful for the many young Indian readers who loved it as *Red Turban White Horse*. This was, and always will be, my debut novel.

The Writers' Loft, SCBWI New England, Boston Author's Club, Onwords and Upwords critique group, and others in my local writing community—thanks for years of friendship, honest critiques, cheering on, commiserating, straight talk, celebrations, and so much more.

Finally, thanks to my family:

My sisters: for being my first readers, then, now, always.

My father: for his pride in his four daughters that is our strength.

My mum: for the space both physical and mental to finish the first version of this book on deadline, for believing firmly that it would have another shot though she isn't here to see it happen, and for her lifetime of love that will last and light the rest of my life.

My husband, Chandra, and my children, Ravi and Anika: for their love, support, and endless patience. You guys are my rock and my world!

My cats, Bikky and Zara, and especially my sweet old dog, Yogi: for being the best companions a writer could have.

The idea for this book came from the real-life hurricane wedding of my sister-in-law—thanks, Urmila and Satish, for the inspiration!

Nandini Bajpai

grew up in New Delhi, India, one of four sisters and many cousins in a family that liked to read. She now lives in the Boston area with her family and a fluctuating number and variety of pets. She is the author of *Sister of the Bollywood Bride* and *A Match Made in Mehendi*, as well as several books published in India.

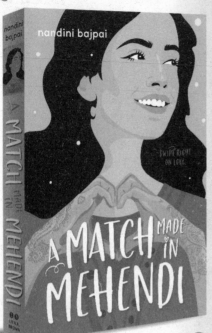
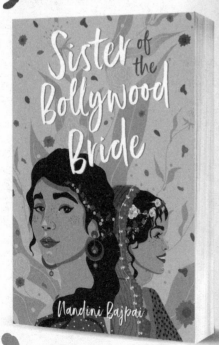